I0738035

"Were you dreaming?" Pharun asked coolly. He drew his foot back only slightly, resting it on the lip of the seat.

"Somewhat," Felix confessed. "It was neither a dream nor a sense of consciousness. It was somewhere in between."

"I see. And what sort of images does your mind conjure when it is idling?" Pharun plucked at the lace on his wrist, draping it over his dark gray knuckles.

"I saw you," Felix said softly, not looking at the prince but focusing on the world passing by their window—what parts of it could be seen through the drawn velvet curtains. "You were being consumed by flames."

II

UNCROWNED

The Draonir Saga: Book One

Sirius

THE LAUGHING MAN HOUSE

This book is a work of fiction. References to real people, events, establishments, organizations, or locales are intended only to provide a sense of authenticity, and are used to advance the fictional narrative. All other characters, and all incidents and dialogue, are drawn from the author's imagination and are not to be construed as real.

Uncrowned

Copyright © 2022 by Cyrus Claude Spears

ISBN: 978-0-578-39018-5

All rights reserved.

No portion of this book may be reproduced in any form without written permission from the publisher or author, except as permitted by U.S. copyright law.

www.uncrownednovel.com

Book design by Just Venture Arts

Cover Design by Jette Ossoba

First paperback edition, 2022

The Laughing Man House

For Janus, for Ellis, for Irene

CONTENTS

1

ENCARZ

An Intimate Introduction into Royal Circumstance

IN THE SOFT, DELICATE hours of the morning, snow fell in great puffs that piled up on the palace windowsills and crowned the grand turrets. It formed steep drifts at every entrance, set to impede morning progress while enticing small children and unpenned royal hounds to fling themselves fully into the piles. A wild breath of ice formed patterns like expensive lace on the colored glass of every window and door. Depictions of roses and dragons tangled in their brambles glistened like stars in the waning moonlight.

The glass in front of which the king sat on a cushioned seat was transparent. The window's slim, arched frame came to a peak at eight meters above the monarch's head, too high for even the curls of smoke from his clay pipe to reach. Encarz's seat looked out over the entire courtyard, the view stretching out toward the tall iron gates which were only a dark silhouette against the snowy landscape. It was a favorite perch of his for this reason. He slid his thumb over the fluted side of his pipe—also a favorite, carved to look like the bowl was being cradled in a reptilian claw.

"And here the royal dragon roosts," a soft voice intruded upon the silence, "gloating over his domain and bellowing smoke."

Encarz had heard the footsteps approaching, so his wife's sudden speaking did not startle him. He pulled his eyes away from the view long enough to acknowledge her presence and was struck breathless by the sight of her in a pale blue dressing gown that draped effortlessly over her figure.

"Do I gloat?" the king asked. "I was thinking I might tear it all down, brick by brick, and start anew."

"Does beauty and prosperity frustrate you so, my liege?" Having been recognized, Lystra approached him, crossing the tile on slippered feet. "Any king would be proud. Your father was. You should be."

Encarz set his teeth against the mouthpiece of his pipe. "Are you now in the habit of chiding me?"

"Generally." She sat down on the seat beside him. He offered his pipe, and she took it without hesitation, placing it against her own mouth.

"I would hazard that you have not slept," Encarz observed. Lystra did not respond immediately. She drew deeply from the pipe and paused before exhaling. Smoke streamed from between her full lips, curling around her chin.

"Neither have you," she countered at last. "You did not come to bed. I waited."

"You kept it empty for me?" He took his pipe back.

"No, but I exhausted the stable boy."

"Pity. You will have to replace him." Encarz leaned back in his window seat enough to draw up his knee and rest his arm. A comfortable silence settled between them once more, stretching on as they shared the pipe and their company.

Lystra was the one to break the silence again. "Do you think your eldest son would believe you, were you to tell him that you lost sleep over his arrival?"

Encarz snorted. "Unlikely," he said, "and it is hardly for joy or the thrill of anticipating his return. I hope he leaves the capital as quickly as he flounces in. I spent several hours, if you must know, with the treasurer. The preparations for this ceremony alone have cost the crown enough. I am not inclined to finance Pharun's pompous tastes in wardrobe, which he will undoubtedly demand."

"You have every right to direct the church to draw from its own coffers," Lystra said. "He is their *Kren Veisten*."

"He is Dragoloth's *Kren Veisten*; that is how they will see things. He presides over the high priests, but he sits on my council." Even the admission brought a sour taste to the king's mouth.

"Perhaps he will heed your advice and appointment a chancellor to represent him for the council." Lystra set a hand on top of her husband's, gently drawing her thumb over the ridges of his knuckles. "He has as little love for you as you have for him. He has no reason to stay."

"No reason other than to gall me, which would be reason enough." Encarz felt tension pull at the base of his spine with the thought. These few hours before dawn had been his only peace, and now he felt a red surge of hatred tighten an existing knot in his stomach. Lystra was an intelligent woman, but she possessed a naïve quality that never allowed her to fully grasp the nature of his relationship with his eldest. Pharun had been only five years of age when she and Encarz were married. She never understood why he was kept away from her, shielded by his nurses and tutors until he finally reached an age where he could be made the church's burden. She thought that giving her husband the son he desired might be enough to start bridging the gap. If anything, it had deepened the divide.

Lystra squeezed his hand. Dawn was starting to chase away the reluctant moon, spilling red across the sky like so much paint. They only had a few precious hours before the courtyard was flooded with palace staff and courtiers alike lining up to receive the prince. Despite his being monumentally unpopular at court, not even the most stalwart of barons was willing to risk divine displeasure by failing to pay respects to the new *Kren Veisten*—the nation's Crowned Priest.

"You must eat," she tried to coax her king. "You cannot face the barons on an empty stomach."

Encarz considered it, tapping the side of his pipe in thought. "If Pharun does appoint a chancellor, it will be because he has managed to find the one person who will nettle me more."

"Let us not worry about it now." She took his hand in her own, urging him to rise. "We have not even made it through the ceremony yet."

Encarz finally stood, offering his arm to his wife. It was a rare gesture, and she knew he would pull away as soon as they entered the public view. Lystra slipped her arm through his, bringing her hand around to rest against the crook of his elbow.

"There is love in you yet, my liege," she said quietly under her breath. His mouth twitched, but he did not quite smile as they walked together down the long, dark corridor.

EARLY DAWN BATHED THE gleaming gold coach in red as it traveled down the wide cobblestone road that led into Seravell. The capital city was known for its magnificent wealth, and yet the carriage had been jostling for the better part of a mile with no end in sight. Pharun learned quickly that he could steady himself by bracing a foot against the opposite seat and, without a qualm, had slipped one from its brocade shoe and planted it right between the legs of his companion. High Priest Felix was not disturbed; the man could sleep through anything. That, or he was at the point where exhaustion had settled in so deeply that nothing short of the final judgment could force him to open his eyes.

Pharun watched the priest sway in his seat, his golden head bumping against the wall with every particularly malicious jerk from the coach. The prince slid his silken hose-shielded toes up the seat and prodded his companion in the thigh. Felix muttered something unintelligible, and Pharun prodded him again, jamming his foot against the high priest's groin.

Felix coughed and made a face, drawing his thighs together and pulling himself upright. He finally opened his eyes, casting a look at the prince across from him before reaching up to touch the holy talisman draped around his throat.

"Were you dreaming?" Pharun asked coolly. He drew his foot back only slightly, resting it on the lip of the seat.

"Somewhat," Felix confessed. "It was neither a dream nor a sense of consciousness. It was somewhere in between."

"I see. And what sort of images does your mind conjure when it is idling?" Pharun plucked at the lace on his wrist, draping it over his dark gray knuckles.

"I saw you," Felix said softly, not looking at the prince but focusing on the world passing by their window—what parts of it could be seen through the drawn velvet curtains. "You were being consumed by flames."

The prince's expression did not change. "Perhaps it was a portent of things to come."

"I sincerely hope not, Your Grace," was Felix's response.

"It could have been a funerary fire," Pharun continued to speculate. "Being burned alive in a dream can also be symbolic of an ascension into power, a sort of shedding of the old self."

"It may also be indicative of priests who have not slept," Felix dismissed his theorizing. "Twenty-one days on a ship and three more by coach from the coast to the capital. I am ready to rest my head where it does not bump or sway."

"It is a journey you will only have to make once should you stay." Pharun tilted his chin up. "That alone should tempt you to accept my offer."

Felix shook his head. "I must return to my temple," he said.

"I will build you a new one. A temple for the three father gods, each one erected in Seravell? Even my father's miserly Secretary of the Royal Treasury would jump on the idea." Pharun kept his eyes fixed steadily on Felix, even as the high priest avoided his gaze.

"I am needed in East Avralaen," Felix said. "I must tend to my flock there and nurture the clerics and chaplains who look to me for guidance."

"Mm, and I am certain it has nothing to do with maintaining your place at the queen's table." Pharun rolled his eyes.

Felix bristled. "You are not the only one with a council seat to consider."

Pharun waved his hand dismissively. "There is no need to get worked up. I am not questioning your integrity."

"No," Felix said, "you are simply suggesting I have none at all."

"I want you by my side. Is that a sin?"

"Serving one's own desires is a sin," Felix said quickly in response. "Abandoning one's vocation for an indulgence is a sin."

Silence rested between them for the duration of a heartbeat.

"So, so," Pharun looked smug, "you admit that you desire to stay with me."

Felix flushed, his bronze skin turning wine red. "I do not know why I bother speaking to you."

"You have had no choice the past twenty-four days," Pharun said, indifferent.

"I have had no choice for the past three years." Felix stroked his talisman harder with his thumb, finding the raised metal engraving somewhat grounding. "You have seen to that much."

"Such a terrible fate you have suffered. I am a wonderful conversationalist." Pharun turned his gaze away from Felix, finally, and toward the passing landscape. The rising sun made the snow-covered country appear bloodstained.

Felix watched his face. "How long has it been since you have seen your father?"

"How old is my brother?" Pharun sucked on his teeth. "Will he not be twenty-three this autumn? It has been almost five years."

"When Shrukian came of age? That was the last time you saw your father?"

"Yes. His name day was an unbearable affair."

"Why did you not return the following year?" Felix tried to remember where he was five years before this moment. He found that he had difficulty remembering anything that occurred in the last five hours.

"There was no point. Besides, I was busy." Pharun crossed his legs primly. "I was anointed in the Temple of Azrael as the divine's chosen for Crowned Priest. I went to the Temple of Saldon after that and spent a year prostrating myself before the altar of my divine father. When I was convinced that I had earned His blessing, I went to East Avralaen."

"Four years in East Avralaen?" Felix stroked his talisman again. "You did not need to entreat Morcant for a blessing for so long."

"There were some distractions," Pharun said, "I am prone to them."

Felix raised his chin, aware of how uncomfortably warm he still was. "I…"

"Besides," Pharun interrupted before he could finish, "High Priest Gwynafor did not want to anoint me. Morcant's blessing or not."

"In light of which, his passing seems auspicious," Felix observed.

"Fortunately, you were there to take his place." A smile danced over Pharun's lips.

"His mantle rests heavily on my shoulders." Felix did not return the smile.

Pharun waved his hand again. "We are nearly there." He abandoned the topic and reached up to straighten his cravat, which had slackened around his throat since their departure from the inn that morning.

"Are you nervous?" Felix asked.

"No," Pharun answered. "Are you?"

"Yes," the high priest admitted. "I fear he will see right through me."

"He will not be paying you any attention, I assure you. He will be far too busy ridiculing me. Besides, my darling Felix, the things he might discover about you would not faze him one jot. He has three absolutely wretched children. By comparison, you should be deified."

"Perhaps you can see to it that I am," Felix said, his anxiety climbing as he felt the coach slow to a more sociable pace.

"Perhaps I will." Pharun tilted his head. "There is no telling what I might do."

PHARUN'S PRESENCE WAS HERALDED by trumpets. Encarz pushed his garnet stickpin into place and then moved his hands so that Lystra's fluttering ones could tug at the lace around his throat and make certain nothing was askew.

"I have servants who dress me," the king pointed out.

"So you do." Lystra pushed herself up on her toes to kiss the king's severe cheek. "I will cease fussing over you."

Encarz held out his arm, waiting for her to take it before starting the long walk down to the front of the palace. Servants clamored all around him, running back and forth from the kitchen to the upstairs to the main hall. Courtiers still in their morning gowns were pressing in from all sides, none too preoccupied with propriety to risk missing a second of the prince's arrival. Encarz felt a stirring sense of irritation, knowing that Pharun was all too happy to create a spectacle.

The entrance doors were thrown open as soon as Encarz approached them. He did not break his stride, gripping Lystra's arm a little tighter as she struggled to match his pace. He swept her out onto the palace steps and then released her from his side, making the rest of the descent by himself. Pharun stepped out of his coach at nearly the same instant, his silver heels clattering against the stone.

Encarz inhaled sharply, coming to a stop only six feet away from his eldest son. Pharun smiled at him, not so much as bending at the waist. The entire present court held its breath as the royals stood, facing each other, neither uttering a word of greeting nor making any gesture of respect.

Finally, Pharun extended his hand. On his thumb was a gold ring bearing an engraving of a dragon. He had three rings in total, but the one on his thumb was an artifact of the god Azrael. Encarz ground his back teeth so sharply that they ached. He reached out to take Pharun's hand, raising it up and bending stiffly so that he might brush his lips against the gold. Pharun's smile widened, and he withdrew his hand, preening visibly before every witness to his holy preeminence.

"Your Grace," Encarz finally greeted him.

"Your Majesty," Pharun returned the etiquette.

"I trust your journey was not an unpleasant one." Encarz watched as a blond man that he did not recognize emerged from the coach. Pharun turned his head when he saw his father's gaze change directions.

"It was not," the prince assured him vaguely. "Allow me to present Felix d'Artion, High Priest of Morcant. He was good enough to accompany me from East Avralaen."

"Quite a long voyage for a single ceremony," Encarz raised an eyebrow. "Surely you intend to remain with us for some time, your eminence?"

"It will be my pleasure to remain here as our new Crowned Priest settles into his position," Felix said, bowing his head to the king.

"Felix has this dreadful notion that I might be in need of some support. I tried to dissuade him, of course, knowing that I will want for nothing now that I have returned home."

Encarz clasped his hands behind his back. It was all he could do to keep from peeling that smug expression off Pharun's face.

"I imagine you are famished," the king said. "Breakfast will be served on the terrace. High Priest Melchiorre has yet to arrive, but High Priest Malhii is already here."

"How delightful." Pharun accepted his walking stick from a footman. "Who else shall be joining us? My sister?"

"Have you missed her at all?" Encarz began to walk.

"No, and I hold no illusion that I am the brother she sits in her window and pines for."

"She does not miss you, but she will be present nonetheless," Encarz said. "If you can tell her something of Shrukian, that will please her."

"Fortunately, I would rather speak on anything else." Pharun glanced up at his sister's window as he passed underneath. He would not put it beyond her to still be abed. If the gods held him in any favor, she would miss the ceremony altogether.

The white marble terrace overlooked the castle gardens of manicured hedges draped in an undisturbed blanket of snow. Pharun missed the roses, for the ground was too cold and their bushes had fallen dormant. Even the winding paths were covered, which made the fountain in the center look as though it had been cut adrift in a sea of clouds. Looking further out, Pharun could see the red shutters of the king's private chapel, the only spot of color aside from the golden snake wrapped around the fountain's base.

Breakfast was a decadent arrangement. There was a carafe of hot coffee waiting to be poured and delicate squares of expensive chocolate to stir into the brew. There were poached quail eggs and airy pastries with crisp, golden crusts. There were apples stewed in spiced Brandywine and candied nuts heaped into a dish, as well as dark pork belly that had been heavily salted and roasted over a flame. Pharun took his seat, and a servant appeared immediately to pick up the carafe and fill his cup. He watched from the corner of his eye as Lystra joined them and took her place by Encarz.

Of all Encarz's wives, she was Pharun's least favorite—possibly because he knew her the best. She always had this soft look in her downturned eyes and a mollifying smile. She liked to mother him.

"It is nice to see you again, Pharun," Lystra said as she tapped her spoon on the peak of a quail egg. "Were the waters calm and the weather fair?"

"Miles of ocean and sky." Pharun picked up his cup and sipped from the thin rim. "Hardly even worth a mention."

"I suppose that is preferable," Lystra mused. "And you were not murdered by Simisolan pirates."

Pharun scoffed softly. "Are there not Simisolans in the castle now?" he asked, directing his question toward his father. "Are you still working out the terms of your treaty?"

Encarz pierced a slice of porky belly with the tip of his knife. "Their Ambassador of Foreign Affairs and their Master of Spies are currently residing within these walls, yes. They have been here for almost a year."

"To listen to you bellyache about your borders?" Pharun lifted an eyebrow. Encarz shot him a look.

"Queen Efemena and I have yet to reach an understanding on the key issues that drive a wedge through our alliance. For instance, the Blest territory."

"Oh, I see. You are both still stuck trying to drive each other's troops off the soil." Pharun popped a candied walnut onto his tongue. "You should let them have it; it is not much. You will find yourself wealthier with Simisola for allies than with a plot of land infested with elves."

"I did not come all the way down here to listen to you talk about politics," a sharp voice interrupted them. Pharun recognized his sister's tone immediately. He sipped from his cup again rather than stand and greet her.

"The Blest territory is as vital as it ever was," Encarz continued as if she had not spoken over them at all.

Olympia sat down near her brother, adjusting the lace of her bodice with her right hand while her left reached across the table and plucked up a pastry. "I hope your chancellor riles up father less than you do."

"Who has said that I am appointing a chancellor?" Pharun asked.

"You will sit and write taxes all day?" Olympia tore off a piece of her pastry. "When would you have time to file your nails?"

"I have no more interest in appointing a chancellor than you have in pinning down a husband," Pharun pointed out mildly.

"My prospects are very slim."

"Every man in Dragoloth would martyr his mother to marry a holy princess."

"Once you take out the old, the ugly, and the dull, they are *very* few." Olympia stirred some chocolate into her coffee. "And once you rule out the witless fops and the dandy young boys who only care for garden duels and poetry."

"Olympia, I very much doubt that you would be able to attract a man of such style." Pharun tapped his nail against the side of his cup.

"I prefer battle scars to lace," she countered. "Just as I prefer the scent of sweat and leather over perfume."

"I will find a suitable man, then," Pharun said, "and you can bed his destrier."

"Baroness Nerissa Ercole has offered up her eldest son as a prospect," Encarz cut in, shutting down the bickering. "And I believe the alliance would be well worth it to bring the Drakkian Province back into the fold."

Pharun sighed. "There you have it, then." He looked at Olympia. "Adriel Ercole has no battle scars."

"Although he is in possession of an unspeakably bad personality," she said disdainfully.

"Ah," Pharun smiled. "Then you will be ideally matched."

"You may as well finish your breakfast," Lystra tried to smooth things over where Encarz could not. "The ceremony is at noon, and I know you will wish to change your clothes."

Pharun's mouth twitched but he nodded, picking up his spoon to dip into his quail egg. "I have a new ruby frock coat for the celebration afterward." He looked at Felix, "perhaps you will dress to match?"

Olympia scoffed before the priest could answer. "Coxcomb."

Pharun kicked her ankle underneath the table. "Shrew."

2

SHRUKIAN

THE DELICATE NAVIGATION OF RIBALD FOREIGN AFFAIRS

MARMALADE SMEARED OVER THE thin blades of breakfast cutlery had been left abandoned amidst half-eaten triangles of toast and porcelain cups of cold tea. Saucers that had been repurposed barbarically as plates were stacked haphazardly atop one another, creating a distinctly inelegant mid-morning tableau and, even though the sun was climbing steadily toward its zenith, Prince Shrukian was still in his housecoat.

"This would be easier," his companion suggested, "if you were also wearing shoes."

"My toes are too bruised. I think it would be easier if I were leading instead."

"You cannot lead if you cannot *Gragetus.*" The young man tightened his arm around Shrukian's waist. "Try the turn again. I will not allow you to fall."

"You nearly broke my back once already," the prince muttered.

"With respect, that is a little dramatic. I have never seen a man break his back from a dip." The young man rotated his heel to lead the prince's body into a turn, carefully keeping his polished shoes out of the way. Shrukian gripped the hand in his and swept his leg out in an inelegant step. It landed awkwardly, but he did not have time to correct it before transitioning into the next movement. His foot came forward, banging against the toe of his companion's shoe.

"Marcellus…!" The prince gripped his companion's gloved hands even tighter. Despite his crushing grasp, the young man did not even flinch.

"That was better than the last time," Marcellus said. "Try that again. Forward, step, good… now back, step-… Part of learning the dance is learning to anticipate my movements."

"You go through great lengths to remain unpredictable," Shrukian countered.

"Yes, but not when it comes to the Vuelzt." Marcellus pulled the prince in once more, pressing his hand against the small of Shrukian's back and leaning in so that their noses nearly touched. "I am going to dip you again."

"Dragoloth declares war on East Avralaen," Shrukian hissed.

"East Avralaen surrenders," Marcellus said smoothly. "Remember to support your weight in your core, or you will fall."

"What will you tell the queen?" The prince's words were nearly cut off when he went back.

"That in dancing I saw what savagery you were capable of. We would fall back. It is a large continent, and your troops would not last long."

"Ten thousand men?"

"You do not have enough ships to transport ten thousand men, let alone keep them supplied well enough to chase us for long." Marcellus finally pulled him up, but did not release his hold.

"Say I bring a thousand," Shrukian shot back.

"A dozen; that is how many are already with you." Marcellus finally relaxed his arms and stepped away. "I thought you were here to secure an alliance."

"I was; I am." Shrukian went back to the table and poured himself a cup of wine from a crystal decanter. "Though I feel as adept in politics as I am in dancing."

"Both take time." Marcellus joined him at the table, picking up the decanter. "If all else fails, it is surprisingly easy to bluff your way out of either."

"You would be the one to know." Shrukian raised his glass to his lips. "How many thousands in gold have you taken Her Majesty for?"

"Nothing that she could not afford." Marcellus' gaze flickered over to the prince as if measuring him carefully. "She favors you already, or she would not have asked you to sit at her table tonight."

"Enough to fund my father's war with Simisola?" Shrukian shook his head. "I will have to give her far more than a dance to acquire that."

"She will never join Dragoloth and East Avralaen in marriage. That is the sort of union that exists only in the throats of bards."

"My father knows that," Shrukian agreed. "He wants better than marriage from my courtship."

"Blackmail?" Marcellus guessed. Shrukian nodded.

"He is using you for your pretty face," the lord said. That was enough, at least, to pull a laugh from the prince.

"It is certainly not for my diplomacy," Shrukian said, amused.

"You have been a soldier for most of your life. Neither soldiers nor young princes have very much use for tact." Marcellus set his cup down. "You came home from fighting your father's holy wars to receive sashes and medals of honor. Even as young as you are, you might have expected some sort of respite after that, marriage and living out the rest of your life as Captain of the King's Guard."

"Something of that kind," Shrukian agreed. When Marcellus spoke of marriage, the prince could only think of his sister. He wondered, always, how Olympia was faring without him. Each of his letters had gone unreturned and without news of anything that might have granted her a change of heart. There had been no summons from his father to attend a royal wedding. "I may still end up captain."

"Or you may end up king," Marcellus said mildly. "Just because you are an extra prince does not mean you will have to spend your remaining days jotting down reports and assigning shifts."

"Pharun would have to..." Shrukian trailed off before finishing that thought, trying to think of a better one. "Pharun has been trying on my father's crown for size since I could walk. When my father passes on to the next life, Azrael keep us, there may very well be a funeral and a coronation on the same day."

"It was only a speculation," Marcellus told him. "I, of course, have little insight."

Shrukian waved his hand. "It is not as though I never considered the possibility. I know my father would prefer me on the throne. Pharun knows it, too. There is no secret. I want to continue my father's legacy and make Dragoloth the greatest dynasty in the world. And you would think that with Pharun becoming *Kren Veisten*, being put in charge of every soul across two continents, it would be power enough." Shrukian drained his cup until he hit the dregs and then tossed them into a little silver bucket beside the table. "I had completely forgotten that he is being confirmed, you know, until just now."

"You have had a lot on your mind," Marcellus offered.

"Yes, but I should have taken the excuse to go home." Shrukian sat down in a chair, leaning forward and resting his hands on his knees.

"It would have been of no use. Your father would have sent you back," Marcellus told him. "And your absence may have allowed for another suitor to captivate the queen."

"Pharun would not have wished to see me regardless." Shrukian sighed and pinched the bridge of his nose. He pushed his fingertips into the corners of his eyes as if he could drive out the encroaching headache by force. "It does no good to dwell. What should I wear tonight?"

"Are you asking me to select your outfit?" Marcellus accepted the change in subject, already stepping toward the prince's wardrobe. "I think yellow satin."

"Bite your tongue," Shrukian grimaced.

"With a pale blue frock coat? You would be very dashing." Even as Marcellus spoke, he selected a deep merlot colored coat. He simply could not resist the tease.

"You will have me looking like a royal parrot. Perhaps *that* would amuse the queen." Shrukian scoffed.

Marcellus chuckled dryly. "If yellow satin could launch a thousand ships, would you bear it?"

"I could, perhaps, bring myself to endure it then," Shrukian said with great reluctance.

"Of course your shoes would have to match."

"I will have you hanged. That *will* amuse her."

"Without a doubt." Marcellus draped an ivory-colored shirt over the back of Shrukian's chair. "Were I you, I would bathe before dressing. You may dance like a barbarian, but you do not have to smell like one."

"Do you think that will put her off?" Shrukian stood to obey. "I thought she had an appreciation for wild men."

"Well, I do not." Marcellus tapped the prince's shoulder.

Shrukian smiled at him. "Very well, very well. As you wish."

E AST AVRALAEN'S PALACE GLIMMERED like a star in the center of a cloudless sky. Spring was smiling upon them and warmed the red cheeks of the musicians whose music flowed from silver balconies, utterly enchanting the guests below. Servants clad in the royal purple and gold livery carried trays of sweet wines and meats, circulating them through the congested crowd while nimbly avoiding squared-off toes and silk-embroidered waistcoats. The palace doors were open wide, emitting an inviting golden glow that enticed the queen's guests inside. Shrukian stood at the threshold, his hands clasped behind his back in a military fashion as his eyes flicked over the crowd. He recognized only a few faces; Marcellus had abandoned him to make his rounds inside, greeting lords and ladies as old friends and working the crowd with natural charm and just enough indifference to be appealing.

Shrukian felt a glass nudge his elbow. He glanced down and caught sight of the queen's gold stater ring, which led to noticing her pale fingers wrapped around the flute and her flame-red hair, coiled up away from her neck and fastened with gold hairpins.

"You seem a thousand miles away," she told him. Shrukian finally turned, reaching out to accept the offered glass.

"There is nowhere I would be in this moment rather than here." He smiled at her. "Your garden is stunning tonight."

"The roses have overtaken it a bit," she said. "I hope that the addition of the Snow Swallow fountain will keep anyone from noticing."

"It is a marvel," Shrukian agreed.

"And it makes seven," the queen gestured proudly. "The Brahntaiste Gryphon, the Death Hand of Morcant, the Painted Fish, the Swordsman, the Rectoress, the Seeking Angels, and now the Snow Swallows. Have you seen it up close?"

"No," Shrukian admitted, "though I would be delighted." He extended his arm, and the queen slipped hers through to rest in the crook of his elbow. Together they descended the palatial steps and crossed the courtyard on stark white pathways. The crowd of courtiers parted down the middle to allow them through. While the gap closed behind them, no one tried to follow.

The fountain gleamed in the center of a cluster of rosebushes, rising above dark leaves and arterial red blooms. Two birds the size of horses had been carved masterfully from the stone, talons and wings entangled with one another. The stone was painted white with accents of gold and soft pink. It must have cost her a fortune. He wondered how many courtiers had turned their pockets inside out to fund the cause and if they thought it had been worth it in the end. Perhaps they never had a choice in deciding.

"It is beautiful," he tried to express proper admiration without becoming repetitious. "Even more so up close."

"It represents us well." She slid her hand down the curve of a wing that was arced in her direction, following the line of feathers down until she touched the throat of the other bird. "We are a monument trapped in brambles and strangled by thorns. Even one crack in the stone would be enough for the whole structure to come tumbling down."

Shrukian reached out and brushed his fingers over the delicate petals of a rose. "Monuments are memories given shape; the bramble bears living blooms. If the stone is being invaded, it is because it is weathered with time."

"Does it then deserve to crumble?" Her tone was sharp.

Shrukian pulled his hand away. "You may erect one structure after another, but you must stand guard as well and prune your bushes. A conscientious queen cannot be a lazy gardener."

Robin gave him a long look. "I have been queen longer than you have been alive, and there are no cracks for Dragoloth to slither into."

"Dragoloth is here offering its hand," Shrukian said to her humbly. "As a friend or as an ally, a ready sword to defend your shores."

"A rose for now." The queen turned her face back to the fountain. "There are other thorns in my side."

"The magus uprising." Shrukian remembered that Marcellus had briefed him on the entire affair, and now he racked his brain for any information that would be helpful to recall.

"Led by Elzbet Riber," the queen spat out the name as though it were poison, "bitter because my father would not extend a royal pardon when she slaughtered her mother and father in their beds."

"She seems to have amassed a large following very quickly," Shrukian said carefully. "Does that give you concern?"

"Only because her followers are the most reckless of her kind. Magi who have fallen out of favor with the crown or who have no formal education to curb their power. Everywhere they go, they leave destruction in their wake. And they have proven near impossible to track."

"It is truly intolerable," Shrukian agreed, trying not to allow for his face to relay that he was losing interest in the conversation. He was thankful for the darkness.

Robin folded her arms. "There are rebels in our Western half that are supplying them with gunpowder. Once they acquire enough pistols and canons to arm those who cannot cast, we will have a real problem on our hands." She let out a breath. "And your father believes he can help."

"In exchange for ships for our war against Simisola."

"Conquering Simisola will more than double his wealth. And he thinks I do not worry about that?"

"He knows better than to challenge the Titan Continent," Shrukian reassured her. "And as Morcant and Azrael were brothers, so are we—ah, so to speak."

That pulled a little bit of a smile from her, though she hid it by rolling her lips inward. "Would you say that makes me something of a sister to you, then?"

Shrukian rubbed the back of his neck, flustered. "If you do not believe that disrupts the manner of our courtship, Your Majesty."

"Of course not," Robin said, "I know how Dragolothian princes value their sisters." She inclined her head at that and turned back to face the party. Properly appalled by her words, Shrukian offered his arm to her once more and together they made their way back to the lights and the clusters of silk-clad bodies.

FOR ELZBET, THERE WAS no moon. It was blotted out by the heavy grey clouds that signaled an oncoming storm. And from the way the wind was making the trees sway above her head, there was not much time before the first raindrops started to fall.

She ducked into her tent and pulled the flaps shut behind her, sweeping the hood of her cloak back and away from her face. Despite having been in one spot for a few weeks, her things were still in complete disarray. She should find the time to organize a few of them–scrolls, battleplans, grimoires–but it seemed pointless knowing everything would be uprooted in a few days. Despite what Ringo said, she knew that Marcellus was getting closer to finding them. *Lord* Marcellus, she scoffed to herself. His ability to keep the queen on a line about the Movement's whereabouts was the only reason he had acquired that title to begin with, the filthy grifter.

They *had* to keep moving. Their numbers and equipment were dwindling. Talented casters had abandoned the cause and been replaced by tramps and rogues who drained the wine casks and incited violence wherever they roosted. Elzbet had been forced to abandon many sympathetic taverns and inns who would have happily taken her in before but were now more concerned over the possibilities of damaged property.

"You need to clean this place up. I do not know how you sleep."

Elzbet looked over her shoulder at Ringo, who had entered the tent without even bothering to announce his presence. She started tugging on the strings of her leather tunic, allowing it to relax enough so that she could breathe unhindered.

"Not everyone is afflicted by your particular malady," she snorted. "They can stand a little disorder."

"A little is one thing." Ringo picked his way across the room and grasped the laces of her tunic, pulling them loose with a jerk of his strong hands.

Elzbet gasped. "I thought you were on watch tonight."

"Something interesting tapped on the inside of my globe," Ringo talked over her. "Do you want to guess at what it was?"

"You have dropped it so many times. It is cracked, it is clouded... Whatever you saw is likely not to be trusted."

"I saw Marcellus' banner," Ringo said, "the black rose. It was tattered and limp."

"I see," Elzbet said, trying to step forward and pull herself away from him. "So?"

He kept a tight grip on her laces. "It means our victory is assured. Let him find us. If we fight, we will win."

"No." She dug her nails into his scarred hands until he pulled them away, and then she sprang forward, ripping off her leather tunic and tossing it onto the floor. "If we fight, we will lose everything—including our lives."

"If we fight together, we are more powerful than he is," Ringo insisted. "He has seen displays of our power over and over again. That is why he maintains his distance."

"He killed our best caster, if you recall—and that woman taught him everything she knew."

"I am not going to run again," Ringo said darkly. "And neither are you. I have already lifted some of the wards that were redirecting his eye."

"You are insane!" Elzbet snapped.

"I will continue to peel back the wards," Ringo belligerently held her gaze as he spoke, "until there is nothing left. And if we are found, we will be prepared."

"Prepared?" She made a broad, exasperated gesture. "He will bring an army, Ringo—or did you think he would come alone? We do not have enough pistols and rapiers to fend off the queen's soldiers!"

"When Marcellus falls, the men will withdraw." Ringo took another step toward her. "You are not focusing."

"I have no interest in being slaughtered." Elzbet picked up a heavy tome, gripping it by the spine as a ready weapon to hurl at his head. "How many days has it been since you slept?"

His lip curled. "What does that have to do with anything?"

"You are out of your mind. Get out of my tent."

"It has been three days."

"I thought as much. You have been snorting so much Glow up your nose that it is eating away your brain."

Ringo aimed a sharp kick at a stack of books. They went tumbling, several of them landing spine-up with the papers jammed.

"I feel you are not taking me seriously." Crackling threads of lightning jumped between his fingertips, giving off a sulfuric odor. Elzbet did not move, still gripping the tome.

"You are unreasonably paranoid," she said. "Go to sleep. Nothing can be done tonight. We will talk rationally in the morning."

Ringo glowered at her for a long moment, his sharp blue eyes offset by the ugly purple scar that sliced open his face. He did not have anything else to say, but the pulses of electricity jumping over his palms died down. He turned away from her, kicking the stack he had already knocked over on his way to the entrance.

When he had gone, Elzbet finally allowed herself to breathe. She lowered her hand and dropped the tome to the floor. She had known Ringo just long enough to know when he was dangerous. Three days without sleep and strung out on drugs was not the worst he had ever been. If he heeded her and slept tonight, he would be somewhat reasonable in the morning.

Elzbet raked her fingers through her thick black hair and walked to the furthermost corner of her tent. She kept her bed roll there along with her writing desk and a small icon of Morcant. The incense bowl was still smoldering from where she had left it burning earlier, weak tendrils of smoke eking out from the holes. She made a mental note to re-light it.

The last thing she had managed to wedge into the corner was a tall wood-and-brass stand. A dark green cloth had been thrown over the top, which she pinched up and pulled away, taking care not to disturb what it was protecting.

What little light there was in her tent was sucked into the mirror-like surface of a large, black orb. Its power thrummed in the air, palpable and heavy, enough that Elzbet felt it throb against the back of her neck and the base of her spine. Being in its presence was like trying to breathe underwater, or like having weights stacked on your chest. Of all who had ever sought to attune to the orb, Elzbet was the only one who could stand before it without crumpling.

She set her hands on the sides. Despite the warm, stormy air, the obsidian was cool. She felt it hum as she explored the smooth surface, her hands gliding over the familiar shape. She closed her eyes and tried for a deep breath, feeling it catch in her chest and leading to a shallow exhale. She was already getting a little dizzy, but her focus shifted to the feeling of phantom fingers crawling up the back of her skull.

"I need to see Marcellus," she whispered aloud. She knew it was a risk, but with Ringo tearing down every defense, she needed to know how much danger they were in. She felt the ground sway underneath her feet, and she flattened her hands against the sides of the orb, holding on in a desperate bid to keep her balance. Her palms felt like they were being scorched, but she did not dare let go. She opened her eyes and was greeted by inky darkness, which lasted only a second before it was broken apart by a spill of moonlight. She saw a canopy of stars and a bright, indifferent moon. The stars turned into lights and became a thousand lanterns. Her view plunged downward, a tilt which nearly sent her plummeting into the stand. She saw the queen's magnificent courtyard and its shapely hedges, its opulent fountains. Dozens of shapes were coming into view, cinched waists and full silk skirts, bare arms and shoulders decorated with glittering jewels. She saw men standing straight with gleaming rapiers by their sides, showy pieces that were not meant for any real combat, with lace cuffs that draped over their knuckles and satin cravats that stuck out from the collars of their frock coats. Elzbet pressed her vision to take her further, seeking one familiar face out in the midst of so many false smiles and glazed-over eyes.

When she finally caught sight of him, it was like running into a wall. If she had been standing before him, she would have been within touching distance, but the vision would not allow her to press any closer. He stood apart from the crowd with his dark hair pulled back, one hand wrapped around a wine glass, the other resting against the jeweled brooch at his throat. Just looking at his face was enough to remind her that she could not breathe. Elzbet tried again to consciously inhale, but her chest ached with the effort, and she could only manage another shallow breath. Marcellus looked like he was carved out of marble, standing perfectly still with half his face cast in shadow.

The ghostly fingers at the back of Elzbet's head suddenly tightened their grip. Pain gripped her chest like her ribs were being forced apart. She ground her teeth to fight back a scream, unsure of how deep the orb had pulled her, whether a sound or a word would be enough to capture the attention of her adversary.

The pressure in her head was enough to make her feel like her skull was being split open. Elzbet felt blood pouring from her nose, running down her mouth so that she could taste copper. She tried to pull her hands away from the orb, but they were stuck fast, and they burned. Panic seized her heart and she cried out, trembling from pain and exertion. At the sound of her voice, Marcellus turned his head, and Elzbet's screams died in her throat. She felt frozen in that gaze, the same deep green as tourmaline. It was as if her heart was being cradled in the palm of his hand, and his fingers were tightening like iron bands around the beating organ.

Marcellus' lips parted. Elzbet strained to hear his words, but none came out. Instead she saw black feathery legs crawl over his lips, followed by a large white body like raw cotton. His mouth opened wider, and the silky green wings of a moth sprang free. Elzbet shrieked, more startled than anything, as the giant moth brushed its wings against her cheek and then began to glide upward. She felt pain ram through her heart like a tent spike, and there was enough force to make her convulse. More blood gushed from her nose, and she tried again to rip her hands away from the orb. This time, she was successful. Her hands were red and raw in places where it looked like they had been burned. She had enough sense left to throw the green cloth back over the orb before curling her injured hands toward her chest and sinking to the floor. She let out a heaving sob, the most she could manage while the pain in her chest and the blood running down the back of her throat made it difficult to breathe.

Elzbet's ears were ringing, a high-pitched keening sound that felt like a needle being pushed through the drums. She drew up her knees to rest her forehead against them, trying to scrub the image of Marcellus from her brain. Like a wine stain, he was difficult to get out. All she could see were those sinister green eyes and the malicious little curl of his lip when the moth came out.

He knew where they were. He had to know. There was no time left to waste.

3

PHARUN

The Utterance of Heresy with a Closed Mouth

FELIX RAPPED HIS KNUCKLES against the door of the room where he thought Pharun might be. He had been wrong two doors down, but he was convinced that he had the correct one now. He was dressed in his clerical robes: blue, white, and gold to honor Morcant. His ornate mantle felt heavy on his shoulders, but he was grateful for it in the viciously dry, freezing Dragolothian air. His sandy-blond hair had been pulled back away from his face and tied off with a blue ribbon, while his matching facial hair had been carefully trimmed and glistened with perfumed oil. He carried his wide-brimmed hat in his hands, unsure whether it was polite to wear it indoors or not. At least it gave him something to fiddle with nervously as he went around skirting people he had never met and avoiding asking for directions at all costs.

He heard the doorknob turn and he stepped back, taking a deep breath while preparing a very good explanation as to why he was late. To his dismay, the man who stood in the doorframe was not the Crowned Priest to-be.

Felix immediately dipped a bow and began to back away. "Your forgiveness," he muttered, turning his hat in his hands while resisting the urge to set it on his head and pull it down over his eyes. The man in the doorway regarded him with icy blue eyes—so light they were nearly colorless—and gestured for Felix to come back toward him.

"You look lost," the man said. He had the thickest Southern Dragolothian accent that Felix had ever heard.

"I am," Felix readily admitted. "I am looking for..." he trailed off, searching his brain for the appropriate title, "His eminence, Pharun Mahtrador."

The man raised a heavy red eyebrow. "You are close. He is a little further down." He smiled, although it did not seem to go all the way up to his eyes. "I am Baron Meridith Traske."

"Felix d'Artion, High Priest of Morcant." He was still having difficulty wrapping his head around that fact.

Meridith inclined his head. "An honor it is then, your eminence." He stepped into the hall, pulling his bedroom door shut behind him. "May I escort you the rest of the way?"

"If you will." Felix glanced down the hallway. "I have embarrassed myself enough already."

"There is no shame. This is a foreign land, and these halls can be quite treacherous." Meridith started his walk, clasping his hands behind his back as Felix fell into step beside him. "I lost my way in them quite often when I was a boy."

"You grew up here?" Felix nearly halted. He was not certain on where he stood with entangling himself further in royals without Pharun being present.

"No, but I spent a great deal of my time here. Pharun and I—we were close in age, and the stories that I could tell you..." He chuckled under his breath, but the corners of his mouth turned down after the fact. "For him to return from such a long absence bearing the title of *Kren Veisten*... it hardly seems real. I have barely had a glimpse of him since he arrived. He seems different. Serious."

"Is he not always?" Felix tried to picture Pharun smiling in any way that was not malicious and found he could not do it.

"Well," Meredith considered, "he was never a jubilant person, but he did have a sort of... levity about his soul."

"As all children do," Felix said, "until innocence is torn away."

"That is true enough, I suppose," Meridith agreed. "And I do not know much about what his life was like when he went to study under Malhii."

Felix knew. There had been many nights where Pharun had woken up in a sweat and found his way into Felix's room, where he would pace and shiver with his sapphire eyes wide and his pale blue-grey hands shaking. Pharun had spent hours muttering words that Felix could only half understand, the other half being in a language that was beyond his learning. Only wine could settle him once the nightmares began and, when he was deep in his drink, he recounted every detail. Felix knew the horror of Azrael's temple and far more about High Priest Malhii's proclivities than he ever wished.

"I could not know," was what Felix said rather than divulge the things that had been confided in him.

The temperature in the hallway felt like it dropped. Felix reached up to touch the holy symbol resting against his chest, although it was largely a reflex. He knew by now how to tell that Pharun was following him. He was not startled when he felt a hand slide down the slope of his shoulder, but it still made his blood run cold.

"I imagine that you are looking for me," Pharun's voice came before the rest of him appeared in Felix's peripheral vision.

"Always," Felix said, drawing himself up straight. "My lord was kind enough to guide me through."

"Poor Felix. You do seem to have a talent for getting lost." Pharun withdrew his hand, looking Meridith up and down and smiling without sincerity. "Cousin."

"Are those all of the words that you have for me?" Meridith opened his arms for an embrace.

Pharun considered, not moving any closer. "I never thought I would see you with a beard."

Meridith reached up to touch his chin. "There was not much I could do for prevention."

"I believe that it suits you, even if you do look like your father." Pharun raised his chin. "May his soul be at peace."

A complicated look flashed across Meridith's face. "I suppose that it is."

"Azrael will have welcomed him through the Unbroken Arch, if for no other reason than to spite anyone else who would rather him not see Firmament."

"If you are trying to be comforting," Meridith snapped, "you are unsuccessful."

"You seem very broken up about the subject." Pharun trailed his long, pointed nails through the air.

"For all my father was—"

"A bellowing drunkard, from what I recall." Pharun lifted a silver brow. "Nothing you can say about his passing will ever fix your nose, for as many times as it was broken."

Meridith took a deep breath as if he considered saying something equally as devastating but then decided against it. "We should speak on other matters."

"Do you feel the years divide us?" Pharun glossed over Meridith's words entirely. "I have a few scars of my own now. I could show you."

Felix pressed his thumb against the engraving of his holy symbol until it started to hurt. "Your eminence," he said, trying to bring Pharun back around to the present, "we should make our way down."

For a moment, the tension could have been cut like a wire pulled tight between the cousins' chests. When it passed, Pharun relented, and Felix felt like he could breathe—although he was unsure of the reason for his relief.

"Of course," Pharun said. He made another idle gesture. "Accompany us, Meridith. Are you not happy for me? Are you not staggered by my accomplishments?"

Meridith cleared his throat but did not make a comment. He fell into step between his cousin and the priest. "I have it on good authority that you will be appointing a chancellor to sit on your father's council in your stead."

"Your authority is middling at best," Pharun retorted.

"You have me, if you want me," Meridith did not miss a beat. "The Traske Barony is not a paltry slice of countryside to have in your corner."

"Want you, cousin?" That was all that Pharun had to say.

THE LAST TIME LYSTRA had seen the palace decorated so extravagantly, it had been her wedding day. The royal treasury was undoubtedly hurting, but Encarz was not going to turn his nose up at a chance to flaunt the family laurels, even those of a disfavored son. Many courtiers in attendance she recognized, and there were just as many she did not know. She liked the wine, however, and stayed close to where it was being served.

She wanted to be by Encarz's side. Dragolothian kings did not flaunt their wives, and she knew she would only be in the way. That did not stop her from following his steps with a watchful gaze: soft, affectionate, and alert. There were guards posted anywhere they would fit on the parapets and in every stone corner. There was nothing she could do that they could not. That did not stop her from scrutinizing her king's every interaction. Poison from a needle would kill him faster than a rapier, and it could happen as quickly as a brush of hands.

Lystra's nose itched with the strong smell of sandalwood. She rubbed the tip with her gloved finger, and the motion was enough to distract her from the person who suddenly appeared by her side. Nkiru's movements were silent. Had she not been wearing the perfume, the queen would not have noticed her at all. Lystra suspected that such a strong application was purposeful for the Spider to make her presence known. Even the muted blue silk she wore blended seamlessly in with her surroundings, flowing soundlessly with every motion of her long, graceful limbs.

Lystra lowered her hand and nodded toward the Spider, who met her gaze with round eyes the same color as a bloody cut of meat.

"He embodies the dragon in every part," Lystra said, referring to her husband. "You can see power in his stride."

"Your dragon has feathers in its teeth," Nkiru replied, her eyes darting toward where Pharun was standing several feet away.

"I would rather he wear that feather in his cap," Lystra sighed softly. "I want Encarz to be proud of his sons. Both of them."

Nkiru's inscrutable expression did not move. "He never will be."

Lystra felt a sudden knot in her throat that she could not explain. "Is it all kings who hold such hatred in their hearts?"

"Simisola does not have kings." Nkiru folded her arms. "I could not tell you."

"Of course," Lystra breathed. "That was a bad question." She turned again to look at the Spider. "You do have men, don't you?"

"No." It was impossible to tell whether Nkiru was joking.

Lystra thought about asking whether that was true, but she did not want to seem dull-witted. There were countless rumors that Simisola was a country entirely populated by women. She could not imagine how such a place would thrive, but she had also never been, so she could not say differently.

"He has a gift for hating." Lystra shook her head. "I have seen his love. Now and again, he will turn his face toward mine, and it is like looking into the sun. He can be radiant—divine in his own right—but then it goes cold in an instant. He keeps the world at a distance, and he pushes me back as well. I feel lost in the crowd sometimes, just another of his courtiers. Perhaps I want for Pharun what I want for myself: just a little warmth every now and again. If he can estrange his own child so successfully, how long before I share the same fate?"

Nkiru looked like she did not want to say anything, but the queen's distress was clearly having its effect on her. She reached up with one dark hand and set it on Lystra's shoulder. "In Simisolan legend," Nkiru began, "the goddess Anais cut off her husband's head and boiled it in spices when he no longer served her purpose. He gave her one hundred children before that."

"I do not want one hundred children." A shiver ran up Lystra's spine. "And I do not want to eat my husband's head."

"She did not eat it." Nkiru turned her eyes back toward the mingling crowd. "She fed it to her dogs."

"Oh." Lystra was starting to feel a little dizzy. She picked up a glass of wine from a passing servant's tray and offered some to Nkiru, who declined with a raised hand.

"It is a beautiful day to find peace." Nkiru tilted her face upward so that the sun made her skin shimmer with a golden undertone. "Anais has hands for welcome, love, and peace as much as war, death, and renewal."

"I have made peace in Azrael," Lystra said. She felt Nkiru's words in her stomach, but she could not pinpoint why exactly they made her feel so uneasy. "When my time comes, I will pass through the Unbroken Arch and find myself exalted in His presence."

Nkiru's eyes flitted up and down, as if she were considering saying something to the queen and held it back instead. "If, when you take your last breath, you utter her name, it will be the same as if you had spent a lifetime devoted to her worship." She pulled her maroon wool cloak up over her shoulder, fingers trailing down the fur trim. "*Quaaheyri.*"

With her final word, the Spider was gone. Lystra could not see even a trace of her disappearance in the crowd.

The queen drained her wine glass and set it down to be whisked away. She had lost track of her husband as well, and now she felt somewhat lost in the sea of elegance. For the countless dinners and ballrooms she had graced, socializing did not seem to get any easier.

She could see Pharun across the courtyard with his blond priest glued to his side. Meridith was with him also, the young Traske baron standing tall and slightly awkward beside his peacock of a cousin. It was strange to see them like this. She remembered a young Pharun who worshipped his red-haired cousin and was ever following him around at his heels. When the Traske family came to visit, Meridith would sleep in Pharun's room. Not even a dedicated nursemaid could keep the boys from talking all night long, trading stories from underneath their blankets by the fireplace. Now, they hardly spoke the same language.

The beautiful pair of glass doors that led out into the courtyard had already been opened. A painted marble elephant had been set in front of each to keep them from closing again. Lystra walked between them, feeling a rush of relief as the palace walls acted as an immediate barrier between her and the cold air. The walls of the ballroom were lined with mirrors, making it appear four times its actual size, and they reflected the light that flooded in from the doors and tall windows. Lystra found it easier to skirt the crowd indoors, only feeling like she was able to breathe again when she had emerged from the other side and stepped in the empty hallway. It was not as bright, but she was grateful for the reprieve. She placed her hand against one of the cool stone columns and leaned against it, her fingers following the lines of its fluted sides.

"It is a joyous day in Firmament, Your Majesty."

She did not recognize the voice. Lystra raised her head to try and pinpoint its direction, her eyes scanning the empty space in front of her. "The Holy Trinity is united under its first *Kren Veisten* in almost a thousand years," she acknowledged. "All creatures celestial, infernal, and natural have reason to rejoice."

"So, so."

Where there had been no one standing before, she caught sight of a man. He was standing in a scattered pattern of light cast from the dark stained glass behind his head. Though his skin was washed in a deep wine color from the glass, she could make out bright red curls that spiraled down around his shoulders and eyes the color of priceless cinnamon. His eyes trapped the light in such a way that they seemed to glow as if illuminated from behind by a lantern flame.

"I must ask your pardon," she said, drawing from her wells of ingrained politeness. "It is nearly impossible to know every courtier by name."

He tilted his head. From the frothy lace spilling down his throat to the brocade shoes with neat golden heels and pale pink bows, he looked the part of a courtier. But from the way he smiled at her, there was something distinctly inhuman. *Feral* would have been a good word.

"I came with something for you," he said. As he spoke, he unpinned a delicate gold chain from his vest and slid his fingers down the length. At the end dangled an ornate mirror—no wider than his palm, with green glass so dark it was nearly black. He held it aloft, and it spun on the end of its chain, teasing her with flashes of bright light and glimpses of her own reflection.

She wanted it. She did not know why. Lystra held out her hand, unable to pull her eyes away from the treasure, expecting him to just place it in her hands.

The man did not stop smiling and did not move to bring the mirror any closer. Lystra felt frustration squeeze her chest.

"What is it?" She took an uncertain step closer.

"Eternal," he answered, "more or less."

"It is alluring," she said, stopping before she could close the distance between them.

"Always," he said, "and you could not grab it if you wanted to."

She cut her eyes at him. "It seems tangible enough."

"By all means, then." He held out the mirror a little further. "You can take it."

Lystra swallowed hard. She reached out again for the mirror, her fingers brushing the gilded edge. It swayed at her touch, and she felt emboldened by the knowledge that it was, indeed, tangible.

"Who are you?" she asked again. He let the chain slither down around his fingers, dropping the mirror into her hand. It hit the center of her palm like a hot coal, and she yelped. She tried to drop the object, but he seized her hand, closing her fingers around it.

"I am a *what*," he said, his voice dropping an octave as his eyes met hers. He ripped the mirror from her hand then, leaving behind an ugly dark burn. "And you will want to hold my hand."

"Why?" Her voice cracked with pain. Her head was spinning, but she felt rooted to her place.

"It is a long way down." He held up the mirror again, and it spun on the end of its chain. Lystra caught every flash of light that glinted off the surface, each one getting brighter and brighter until it consumed her vision. Three in a row, brighter, brighter—and then darkness, snapping down like the jaws of a dragon.

The world was cold, and she was falling.

"**Y**OUR MAJESTY," THE SERVANT'S voice was shaking.

Encarz did not turn his head immediately, rather he waited for the lord across from him to end his long-winded account of the duel that had taken place in the middle of his garden party the week before. Only when the lord had finished did the king turn to acknowledge the servant, who immediately dropped into a deep bow.

"What is it?" Encarz asked.

"Forgive me, Your Majesty," the servant boy said, clasping his hands in front of him. "It is urgent. The queen…" He did not sound like he could complete his thought. The words died on his tongue.

"What about the queen?" Encarz gripped his glass tightly, practicing every ounce of restraint he had in not smashing it against the boy's skull. "Spit it out."

"You have to come see!" the boy cried out, backing away a few paces before making an urgent gesture. "Queen Lystra, she—I was bringing up a tray from the kitchen, and she…"

Encarz lost all patience. He flung his cup down and made quick strides toward the palace, turning several curious heads with his visible fury. The servant scrambled after him, keeping a fair distance to mitigate the risk of being struck. A few courtiers began to follow as well, keeping an even further distance from the king.

The only person who dared fall into silent stride beside his majesty was Pharun, and they did not so much as exchange a glance.

A crowd was starting to gather in the hallway. Encarz ground his back teeth, a snarl rising from the base of his throat. "Move!" The crowd broke like water against a stone and drew back against the walls. When the flurry died down, all that was left was Queen Lystra, lying on the ground with her head twisted so far back that her contorted face could be seen even though she was lying on her stomach.

Pharun watched his father's face carefully. He watched as the king went down on one knee and reached out to touch the corpse in front of him. The state of the queen's body was repulsive; it was vile. The position of her head, the necrotic state of her hands, the smell—as if she had been dead for weeks--was overpowering. It all reeked of black magic. The prince remained standing, grateful for the sachet of lavender sewn into his sleeve that kept him from gagging on the stench. Encarz's expression did not move. Pharun had to wonder how much of that was kingly decorum, and how much of that was a true lack of anything resembling feeling.

"I want the castle purged," Encarz finally spoke, and in a voice so low it could hardly be heard.

"It will be," Pharun assured him. There was no point in stating the obvious. Whatever mage or creature had done this was long gone. Whatever poor soul paid the price, from the kitchens to the ballroom, would not be the assassin.

Yet someone would pay so that the public mind could rest at ease. Pharun already had an idea of who that scapegoat might be.

"I will call the undertaker." Pharun extended a hand, bidding his royal father rise. "A king should never kneel, not even for grief."

Encarz looked up at his eldest son. For a moment, the king's purple eyes were only filled with that silent, dark rage that Pharun was so familiar with. Then he blinked, and the rage had dissipated, replaced by armor.

"I can stand well enough," Encarz said, "without a priest to hold my hand." Even as he spoke, he rose, pressing his hand against the floor to lift himself up rather than take Pharun's hand. "Send word to the palace guard. I want every entrance sealed; I want every head accounted for. Servants, slaves, and courtiers—I will hold none above suspicion."

"It will make for a long night, my liege," Pharun said, "and will be such a disruption to your guests."

"I feel as though this," Encarz gestured sourly to the queen's body on the floor, "was disruption already."

"Exactly so," Pharun said. "It would be unseemly to allow further disturbance." He took a moment to allow Encarz some thought and then continued. "Allow me an hour to consult with the gods. Such a grievous offense on a day meant to honor their Crowned Priest and bring glory to Firmament and Inferno? Surely they will feel inclined to generosity toward me if I ask for their aid in naming the assassin."

Encarz liked that idea less. He drew in his lips for a moment and considered, rubbing his fingertips together in thought.

"You have one hour," he finally relented. "You may burn your incense and make your case to the Most High. If they do not see fit to humor your pleas, then we will do things my way. In the meantime, no one will leave this castle."

"A fair exchange." Pharun swept a curt bow. "One hour." He turned away from the king and traveled back down the hallway, glad to leave the foul odor behind.

FELIX HAD BEEN LEFT lingering on the edge of the courtyard. Meridith Traske had not moved, either, but neither had much to say to each other since watching Encarz storm into the palace and since Pharun had removed himself to join him. Nearly half an hour passed before anything happened.

Pharun was the first to emerge, shedding his holy robes and flinging them over a curved banister. His coat came next, peeled effortlessly from his shoulders and thrown at the nearest servant, who dropped a tray of cakes to catch it. He beckoned for Felix to follow him as he passed, and the high priest did not think twice.

The chapel on the palace grounds was a decent distance from the courtyard. It was big enough to accommodate only three or four people and stayed nestled in a grove of weeping cypress trees. Even though it was clearly a chapel dedicated to Azrael, Felix felt a twinge of peace as soon as he stepped foot on the consecrated ground. He appreciated the well-maintained flowers and rose bushes that lined the short walkway up to the door. He admired the dark, oiled wooden beams and the golden icon that rested on the roof's peak. Pharun pressed his fingers against his forehead and drew a serpent pattern, reverence to Saldon before he grasped the handle and let himself inside.

Felix followed suit. He placed his hand against his chest and then drew it up to his lips in devotion before stepping over the threshold. There were no benches for prayer as there were in larger temples, but there were two velvet pillows by the altar with impressions left behind by royal knees. Atop the altar, there was a bowl of smoldering incense and a series of golden candles, some of which still burned and some that had put themselves out hours before. Another icon, black marble with painted gold attributes, rested sternly in the center of it all.

Pharun made a face and *tsked* his tongue, bringing up his hand and flicking his fingers toward the door. It was not necessary, but he liked the dramatics. The door pulled itself shut and Felix heard the handle jam.

"What has happened?" Felix asked. He brought his hands around to rest, his thumbs and forefingers touching lightly as he kept his posture relaxed, non-threatening.

"Queen Lystra is dead," Pharun said.

Felix made another reverent gesture. "May Morcant guide her peacefully over the River Balam."

"I am not so certain she is Morcant's problem." Pharun turned toward the altar, studying the curls of white smoke that rose from the incense bowl. "Or Azrael's, for that matter. I saw the state of her body. It was hideous."

"Something you have seen before?" Felix could all but see the cogs turning in Pharun's brain, but that was an impossible knot to tease apart.

"She reeked of sulfur."

"Demons?" Felix felt a chill.

"Perhaps." The tips of Pharun's pointed nails slid back and forth over his thumb. "I will have to pray about it, but not now. Encarz is going to try and turn this around on the Simisolans."

Felix's cornflower blue eyes widened. "His guests? Those are trade routes that he surely does not wish to shut down."

"He has been trying to start a war since the beginning." Pharun turned all his focus onto Felix, as if the answer was sitting behind the high priest's hardly composed expression. "Queen Efemena's Spider and her Ambassador are both here. It is a violent storm in the making, and..." He paused, trailing his fingers through the air as if trying to collect all of his thoughts at once. "That is not suitable for my purposes."

"Your purposes...?"

"He is not interested in the truth, and he cannot be allowed to point fingers on his own. Another likely cause would be an assassin. The Ercoles are the obvious choice, but that is another relationship I do not wish to fracture so soon."

"Your brother has been courting Queen Robin Brahntaiste," Felix reminded him. "Perhaps—"

Pharun held up a hand to cut Felix off. "When we had just docked, and we had to stay at that dreadful inn. What was that gentleman at the bar saying… he was going on about firearms?"

Felix nodded. "He said that a group of Avralaenians was causing a stir, penetrating Dragoloth's underground to try and sell weapons. They bring them over on a boat, he… did not know what it was called, but it was something like the *Daydream.*" The words that the bartender and local patrons had to say about Avralaenians had not been so kind, but Felix graciously left that part out.

"We can use that, then," Pharun said decisively. "If Robin Brahntaiste can even be implicated in having a hand in Lystra's assassination, then Encarz will be forced to draw back his efforts in courting her for the time being. With her guns on our shores, and Dragoloth's queen dead, war will be inevitable."

"East Avralaen is already fighting a war," Felix felt the need to remind him. "The civil unrest with the magus uprising already has her on edge."

"So she will be fighting war on two fronts, which is going to be exactly what I need." Pharun took a deep breath. "I am glad we could talk. You always have such valuable insight."

Felix lowered his gaze. He was not sure if, from barely a few feet away, Pharun could still sense his racing heart. East Avralaen was his home, and Felix felt that, by virtue of existing in the same room as this man, he was betraying his queen and country.

He knew that Pharun liked it that way, whether it was just because he liked seeing Felix squirm or because he wanted to test his loyalties.

Because his eyes were downcast, he did not see Pharun approach him. Rather he felt fingertips brush against his face and pointed nails slide down the line of his jaw until they were pressed against the soft flesh underneath his chin. Felix lifted his face with the prompt, his soft blue eyes locking with Pharun's bright sapphires.

The blond priest's lips parted nervously, a neat dark line forming the opening between the mounds of shell pink skin. Pharun brought up his thumb to stroke across the bottom lip, the supple flesh easily pulled.

"You always go quiet," the Crowned Priest remarked, "whenever you have something to say."

"Nothing, your eminence," Felix vowed, his words skating out on a shivering breath.

"It cannot be easy choosing between your cloth and your queen." Pharun made his voice sympathetic as he continued to stroke his thumb over Felix's lip.

The blond priest swallowed. "The choice, for me, is clear. I gave my life to my calling. Her Majesty acquiesces to the church, and not the other way around."

"I fear it shall not always be so cut and dry for you." Pharun pressed his nails into Felix's chin to raise his head up a little higher. "I trust you. Did you know?"

"I will always strive to be worthy of such trust." Felix wanted to pull his face away and break the eye contact, but Pharun's nails kept him well-pinned. After a few more moments, the Crowned Priest slid them away, and Felix's chin dropped. He released a breath he did not realize he had been holding.

"We should return," Felix muttered. "The hour is nearly past."

"That it is, and I do not trust my father to give allowance for a minute later than he allowed." Even as he spoke, Pharun was making his way toward the chapel door. "*Dormez Salvut.* May Saldon be with us both."

"*Dormez Salvut,*" Felix echoed as he made the sign of Morcant yet again. Although this time, he was not sure why.

4

FLORINDEL

The Exacting Devoir of the Master of the House

"Y**OU SEEM A LITTLE** rushed." Tybalt, who was in no such frenzy, leaned back in his chair until it was balanced on two legs.

"There is a large function at the palace," Florindel said, keeping his mirror carefully balanced on one knee as he used both of his hands to braid his long flaxen hair. "My guess is that we will have double our usual clientele tonight, perhaps even more."

"And an influx of foreign coin," Tybalt added. "I can make those exchanges for you."

Florindel's reflection gave the arms-dealer a look. "I said that you could stay the night; I did not say you could show your face. You sully the ambience."

Tybalt rested a hand against his hairy chest while tipping the last of his mead into his mouth. "I would never dare step foot past your kitchen door. Not that I would need to just to slip your bookkeeper some coin."

Florindel pursed his lips. He tied off the end of his braid with a red ribbon and leaned forward to make certain that the rouge on his cheeks and lips had not disappeared. "I thought that you had a meeting with the Black Rose Company."

"I did. I do. Are you telling me to go?" Tybalt set his cup down on the table in front of him and straightened his posture.

"I am simply passing on the reminder that you have somewhere you ought to be." Florindel grabbed the side of his mirror and brought it closer to his face. "Besides, I hear that Amnas does not like being kept waiting."

"He does not," Tybalt confirmed, "but he also answers to me, and I always take my time."

"Certainly," Florindel set his mirror down at last and picked up a pile of golden rings sitting on the table, slipping them one-by-one onto his slender fingers.

"Is Quin working tonight?" Tybalt shifted the subject.

"Tarquin is, yes." Florindel stood, sweeping his hand across the table to make sure he had not missed anything before picking up his mirror.

"I want to be his last client." The arms-dealer dropped his hand down to the purse on his belt—which was not his real purse, but it carried enough gold.

"If you buy him out, perhaps," Florindel said, resting his hand on his hip.

Tybalt huffed through his nose. "I will come back long after the doors are closed."

"Yes, I know. I have also been paying attention to my logbook. You spend the night with him every time you come into town."

Tybalt's smile was a little faded. "Is it against the rules to choose favorites?"

"No, but I am going to discourage you from getting too attached." Florindel did not hesitate. "In another year or two, I will have to cull him from circulation."

Tybalt did not flinch, despite feeling like the bottom of his stomach dropped out. "If I buy him out, what will he do with himself all evening? The other boys will make twice as much coin tending to your foreign lords."

"It is at your discretion." Florindel tilted his head just a little. Tybalt had never met anyone else who could look so profanely submissive and yet exude such a dominant presence.

He gripped his purse a little tighter, feeling the lumps of coins through the leather. "You are a hard man."

"You are harder," Florindel said.

Tybalt could not help but laugh. He bit back his frustration, releasing his purse and letting the laugh fade into a weary chuckle. Far be it from him to impede anyone's earnings, despite his inability to get those soft grey curls out of his mind. "Well," he lifted his hands to signal his defeat, "I will not interfere with his profit. Although my offer stands regarding your foreign monies."

"I will have Franciscus connect with you in the morning," Florindel said, nodding. "If any coins need be exchanged, it may as well all be done at once."

"Of course." Tybalt extended his hand. Florindel rested his light fingers against the arms-dealer's palm, and Tybalt smiled, pressing his lips against the brothel master's dainty knuckles. "You are a king amongst our kind."

"Flattery only gets you most of the way," Florindel said, although he returned Tybalt's smile.

"The day I go *all* the way with you, Master Florindel, is the day I see Firmament—for I will have died and gone to paradise." Tybalt winked as he pulled his hand away. "If Balshett denies me the privilege of your beautiful face for the rest of the evening, I hope to see you in the morning before I am off."

"I will see you off perhaps," Florindel said. "We will see how you behave." With a twitch of his translucent wings, the sylphestine brothel master turned away and left the kitchen. Tybalt watched him depart before making his exit the opposite way through a silent wooden door that emptied out into a narrow alley.

T HE BLACK ROSE COMPANY had its origins in Western Avralaen, which was how Tybalt had come to know them in the first place. Like him, they had expanded overseas, although they had a great deal more money to show. The business used to be all street drugs, things like Red and Glow, and a little bit of the flesh trade with a little bit of smuggling. Then the Red got watery, the Glow got cut with flour, and the demand was for Poppy and tobacco amongst the rich. The wealthy wanted drugs and they wanted weapons, and suddenly nothing else mattered. The

Black Rose Company was perfectly happy to shrug off the responsibility of maintaining order in the underbelly. Tybalt, for his part, did not enjoy dealing with nobles of any kind. He did not trust any nor had he ever met one he really liked. He brought the weapons from West Avralaen and sold them to Black Rose, who would turn around and sell them to some milksop in a cravat for more than triple its worth. And all of that was perfectly fine with him.

His seat on an upside-down orange crate was getting uncomfortable. Tybalt shifted his weight, crossing him arms over his chest. He was glad for his gloves and his striped wool jacket, however thin. He missed the sun in both Avralaens, on parts of a continent that almost never made him step over an icy patch.

Something popped underneath a heeled boot. Someone was approaching, and they were only a few feet away. Tybalt did not move, although his pointed ears twitched at the sound and he placed both feet against the cobblestone, ready to spring up and run. He heard more footsteps coming from both sides and could not even force himself to relax when he finally caught sight of three blood red cloaks. They brushed past him, close enough that he could see the gold roses embroidered on the fabric.

"Well," Tybalt said, sliding his arms down to rest his hands on top of his knees. "It is good to see you gentlemen again."

The one in the middle rotated on his heel and turned to cast a look down on the half-sylphestine man with eyes that were too bright to look upon. "You brought no one with you."

"You said to come alone," Tybalt shrugged. "I can follow instructions."

The leader snorted, a soft abrupt sound. "You are being tasked with a duty—by Lord Marcellus."

"There you are mistaken," Tybalt said almost immediately. "I do not work for Lord Marcellus."

"It is a simple job, and it pays well." The leader held up a gloved hand, and the late day sun glinted off the surface of a gold stater coin. "Are you really too good for his money?"

Tybalt narrowed his eyes. He held out his hand, and the leader dropped the coin into his palm. It was heavier than the coins he usually carried. Tybalt turned it around in his hands, looking for any chips or signs of forgery. "I might be. What is the job?"

"Guarding a weapon," the leader said. "As I told you—simple."

"Then he should get a simple man to do it." Tybalt looked up. "Why does he need me, Amnas, when he has you?"

Amnas' angelic mouth twisted into a sneer, his fine upper lip curling as if he had tasted something sour. "Do you want to see what you are being asked to guard?"

"I might as well." Tybalt closed his palm around the coin, and it disappeared by the time he opened his hand again. "I hope he has several more of those."

Amnas brought his hand out and tossed his cape over his shoulder, the hood slipping back far enough to let his auburn curls come tumbling out. With the material out of the way, Tybalt could make out a dark leather holster slung around the man's slim hips. Amnas reached down and unclipped a strip of leather that released the handle of a pistol into his hand. Pistols were almost unheard of in Dragoloth, but in East Avralaen they were considered the gentleman's weapon, and most were decorated as prettily as a fencing sword. This handle was just dark wood, although beautifully polished. The barrel and its flared muzzle were silver—etched with whirls and flourishes—but nothing Tybalt had not seen before. When Amnas handed him over the weapon for inspection, he studied every inch to catch a glimpse of what might make it special.

His puzzlement must have been visible on his face. Amnas finally took pity. "Marcellus calls it *Briohnemach*. It is the God Slayer."

It was Tybalt's turn to snort. "What god is being felled by a shot?" He shook his head. "It is not only heresy, it is ludicrous. He will end up in an asylum for that."

Amnas handed Tybalt something else. It was a wooden case held closed by a latch. When Tybalt slid the latch, the boxed opened to reveal three gold bullets. They rolled around on dark purple velvet, each one etched with the same filigree that adorned the gun's barrel.

"Three blessed bullets," Amnas said as if that explained it all. "Tempered over a blue angelic flame."

Tybalt did not know what to make of this information. He shook the box a little just to watch the bullets spin around inside, which was absurd but oddly comforting. "Killing gods is not my business." He believed in a sort of natural order of things, and blowing a hole into the back of a god's skull flagrantly violated that order.

"He is not asking you to do anything other than make it disappear," Amnas said, pulling his hood back up.

Tybalt shook his head and closed the box. "Whatever he wants to pay me, it isn't enough."

"He thought you might say so." Amnas made a quick gesture, and the robed man next to him took a step forward. They dropped a heavy purse down onto the ground. The strings around the mouth came loose and the purse vomited gold onto the cobblestones. The heavy gold staters gleamed obscenely rich orange. The man standing on the other side of Amnas stepped forward and did the same thing, his purse bursting with gold before it even hit the street.

Tybalt did not appreciate having money thrown at him like he was some sort of street corner dancer, but he was too focused on the sheer amount to complain. All of those coins, all at once, were enough to make him salivate.

He kept that to himself, still sliding his fingers over the box in his hands. Amnas unbuckled the holster that was slung around his hips and held it up for just a moment before dropping it also at Tybalt's feet.

"For how long?" the dealer asked as the three robed men started to walk away, their soft cloaks brushing past him.

"Until he comes to collect." Amnas' voice sounded farther away than it was as he left Tybalt to pick up the money and his pride off the ground.

W HEN THE GILDED LILY closed its doors for the night, the only way in or out was through the back of the kitchen. And when Florindel doused the lamps, it meant that no one was to move until the first rays of dawn. The resident boys and their clients typically had an hour to settle down, whether that was taking a luxurious bath or simply sipping tea and snacking on thin, sweet honey cakes. If a client had to leave in the middle of the night, they had to wake the bookkeeper Franciscus, because he was the only one who knew how to reach Florindel's chambers—and Florindel was the only one with a key to the front door.

The lamps had been darkened hours ago. The only light came from the scattered fireplaces that were fed throughout the night by the servant boys in the attic who slept in shifts. Tarquin had excellent night-vision, a trait which had saved his life almost as often as it got him into trouble.

He was fairly certain that he was the only one awake. He had left his client in bed. The old lord had fallen asleep almost as soon as they finished their business, despite paying for the privilege of an entire night. That suited Tarquin just fine. He had waited at the top of the stairs until he could no longer hear Florindel's voice carrying out hushed commands for the next day's preparations. Once Florindel had gone to bed, he waited another hour to make sure he could no longer hear Franciscus shuffling around. The Calvarian bookkeeper was something of a night owl, but he preferred to keep to his chambers for the majority of his time. In any case, getting caught by Franciscus was never as dire as getting caught by Florindel. Franciscus would show mercy.

He had no idea of the hour, but it did not matter. Tarquin tiptoed downstairs on satin feet and slipped into the kitchen without so much as a rustle of fabric. The kitchen backdoor was bolted, and he had to move the bar back slowly, turning it just a hair every half inch or so to make certain it did not squeal.

When he got it free, Tarquin opened the door just a little, enough for a cold breeze to squeeze in and bite his cheek. He dropped a worn brick down on the other side so that it would not open any further than he allowed before resting his back against the frame and sliding down to the ground, breathing a sigh of relief. The night air was just what he needed, despite the fact that it made his nostrils burn. A sleight of hand by his crafty fingers produced a rolled cigar that he had pinched from a client's pocket a while back. It was burned down halfway already. He cursed himself for not bringing a match.

He considered going back to fetch one, and that had him weighing the odds of survival. He rolled the cigar around in his hands as he considered, the motion strangely pleasing, the texture of the frail paper oddly satisfying.

Before he could make a decision, he heard the brick move on the other side of the door. Tarquin scrambled to his feet, dropping the cigar to the ground and kicking it as far away from him as possible. If he was caught with such a thing, Florindel would snap his neck. Stealing from clients was the unforgivable sin of the Gilded Lily, and not even Balshett— the lover of thieves—could stop the brothel master from taking a mallet and a spike to the back of his skull.

Though his heart was racing, Tarquin felt frozen to his spot. He watched the door slide open and a head poked in. He recognized Tybalt's dark brown curls immediately, and the look on the man's face was enough to make Tarquin laugh in relief.

"What are you laughing at?" Tybalt whispered crossly, reaching in to snatch the boy by the arm and drag him outside.

"Your face," Tarquin hissed as his bare toes touched the cold ground outside. "Balshett take you! It is bleeding cold."

"Should you not be in bed?" Tybalt shut the door behind them, leaving just enough of a crack that they could open it back up without fear of being locked out.

Tarquin shrugged. "You could take me back to it, if you wanted—but there is another man under the covers."

Tybalt rolled his eyes and took off his wool jacket to drape it over the boy's slender shoulders. "You should be more attentive to your clients."

"You sound like Florindel." Tarquin grabbed the edges of the jacket and pulled it tight, looking up at Tybalt with soft hazel eyes.

Tybalt muttered something and rubbed his face, heavy stubble scratching against his palms. "Maybe Florindel and I should spend some time apart."

"I heard that you were here," Tarquin said. "And you did not come up to see me."

"I had a meeting," Tybalt said half-heartedly. "Besides, I would have paid for your night, but I wanted you to have a chance to make some decent money. I know it is only..." He could not bring himself to mention what Florindel had stated earlier. "I knew that tonight would be a good opportunity."

"I do not care about money," Tarquin said.

"You should," Tybalt snorted back. "You should care about money a lot. You will not always have the Gilded Lily, where Florindel feeds you thrice daily and makes certain you have soft silks to wrap around your body and expensive oils in your baths."

Tarquin shrugged. "I would rather see you," he said, "than have silk around my waist or oil in my hair."

Tybalt exhaled miserably. "You are going to get me killed."

"I do not think so." Tarquin stepped a little closer until there was no room at all between them. He placed his icy hands on Tybalt's hips and wormed them underneath the man's shirt. Tybalt jumped a little with the contact made against his hot skin. He swallowed hard and touched Tarquin's hands, warming them with his own through the thin linen shirt.

"I," Tybalt's voice was nearly a whisper, "do not want my tongue roasting on a spit."

"I rather like your tongue, so I am inclined to agree," Tarquin responded impishly.

Tybalt made a pained sound. "Quin." He reached up and brushed his thumb over the boy's cheek. "You have to go back to bed. I have to go to my bed—alone."

Tarquin looked like he was going to protest, but he stopped just short. He pulled back as he was bid, standing there just a moment longer before pulling Tybalt's jacket away from his shoulders and offering it back.

Tybalt almost told him to keep it, but quickly realized what a grave error that would be. He took the jacket back, reluctantly, and draped it over his arm.

"I suppose I will see you at breakfast," Tarquin said. He kept his words curt. The injury behind his eyes was *almost* enough to make Tybalt retract his words and take him to bed.

"If Florindel is cooking, you will." Tybalt tried to stay light-hearted, reaching out to tuck one of Tarquin's downy grey curls behind his ear. The boy puckered his lips and turned his head away.

"See you then." Tarquin slipped his hand through the crack and opened the kitchen door, vanishing behind it without a sound. Tybalt waited a few moments to give the boy time to get across the room before following suit.

The look on Quin's face would not leave his mind, but the priceless pistol strapped to his thigh and the box of god-slaying bullets that rattled on his belt reminded him that he had bigger problems.

5

SHRUKIAN

A BITTER OUTCRY OF GRIEF

THE LETTER APPEARED WHERE nothing had been before. If Shrukian had not been searching for his cufflinks, he never would have noticed. It rested in the center of a silver tray, smelling faintly of sulfur (as things passing through the astral realm often did) and overwhelmingly of perfume. His initials were written on the front in flowing script, each character dotted very pointedly. E.S.M.

Encarz Shrukian Mahtrador.

He nearly did not dare to pick it up. It was never a good sign when news had to be rushed to him so hastily that Pharun would squander a charm. And it had to be Pharun—who always smelled of cedar and lavender, and who always soaked the corners of his envelopes.

Shrukian glanced over his shoulder, suddenly suspicious of the idea that someone might be standing behind him. He picked up the letter, flipping it over to reveal the deep blue wax seal and the imprint of a peacock that he knew so well. The prince's breath got caught in his chest as he felt blindly around the surface of the desk for a letter opener.

He finally found one and worked the tip under the corner of the envelope, slicing it all the way across and breaking the careful seal. The letter inside was beautiful stationery, but his eyes were drawn immediately to what was written. Pharun was not one to waste words on him, so there was not as many formal, flowery paragraphs as he would expect. The message was simple, cold, and informative. Shrukian still had to read it three times before he could rightfully process what his brother was saying.

It does grieve me to inform you of your mother's death.

Shrukian realized that his hands were shaking. Without thinking, he reached out to grab the back of his chair and pull it closer so that he could sit down. He was gripping the letter so tightly that his sweat was beginning to soak through the paper. He read that same sentence over and over again. Yet, no matter how many times or ways he read it, nothing changed.

His throat was dry, but his skin felt so clammy. Shrukian reached up and dragged his fingers over the corners of his mouth, trying to make sense of it all. Pharun did not bother to elaborate on how Lystra had died. He said something, vaguely, about how the crown would be taking matters into their own hands regarding justice. Pharun never once mentioned anything about Encarz and how he was handling it, he only gave a few scarce details about her funeral. Her rites would be carried out and she was going to be burned long before Shrukian would have the chance to arrive. They could not store her body for him, he knew that, but it did not stop him from wishing that it could be done. To see her face and hold her hand one final time before giving her soul over to Azrael, to recite a prayer and a poem as her body was laid out on its pyre.

Shrukian tried to take another deep breath, but it hurt his chest to do so. He could not force himself to set the letter down even for a moment. Suddenly, in one desperate and all-consuming moment, it was everything he had.

Your mother's death. His nostrils and eyes burned, and his head was starting to pound from the sudden rush of emotion that he was trying desperately to repress. When they were boys, he used to think that she was Pharun's mother too. Lystra told him the truth, eventually, but never without a reminder that she loved Pharun as one of her own. She wanted to be close to him and strained every nerve for many years to try and foster a kind of closeness. Shrukian never understood why Pharun did not want her. She was so beautiful and warm, so graceful and ferocious. There were many nights where Shrukian would lay his head in her lap, and she would tell him stories as she braided his long, curly black hair. She would weave ribbons through the strands and tell him that he looked like he belonged with the traveling fools and fire-eaters. *Your mother.* How could Pharun not love her, too?

Shrukian buried his face in his hands. He could not breathe anymore. His salty tears were too painful to keep back. He crumpled up the letter until the edges pressed into his palm and let out a hard, wretched sob. He bowed his shoulders and nearly doubled over in his seat, moaning miserably into his own hands, tears flowing undammed.

He did not keep track of how many minutes passed. It could have been hours. All he knew, when he started to come around, was that his head and his stomach hurt.

Eventually, he managed to sit up right. It was all he could bring himself to do to grab a piece of paper and drag it across his desk. His fountain pen sat at the ready, and he picked it up long enough to write out a desperate plea. The paper was covered in ink blots and streaks of tears from his hands as he begged his brother to use his magic, if it was even possible, to bring him home to see his mother's funeral.

He did not even place it in an envelope. There was no beautiful wax seal. He folded the paper in half and placed it on the silver tray. Shrukian slumped in his chair and watched it intently, waiting.

The door opened behind him, and he sat up straight like a rod had been shoved up his backside. Shrukian twisted around in his seat, his hand going down to his side for a sword that was not there. He tried to force himself to relax when he saw Marcellus walking toward him, but his posture was too tight for him to unfurl in front of the man.

Marcellus raised an eyebrow in question but did not speak a word until he was standing by Shrukian's side. Shrukian waited for the inevitable, already humiliated by the knowledge that Marcellus could clearly see the red tearstains on his face. He waited for 'what is wrong with you?,' unsure of how he was going to answer.

Marcellus flicked his green eyes up and down, taking in the scene before finally opening his mouth. "Are you coming downstairs?"

Shrukian nodded. He did not trust his voice, and he knew that if it cracked it was over. Marcellus let another quiet moment pass before he reached out and rested a hand on Shrukian's shoulder.

"Do you want to tell me?" he asked. Shrukian opened his mouth and closed it again, unsure. When he opened it the second time, his words came out in an incoherent babble, and he came dangerously close to sobbing again. He leaned forward, grabbing Pharun's crumpled letter from his desk and pressing it into Marcellus' hand. The ambassador unfolded it carefully and smoothed it out with his elegant fingers to read the contents. Shrukian searched his companion's face for any sort of change in expression, but it never shifted.

Marcellus must have read it over twice before finally setting it back down on the desk. Then he knelt in front of Shrukian's chair and opened his arms. The prince fell into them, pushing his face into Marcellus' shoulder and letting out another despairing, broken sound.

"There is never a proper time," Marcellus said in his most even tone, "to experience the loss of one's mother."

Shrukian nodded. He could not bring himself to pull away, and Marcellus did not make him. His tears were flowing silently now and soaking through the fine fabric of Marcellus' doublet. He knew it would stain, and he felt badly about that, but he could not bring himself to even lift his head.

However much time passed, neither man was keeping track. Finally, Shrukian's tears stopped coming, and he was able to pull himself away and settle back into his chair. He sniffled a few times, and Marcellus handed him a handkerchief after standing once more.

"Will you be returning home?" Marcellus asked.

Shrukian nodded, dragging the linen handkerchief over his nose. "I wrote my brother. I asked if there was a way that he could..." He trailed off, glancing at where the silver tray had been. Both it and the letter had vanished. He felt the smallest spark of hope. "He is very powerful," he tried to finish his thought. "I asked if he could bring me home. Sometimes he can travel the astral planes. I have seen it done."

"It takes a great deal of power at such a distance," Marcellus remarked. "And a letter is not so cumbersome as a prince."

Shrukian nodded, even if he did not fully understand. "It will be nearly thirty days before I can be home again otherwise."

"I may know someone who can abet your plight." Marcellus reached out and brushed a strand of Shrukian's hair away from his sticky forehead, tucking it behind his ear. "I know nothing of your brother's ability, but I know of what this person is capable."

Shrukian licked his lips. "Whatever his price for such a service, I can pay it, of course."

"Hm." Marcellus did not remark. A ghost of a smile graced his lips as he reached out and squeezed Shrukian's arm. "Make your preparations," he said. "I will relay this information to Her Majesty and make certain to give her your regards. It would be correct of you to say your goodbyes to her yourself, but I believe you can be forgiven in this instance."

Shrukian shook his head. "I can still perform." He rose from his seat while gripping the arms of the chair a little too tightly perhaps. "I will carry out my obligations as expected."

"As you say." Marcellus turned toward the door. "We can make our way down together then."

"Thank you," Shrukian said. Words that felt like too little, considering all he had to thank Marcellus for.

All he received in response was another glance from those shimmering dark green eyes before they made their way out into the hall.

THE QUEEN'S SOLAR ROOM was a haven of rich green velvet drapes and dark, elegantly carved wooden furniture. Like most of the palace, it embraced East Avralaen's golden sunlight, dedicating an entire wall to intricately framed slices of glass. Marcellus had been privy to its quiet sanctuary many times, but never with the prince in tow.

In his uncertainty, he left Shrukian standing in the hallway. He had no desire to take his eyes off the grieving prince, but his urge to observe proper decorum was stronger. Constance, the queen's dark-haired attendant, opened the door for him as he passed through the entryway. She peered at Shrukian from underneath her maidenly lashes, and Marcellus felt a twinge of anxiety at the idea of leaving them to their own devices.

The queen was waiting for him, standing in front of her enormous window and looking out toward the lush green moorland that was covered in a blanket of fog. Marcellus bowed from the waist, touching the jewel at his throat. The low pulse of its magic against his fingertips always brought reassurance, and touching it had become something of a compulsion over time.

"Your word almost did not reach me before you did," Robin said. "Constance tells me that some great tragedy has occurred."

"One such tragedy that was out of our hands entirely," Marcellus replied. "The foreign prince has freshly received word of his mother's death, and it has sent him to grief."

"What a terrible thing," Robin expressed compassionately. "I assume that he will be sailing home on the next tide?"

"If I can do better for him than that, I will," Marcellus said. "Regardless, he came to bid you farewell and give his thanks for your hospitality. He sincerely hopes that this will not sully your good favor with Dragoloth and its aspirations."

"No, of course not." She pinched a lock of her red hair between her fingers. "I will extend my condolences to Dragoloth's king as well. What would be becoming of me to send, do you think?"

"His Majesty has been expressing interest in expanding Dragoloth's navy for some time," Marcellus said after a moment of consideration. "Now may be an appropriate time to send them the ship you have been saving."

"The *Kestrel?*" Robin smiled. "And its captain, as I would never part them."

Marcellus resisted the urge to rub his temples against the headache that threatened to surface at the mere mention of the *Kestrel's* capricious commander. "As Captain Cillian was born near the shores of Dragoloth, I am certain he would be pleased to return."

"That is settled, then." The queen seemed satisfied. "Prince Shrukian will be returning home, and I will see that the *Kestrel* is equipped for its journey. I must say that I am not entirely displeased at the idea of having you all to myself once again, Lord Marcellus. I will need your full attention on the South as we track the latest movements of the rebellious Magi."

Not that he had considered it very heavily in the last hour, but the thought of not being able to follow Shrukian home left a sharp pang of disappointment. Still, Marcellus brushed it aside. There was no time to linger on regret, and he certainly did not want the queen to sense it.

"Of course," he said automatically. "I am entirely at Your Majesty's disposal."

Robin extended her hand to Marcellus. He took it without thought and brushed his lips over her emerald ring.

"Do you wish to speak with the prince before his departure?" Marcellus asked when he straightened. "Or are you satisfied?"

"I am satisfied," Robin told him. "I see no reason to prolong the farewells for propriety's sake. If it puts him at ease, make it clear that I expect to see him back." Her lips twitched with good humor. "And send my love, of course, along with my sympathies."

"As you wish." Marcellus' mind was already in several different places, moving all the pieces where they needed to be so that everything fit in place according to her majesty's command. When he left the solar room, he had already constructed a concise agenda in his head. All that remained was to see it through.

Much to his relief, at the very least, Constance and Shrukian had not moved any closer than they were when Marcellus had left them. They looked as though they had been talking, but all conversation ceased once the door opened and the ambassador stepped out.

"All is well?" Shrukian asked, looking up as his friend approached. Marcellus nodded, clasping his hands behind his back as he maintained his pace down the hall. Shrukian fell into step beside him.

"The queen extends her deepest sympathies to you and your family," Marcellus said, "and regrets that her duties keep her. She sends her best wishes and offers reassurance that there are no hard feelings between her and the crown of Dragoloth. More explicitly, she stated that she expects to see you again very soon."

Shrukian allowed himself a small, relieved smile. "Well," he said. "I am relieved she has been so gracious."

"Yes." Marcellus gave a perfunctory nod. "Now we must make certain you arrive home."

"I have heard nothing from my brother," Shrukian said.

"That is all right." Marcellus rounded a sharp corner, reaching out to grasp Shrukian's sleeve so that he did not miss the turn. "I have my own ways."

P ACKING WAS NOT AMONG her favorite things to do. Elzbet, despite having received many lectures in practicality from Ringo, had not yet mastered the art of traveling light. Her servant girl, Katrina, was an efficient little thing—but the short morning hours were draining into the afternoon and the tent still had to be broken down. The rest of the camp was doing their part in uprooting, and Elzbet was hoping to be on the move before long.

Her orb was the first thing she had packed away, and she had checked on it twice since closing the trunk lid. She had wrapped it up in yards of thick fabric and filled the spaces around it with books so that it did not roll. Every time she opened the trunk, she had to reach down and nudge the fabric to make sure she still felt something solid underneath. As many attempts as had been made to steal it from her, she felt the paranoia was justified.

"You are not ready yet?" Ringo's voice snapped through the air like lightning. "This is all your doing."

Elzbet stood and rotated on her heel, pinning him with her dark eyes. "I was not the one who tore our every defense down. The queen knows where we are. If we do not move, we will die."

"If you continue to make decisions without me, you will see where that leads." Every word was a threat. "I did not pull you from that hell you were stuck in just to be disrespected so."

Elzbet's nostrils flared. "Would you put me back if given the chance? Because I will gladly go back to the life I had, rather than be—" she did not get the chance to finish her words. Ringo's immaculate silver gloved fingers were gripping her by the face, squeezing her cheeks like a child.

"All I am hearing from you," the warlock said, "is a lack of gratitude."

Despite the grip on her face, Elzbet sneered. "How is it any better now? I am still on the run for my life."

"Only because you have such narrow thoughts!" Ringo used his grip to bring her closer to him until she could see the raised edges of his scar. "You are acting like a hunted animal, and so they are treating you as such."

"If I am to be hunted, better a fox than a rabbit." Elzbet tried to pull her face away, but his grip was iron. "And you are like hunting a grouse. A stupid grouse. Let me go!"

Ringo obliged, his hands leaving behind discolored imprints on her face. "If the queen was here now, would you run?"

"No," Elzbet said. "I would rip her heart out through her throat, but I would be annoyed that I had to do it."

"I think you would run, and you would do it with the orb shoved up your petticoats."

Elzbet's lip curled, and she touched the spot on her cheek where his hand had been. "How many more people have to die trying to pry it from my hands?"

"What is one more?" Ringo brought his harrowing gaze around to Katrina. The maid shrank back, pressing Elzbet's folded blanket against her chest before quickly shoving it into a trunk. Ringo dragged his tongue over his teeth, the tip lingering over a single gold incisor.

"The whole camp is moving," Elzbet brought the topic back around, taking advantage of his pause, "you can come with us, or get left behind."

"You need me, and do not pretend like you do not."

"I needed a mentor when we met. I need a partner now. I am no longer a maiden, and you have nothing left to teach."

Ringo drew himself up indignantly. He was not carrying his cane, and without the support it was hard for him to stand entirely straight, yet he still towered over her.

"The route you have mapped takes us right past where your old lover is buried," Ringo finally said. "Do you mean to pay your respects?"

A sharp pang she could not describe hit Elzbet in her belly. "I had not considered stopping. I only thought to pass through."

"Maybe consider it," Ringo told her. "Better to make peace now than in the afterlife. And you seem determined to meet him so soon."

SHRUKIAN KNEW THAT MAGIC was a gift from the gods, and therefore was one of the most natural things in the world. The man standing in front of him, however, did not appear natural by any means. He was a little too beautiful and a little too strange. His eyes, the color of coveted spices, tracked every movement with flawless precision. He was dressed as a courtier; but the soft lace, supple satin, and stiff brocade only served to accentuate everything he was not. He sat perched atop Marcellus' desk with one leg dangling off the side and one gold heel resting on a stack of papers, holding a gleaming penknife, and slicing through the rind of an orange while dropping curls of peel onto the floor.

If Marcellus had not been standing beside him, Shrukian would have turned on his heel and moved swiftly in the opposite direction of this man.

"I trust Amnas implicitly," Marcellus assured the prince, despite being unable to tear his eyes away from the scattering of peels on his rug.

"And I trust you," Shrukian responded, "with my life." A trust, he was starting to hope, was not misplaced.

Marcellus placed a steady hand against Shrukian's back before addressing Amnas directly. "Do you care to explain to his Royal Highness anything about how this works?"

"Are you asking me to explain myself? I do not do that." Amnas popped an orange slice into his mouth without breaking eye contact. "And it is not as though he would understand a word anyway."

"You know," Shrukian said, "he is not wrong."

Marcellus internalized a sigh. "I hope to see you again soon," he told the prince.

"You make it sound as though the odds are bad," Shrukian said, liking this idea less and less.

"I know who your brother is," Amnas said, spearing the rest of the orange with his knife and leaving it on Marcellus' desk. "Of the two of us, the better likelihood of coming out in one piece is with me."

"Ah." Shrukian did not doubt *that* for a moment.

Amnas descended from his perch in one smooth motion. Shrukian towered over the man and was still glad for Marcellus' grounding hand against his back.

Amnas reached out to the prince, beckoning with his sticky fingers. Shrukian reached out, somewhat hesitant, and set his large hand against Amnas' fine fingers. They curled inward, gripping his hand tight like iron bands. Shrukian felt a pull against his chest, as if someone were wrenching apart his ribs and pulling his lungs out on a line. The world around him was sinking, sand being pulled rapidly by the tide, as the walls vanished, and he could no longer feel Marcellus standing behind him. Above his head, the sky was dark. He could see nothing except silver wires crossed through and around one another with the intricacy of a spiderweb. To one side he could see trees, taller and grander than even the firs that surrounded the castle. Their trunks were as thick as eight or ten men, and so great were they in number that he could hardly see anything else—other than the occasional ghostly figure, paler than sea foam, drifting and directionless. To the other side he could see grey plains: flat, barren land that stretched as far as the eye could see. Somewhere in the distance, the monotony was interrupted by a walking figure. Shrukian was not sure, but it looked something like a man of impressive size with pitch black skin and horns like an antelope that dragged across the bellies of storm-clouds above its head.

The pull against his chest tightened again. Shrukian almost choked on his own breath. Amnas' hand was gripping his own so tightly that the tingling had come and gone, and all that was left behind was numbness.

The world came to a stop. Amnas released his hand. Suddenly struck by the weight of his own body once more, Shrukian fell to his knees, nausea gripping him. He leaned over, bracing himself against the ground with his good hand, and unleashed the contents of his stomach until his nose and throat burned and his eyes watered.

"Where—?" It was all he managed to gasp out, but there was no one around to answer his questions. Amnas had disappeared.

The feeling was starting to come back to his right hand. Shrukian remained hunched over until he was certain he was not going to throw up again. When he was able to gulp down a few shaky breaths, he sat up on his knees, pushing both hands through his mane of black curls to get them out of his face.

At first, he did not know where he was. There were fir trees around him and snow on the ground, so it had to be home. Exactly *where*, in the great expanse of Dragoloth, remained to be seen. He could only hope that he did not have to walk far. He was still wearing his court attire, and while he had possessed enough foresight to throw on a wool cloak, he still missed his furs.

Shrukian dragged his sleeve across his mouth and waited to see if his stomach would betray him again. A minute passed and nothing came up, so he picked himself up off the ground. Once he was standing, he grabbed the edges of his cloak and shook off what snow he could. He reached for the drawstring pouch tied at his waist and pulled out a folded pair of leather gloves. They were his favorite pair, though a little worn, taken out often for riding, hunting, and practicing with his broadsword. He slipped them on, their cozy snugness around his fingers bringing some comfort as he began his traipse ahead.

6

ENCARZ

THE WITHERING VIVISECTION OF MODERN POLITICS

IN THE HOURS SINCE his wife's death, Encarz had found no comfort. The last words he had exchanged had been with Pharun, when the newly vested *Kren Veisten* flashed his opal status ring and said, "Trust that the arrangements shall be made."

Pharun had made his insultingly dismissive utterance after returning from his prayer with his clothing half-discarded and his cheeks bitten by the wind. Encarz had seen him vanish with the meek blond priest and could only spitefully wonder which of the two had spent their time on their knees being filled with divine providence.

As king and Crowned Priest, they were expected to bend to one another on occasion.

As father and son—*bastard son...*

If he had stabbed the baby in its cradle all those years ago, instead of Anastasia, perhaps his problems would be far fewer.

"You look troubled," Malhii's reedy voice overtook the silence in the drawing room. Encarz glanced over at Azrael's high priest, having completely forgotten he had invited him in. Nothing had been said between the two of them for over an hour.

"I was thinking about Anastasia." Encarz straightened up a little in his chair, his shoulders aching from an upset slouch. "And how Azrael seems to have a penchant for taking all my wives in a tragic manner."

Malhii nodded. He had been in the room when Encarz drew his dirk from its sheathe and put nine very sizeable holes into his wife. The night Pharun was born, he was baptized in arterial blood. And Encarz had always treated that boy as though he wielded the blade himself.

"Lystra was a blessed woman. Your favorite, I recall." Malhii wove his fingers together in front of him, watching Encarz from deep-set, hooded eyes. "Nothing like Anastasia. Nothing like Daphne."

The latter he barely remembered, although he had presided over her funeral.

"She gave me Shrukian," Encarz said, picking up his glass to drink deeply from his wine. "My son. My heir. I never asked her for more than that."

"She would have given you more," Malhii said, "had they not been taken in their infancy. Blessed be his mercy."

"Blessed be his mercy," Encarz muttered, taking another drink before finally lowering his glass.

Malhii leaned forward far enough to pick up the decanter and offer the king more wine. The heavy sleeves of his robe muffled the clinking of his opulent jewelry. "And now, what will you do?"

"About Pharun?" Encarz watched the firelight glint off the stream of dark plum wine.

"Mm." Malhii did not volunteer anything, he simply pulled back and topped off his own glass.

"I came back into my senses while he was… consulting with his gods." Encarz rolled the words around as if they were blasphemy to consider. "I know that his solution has some merit, though it galls me."

"He did not allow you to destroy yourself, and your kingdom, in one swift gesture," Malhii proffered. "That is something."

"It was to buy time to further his own agenda, nothing more," Encarz dismissed that. "We are at odds when it comes to war, and with whom, and I unwittingly gave him the upper hand."

Malhii held back a smile. "I remember the turmoil after Anastasia's passing."

"I kept the land from her dowry," Encarz scoffed. "Nothing else mattered."

Malhii turned his glass around in his hands. "Daphne...?"

"Hm?" Encarz could not separate himself from his thoughts long enough to keep up with the high priest's constant rabbit holes of thought.

"Your second wife," the high priest said patronizingly.

"I remember her," Encarz gave him a look. "You are asking how she died? The physician said it was a case of hysteria. She threw herself off a parapet."

"They say childbirth tears holes in the mind of a woman," Malhii shook his head.

"And if the child is a girl, such tragedies are three times as likely," Encarz added. "Or so states the latest medical journals."

"Such things are beyond me, I admit," Malhii said humbly. "I place my trust in Azrael and His will. If the sacred mind or heart are meant to be torn asunder, who are we to try and stay the inevitable with medicine and half-cocked speculation?"

"I am not here to argue the divine and modernity with you," Encarz said, putting a blunt end to the discussion, "when you are three times my age and Azrael's will is the only explanation for why you are yet walking this plane."

"I consider it a vestige of His favor," Malhii said, stroking the front of his robe. "Six decades have I been High Priest. And there will be six decades more, as He pleases."

"I have seen many of your hopeful successors fall to the wayside in despair, waiting with bated breath for your dying day," Encarz said. "You give them false hope."

"One's final day cannot be foretold. I must always have a successor prepared." Malhii's dark eyes shone in the low light, the predatory gaze of a vulture.

"I suppose we all rear our heirs without intention of ever dying." Encarz looked down at his wine, which was nearly empty yet again. "I did not stand in the way of Pharun's rise to *Kren Veisten* because I knew it would mean he can never sit on the throne. A man cannot be a Crowned Priest and a crowned king. I could never publicly disown him because he was marked by the gods for greatness. A blessing and an honor, several of your priests had the gall to tell me."

"Their final words," Malhii reassured him, "before their tongues were removed."

Encarz made a noncommittal sound. "A baby with silver hair and stone-grey skin. The nurse thought he was born dead until he cried. And when he opened his eyes, I wished he had been born dead, because he looked like Anastasia, and at the same time a bewildering wild fey. Barely human, certainly not Verian. I had no hand in his creation, and yet I had to raise him as my own. The ultimate insult to my line and to Azrael."

"He serves Azrael now, and Saldon, and Morcant. He will never sit on your throne."

Encarz pulled himself back from his thoughts enough to shake his head. "No," he agreed. "It is for Shrukian now. My boy." He went to finish his wine, but there were only dregs. Malhii moved to pick up the decanter, but Encarz refused it with a wave.

"I should not," the king said. "There is much to be done in the morning, and I must prepare."

Malhii obediently set the decanter back down. "I have ordered the funeral pyre to be constructed. They are decorating it for her now at the temple."

"With white roses," Encarz said.

Malhii bowed his head. "Of course."

"Leave me," Encarz said with a sharp, dismissive gesture. Malhii did as he was told once again. He stood and bowed to the king properly from the waist before walking around his chair, bringing his hand down to rest on Encarz's shoulder as he did so.

"*Dormeche salv, min kren dragg.*" The high priest leaned over, long oily braids forming a curtain around their faces as he pressed his dry, thin lips against the king's forehead. Encarz did not flinch, even as he reached up to grasp Malhii's hand and give it an iron-tight squeeze.

"I will see you in the morning, *fadir.*" There was no fondness in his tone, so the affectionate, familiar words were wasted between them.

"As the sun rises." Malhii pulled away and left. Encarz did not make another move until he heard the door close and the footsteps fade.

Once Malhii was gone, Encarz reached for his silver pinchbox. The tobacco inside was from a recent Avralaenian shipment, and the sharp, slightly sweet smell was an immediate comfort. He pinched up enough to pack into his favorite pipe and flipped the lid shut once more.

He had conducted this ritual a thousand times, almost always alone. It felt strange to him now, knowing that there would be no interruption. There would be no one sitting on the arm of his chair, no one taking the pipe from his hands to draw from it with their own lips. The fire, as it dwindled, allowed the cold to sink in through his thick velvet housecoat.

There would be no one in bed, either, although the sheets would still smell like her. That space he could not even fill with another body, because her perfume would cling to their hair and skin, too disconsonant for pleasure.

He took a long drag from his pipe and let the smoke burn his throat before pushing it out through his nose.

Of all his wives, he had loved her the most. As far as he was capable of loving. The ache in his chest was an unfamiliar one. If grief had ever been meant for his experience, surely it would have been present when his mother speared herself on the castle gate. Or when his father vomited black bile onto the dinner table, or when the church unwound his younger brother's intestines and filled his stomach with hot coals.

He drew from his pipe again. The flames were shrinking in the hearth, and his fingers were feeling a little numb. Numbness he could accommodate.

The door opened behind him again. Encarz drew himself up in his chair, ready to bite off the head of anyone who walked through. He expected that Malhii might have come back for something, or else it was his manservant trying to usher him into bed.

Neither option, though viable, was the case. He saw pale fingers flit down and touch the lid of his pinchbox, tracing over the ivory-inlaid engravings. Encarz looked up and saw his daughter, her beautifully structured face set with a dour expression he did not care for.

"Olympia," he said, catching her hand in his and drawing it to his lips, "you look sullen."

"You look cold," Olympia countered, "and not sullen enough."

"Am I to be morose *and* kingly?"

"You are supposed to be possessed of a regal melancholy, so I am told." She moved around his chair to settle at his feet, tucking up her knees and adjusting her skirt so that it fell in dark folds around her. "Something in between prostrate and upright."

"A hunched king." Encarz looked down at her, taking in the welcome sight of her lavender eyes and her apple-shaped cheeks. "You grow more beautiful every day."

"'*Blooming*,' as General Ferris would declare. Or '-*simply glowing*,' according to Baron Nicos." Olympia rolled her eyes. "Oh, '*as beautiful as your mother*'—Lord

Clotaire said that to me. I would have struck him for it, if not for my miraculous restraint."

"What I am taking from this is that you do not wish for me to make such remarks." Encarz filled his cup with wine again for the sole purpose of passing it down to her.

"It is one thing from you. It is another from your lords. I wish you would inform them of how tiresome it is getting."

"Old men are tiresome, dear."

"Especially when the hand of a holy princess is placed up for declaration," she scoffed and put the wine glass to her lips. "What Lord Clotaire said put me off more than the rest."

"Your mother was a beautiful woman." Encarz took another drag.

"I never knew her. So she is dead, she was mad, and it only serves as a reminder that Lord Clotaire is at least as old as you."

Encarz raised an eyebrow. Olympia met his gaze without flinching, even as she drank.

"If he speaks again, you may have him beaten," Encarz promised. He reached out and touched her long, wavy black hair, coiling it around his fingers. Olympia rested the glass in her lap as she leaned into his hand.

"A small consolation," she allowed.

"Mm." Encarz leaned back into his seat. "You did not come to talk to me about Lord Clotaire."

"No," Olympia said, "I wanted to see how you were handling everything."

"About as well as can be expected of a grieving husband," Encarz responded somewhat candidly. "I should be asking the same of you. She was as much your mother as Shrukian's."

Olympia bit the inside of her cheek. "I suppose it has not struck me yet," she said. "I keep thinking that when I turn the corner, she will be there. When I think of breakfast in the morning, I do not think of how she will be missing from her place at the table. It feels as though everything will be normal, and this nightmare will be at its end. Although I know that the nightmare is far from over."

"Indeed." Encarz could not help the bitterness trailing from his words.

"Pharun said that he would get word to Shrukian." Wherever Pharun was involved, Olympia usually refrained from bringing it up around her father. In this case, however, her concern rose over her more diplomatic instincts. "Did he say anything to you, about whether...?"

"Pharun has not said anything to me regarding your brother." With the very mention, Encarz's expression shuttered once more. Olympia could no longer read even the slightest trace of fatherly affection in his eyes or in the lines around his mouth. Resignation took a heavy breath from her, muffled by the wine glass.

"He will want to see her," Olympia said, lowering her voice in deference to her father's shift in tone.

"Her funeral is in the morning, and he is in East Avralaen." Encarz rubbed his fingers against the grooves of his pipe. "It is as much impossible as it is unfortunate."

Olympia knew better than to argue. Pharun had magic—he could whisk Shrukian across the sea if he wanted to. She had seen him do impossible things. The physical toll might be great, but a small price to pay, in her opinion, for Shrukian to have a chance to do what she and Pharun had been denied.

She was barely three when her mother split her skull open on the castle pavement. Pharun never even knew his own. Shrukian deserved to say goodbye; he had a right to it over any of them.

"I know your emotions toward your brother run high," Encarz said, "but you cannot lose yourself before the proceedings tomorrow. Grieve when it is over, and when the public does not have its eyes on you."

Olympia took a deep breath and nodded, rising on her knees. She set her half-empty glass on the table beside her father as she did so. "Will the procession begin at sunrise?"

"The funeral party will begin drilling in the courtyard an hour prior. And then at sunrise, yes, we will make the procession to the Temple of Azrael."

"I will be ready." Olympia stood. She looked as though she wanted to say something further, but she did not. She considered embracing her father, but she did nothing more than take his cold hand in her own and kiss his imperial ring.

When Olympia left, the fire reached its end. The final flame snuffed out and cast the room in near-complete darkness, save for a single lamp. Encarz lingered in the dark and cold long after, thinking on all that was possible and what was to come, while all that was lost sank into the shadows behind his chair, already forgotten.

✦⊷————⊷✦

DAWN BEGAN TO PAINT the sky dreamy orange. It was barely enough to crest over the snow-capped mountains, so Pharun was in no rush. Funeral proceedings would not begin without him,- and he could comfortably, smugly, take his time.

Nkiru, the Spider, sat comfortably in one of his chairs. With her legs drawn up and crossed and her shoulders pulled forward, she looked impossibly small. If she tucked her head down, she could have vanished from his sight altogether. Of course, he had learned at an early age to never underestimate Simisolans, and especially not one with such a formidable reputation.

"I regret," Pharun was saying, "that there is not adequate time for you to fully inform your queen as to what we have discussed here."

"I have my ways of speaking to Efemena," Nkiru's brilliant blood-red eyes never seemed to blink. "Ocean or no ocean. Arendse and I are here for the same reasons. We want to stave off a war."

"You make it seem as though war is inevitable." Pharun adjusted the skirt of his robe over his knee.

"The dragon seems to want it," Nkiru said. "And what the dragon wants, he pursues."

"Even unto his end," Pharun agreed. "Which is why I believe East Avralaen to be a far more tempting lure for the time being."

"Simisola has wanted its share of the Titan Continent for centuries." Nkiru wound her fingers in the fabric of her loose pants. "Throwing our hand in with you, we expect our cut."

"You will have it." Pharun stood. He crossed over to his desk in a few easy strides, picking up a leather satchel and tossing it over to the Spider. She caught it deftly and then lowered it into her lap to peer inside. There were several stacks of folded papers, which she was quick to pull out, inspect, and then fold back up before sliding them back in place. "This is all of the information I could gather on Avralaenian presence in the city in under a few hours," Pharun said. "I have faith in your ability to take it and turn it into something useful."

Nkiru's lip curled as she pulled out another piece of paper, unfolding it in the same way she had the others, and scanned the contents. "You are not making this easy."

"Lystra was not poisoned," Pharun said, "she was not stabbed, or strangled. It was an unnatural cause of death that I need to find a natural explanation for.

Someone will swing for a crime they did not commit, but is that not the way of things?"

Nkiru shrugged. Sacrificing an innocent did not sit well with her, but she had done it before. She would do it now for her queen. "You are putting me out of my element. I am not the assassin here; I am the storyteller of your play. You want me to bring the players together and assign their fates. You are the one holding the axe."

"Hardly I," Pharun said. "I am not cutting off heads. I am presenting a package with every detail nicely wrapped. My father will dole out justice as he feels it is merited. Does that make you feel better, knowing you are absolved of any blood on your hands?"

Nkiru gave him a dark look. "These people," she raised the satchel, "are every one of them dead. My hands are bloody, bearing their corpses."

"A burden well passed on, then, as it would seem." Pharun sat back down and crossed his legs once more. "My gloves are too fine to bear a stain."

Nkiru left her chair. Pharun hardly saw her move, her movements were so quick and light.

"You have a funeral," the Spider said. Pharun's eyes wandered to the window, where the sun was making its steady climb and spreading its dreamy color.

"I suppose so." He turned his gaze back toward her. The spot where she had been standing was empty. Nkiru had gone and left Pharun in the quiet of the morning.

Pharun drew in a deep breath before setting his hands down on the arms of his chair. It was going to be a monstrous day, and he had not slept at all. Once it was all over, he would collapse. For now, he had to dress, and his priestly vestments weighed heavier than a crown.

Pharun rose from his seat and rang the bell for his servant.

SNOW CAKED ONTO SHRUKIAN'S boots and did not shake loose until he scraped his heels against the palace steps. Dawn filled the sky with swaths of orange and romantic blue, though—as beautiful as it was—he could not bring himself to admire it. The guard was changing shifts, and the servants were just beginning to rouse. The guards at the gate had recognized him, but they had been the only ones. No one had appeared to make a fuss over him so far, and he was not sure whether he preferred it that way.

Shrukian circumvented the front entrance entirely, walking nearly all the way around until he found one of the servant entrances close to the kitchen. It was a narrow door that was unlocked when he tried the handle, and it swung open to reveal a dark wooden staircase leading up into the main level. He waited a moment to make certain that no one was coming down before he started up, the stairs groaning underneath his weight.

The stairs emptied out onto a landing which was met by another door. When he opened it, the world changed from warm wood to cold marble as he stepped into what he recognized to be the largest main hallway of the palace.

Only then did he stop to get his bearings. He wanted a cup of hot cider and a bath, but urgency pressed him to find his father or brother first. Although he trusted Marcellus, he knew nothing of magic and did not know the time or the day in which he had landed. If his mother's body had not been prepared, then he wanted at least one final glance.

Shrukian pulled off his soaked gloves one after the other and then stuffed them into his pocket as he walked. At the end of the hall, he thought he caught a glimpse of silver hair. He picked up his pace, all but running the last few steps, before turning the corner and nearly barreling into his brother.

Pharun was draped in brocade and lush velvets, exactly as a priest of his standing should dress. He rotated on the spot and cast a haughty look up at his brother, who towered inches over him even though the Crowned Priest was wearing heels.

"Well," Pharun said, drawing his hand down the edge of his tall lace collar, "it is certainly a surprise to see you."

"I returned your letter," Shrukian tried not to sound bitter, "but you never returned mine."

"And you found your way home regardless. You have the instincts of a hound, and they never fail." Even as Pharun spoke, Olympia appeared and pushed her way past him, opening her arms to throw them around her younger brother and draw him close.

Shrukian felt a lump form in his throat at the sight of his sister. He wrapped his arms around Olympia and squeezed her tightly, burying his face in her neck. She smelled like rose water and myrrh, and it took everything in him not to break down on her shoulder.

Olympia rested her hand against his head, holding him close to her chest and rocking back and forth slightly, comforting. She pressed her lips against his ear, humming softly. "It is good you came home," she whispered.

Pharun took a step back. "If you hold him any tighter, Olympia, the servants will have to mop."

"There is no compassion in you." She pulled back just enough to hold Shrukian's face in her hands, swiping her thumbs underneath his eyes, although there were no tears in them yet.

"Compassion is for mothers and philanthropists," Pharun sneered, "I am neither."

"Gods willing, you will never sire a child." Shrukian put a little more distance between him and Olympia, breaking the embrace for the sake of cupping her cheeks and giving her a grateful kiss.

"Does that leave bearing on the table?" Pharun looked his brother up and down. "My form can be as fluid as my expression."

Shrukian bit his tongue. "Where is father?"

"Upstairs," Pharun answered, glancing at his nails.

"And... mother?" Shrukian felt his chest burn.

"In there," Pharun tilted his head toward a door. "They have already prepared her body and are about to bear it to the temple."

"I want to see her first." Shrukian was already taking steps. Olympia started after him, but Pharun held out a hand enough to block her path.

The room was dark, lit only by a few dozen candles. Trails of incense curled in the air, scents of death that he recognized: myrrh for Morcant, the lord of death, dragon's blood for Azrael, and vanilla for peace. A large wooden table had been erected in the middle, and an elaborate funeral bier had been set atop that. The base of the bier was gold inlaid with carved ivory dragons, and the glass dome that would rest over the queen's body as they carried her to her pyre had been set off to the side.

Lystra laid on a bed of purple satin, her head resting on an embroidered pillow. Most of her body was covered by cloth of gold, with her hands only visible as a lump positioned against her chest. Her hair had been styled in courtly braids and sewn through with ribbons, the foul stench of death drowned out by incense and heavy perfumes.

An ivory mask rested over her face. The details bore a striking likeness, all the more impressive for how quickly it had been made the night before. Shrukian reached out, able to see his hand trembling as he went to remove the mask, but he pulled it back before he could touch it. Masks were only placed over the face to hide gruesome attributes that the undertaker could not patch. His mother was—had been—beautiful, and the image of her beauty and her kind face was cemented in his mind. Whatever was underneath the mask might be too horrible to bear.

Shrukian took a deep breath. He did not know why he was hesitating. He had seen war. He had seen men die on the end of his blade, he had sat with his own men and listened to their dying words, and yet this was different. He loved her, by all the gods. Did he not owe her at least as much honor as a dying soldier?

Without giving himself a chance for another thought, Shrukian reached out and grabbed the mask by its face. He ripped it away and immediately dropped it, feeling like the wind was knocked from his chest at the sight of her face. The undertaker had done what he could, but the ghastly horror that had contorted her face in the end was all that the prince could see now staring at up at him. Her cloth-of-gold covering and soft satin bed seemed less now a cradle and more of a casing, wrapped tight around her body to keep it from twisting in all directions.

Shrukian fell to his knees. He dragged the mask down with him, pressing his face against the ivory, his own hot tears coursing down his cheeks and streaming into the carved features. "*Mamma*," his cry was that of a young boy, lost and alone in the darkness without his mother. "*Mamma...min mamma...*" He could not stop. He felt like he was going to vomit.

His stomach churned and the tears would not stop coming, and his sobs tore away from his chest in a ragged scream that echoed through the arched ceiling.

Someone tore the mask from his hands. Shrukian looked up, startled and furious. He had not heard anyone come in. Encarz stood beside him, scowling his disapproval as he brought his hand down against his son's temple, the hard stone of his imperial ring cracking against the prince's skull.

"Will you stand?" the king snarled. "Your mother would be ashamed of you."

His words struck more viciously than his hand. Shrukian stared up at him for a moment in stunned silence, a bead of blood forming through broken skin and trickling down his temple in a hot red trail. He gathered his composure quickly, his training as a soldier and his princely breeding kicking in as he rose to his feet, leaving the last of his tears to dry on his face as he raised his chin and tucked his hands behind his back, meeting his father's eyes.

"Forgive me, sir," he said, despite his throat still being tight. "I do not wish to dishonor her memory."

"That disgusting display should get you sent from her final bed altogether." Encarz wiped his son's tears away from the ivory mask before setting it down over

Lystra's face, covering the shriveled tragedy. "Do I want to know how you made your return from East Avralaen so quickly?"

"With the swift assistance of a friend," Shrukian responded, "and the blessing of Her Majesty. She sends her assurance that there is no ill will, and she extends her sympathies as well."

"Mm." Encarz finally turned his eyes away from his wife's body to look at Shrukian. "She would never, of course, say any differently. This afternoon we will speak on how to return you to court as quickly as possible."

Shrukian bowed his head. "Of course."

There was a pause. Encarz reached and grabbed his son's shoulder.

"You are no longer a boy," he said. "When people look at you, they do not see a prince. They see a future king. Any display of weakness within you reflects weakness back onto the throne. Onto me. If a king cannot bear a loss such as this, is he capable of making any sacrifice for the greater good of his kingdom?"

Shrukian shook his head. "No, sir."

"When you led my armies during the Great Cleansing, you could not stop to grieve your fallen brethren. Yet you stood proudly by their pyres as their souls were sent to Azrael. You were only seventeen then. If your heart could bear it then, it can withstand the weight now."

Shrukian felt shame wash over him, sitting heavier on his chest than grief. He did not feel as though his heart could take much more burdening, and that his father's faith in him was grossly misplaced. Still, he kept his shoulders back and his jaw tight. He could not look at his mother's body again, even as it lay completely covered. But he could keep his eyes trained forward; he could keep his composure for his father's sake. For Dragoloth.

"Should I change for the procession?" Shrukian asked. It was all he could think that was potentially useful.

Encarz shook his head. "There is not enough time before they come to collect your mother. What you are wearing is fine enough."

Shrukian bowed again, at a loss for further words. Father and son stood in complete silence beside the woman they had both loved, whose spirit yearned to embrace them both, and so filled the room with melancholy.

7

FLORINDEL

The Hand That Takes

THE GILDED LILY WAS a house of rituals. It began at sunrise with Florindel walking through the hall, knocking on every door before slipping the client's bill underneath. It was well understood that he expected overnight patrons to linger no longer than an hour after dawn as a courtesy. At the half hour mark, he would knock again. Once an hour had passed, he would enter the room and send the remaining patrons downstairs no matter what state they were in.

Once the house had been swept through, Florindel closed the Gilded Lily's doors. After the front entrance was locked, it would not be opened again until midday. His bookkeeper, Franciscus, would be awake as well and ready to trot all the boys down to the kitchen with a ledger tucked underneath his arm.

This morning was no different from any other. Franciscus was tired, having stayed awake long hours into the night trying to make sure every coin was accounted for. Florindel was very scrupulous with money and would pick the notes apart if every transaction was not exhaustively recorded. Franciscus, for his part, abhorred numbers and knew very little writing. He never looked forward to explaining himself when his master went over the ledgers.

The Calvarian scooped up a handful of dried fruit and dropped it into his bowl of yogurt. He plucked a dark roll from its basket and balanced it on the rim of his bowl in order to grab a cup of milk at the same time. Very carefully, he moved to sit down at the breakfast table where several of the boys had already found seats. They were all talking about the night before, swapping vulgar and embarrassing stories about their patrons. Franciscus set everything he had down, including his ledger, and tore off a piece of his roll first thing. He did not immediately see Florindel, but that did not worry him.

Who he *did* see was Tybalt, staggering into the kitchen while looking like he had been sleeping in the drainpipe. Franciscus took another bite of his roll, watching the man struggle to get his bearings. Like watching a dog try to stand up on its hind legs.

Tybalt bypassed food completely. Instead, he grabbed a bottle of wine by the neck, rotating it in his hands to see if it could be identified in any way. Not finding any markings, he uncorked the bottle and tipped it over his cup. Franciscus flipped open his ledger and pretended to be engrossed, even though the page was half-empty.

He felt movement next to him as Tybalt sat down, bringing his cup and what remained in the wine bottle with him. Franciscus pressed his lips together until they formed a thin line and turned another page. It was blank, so he flipped it back.

"Were you up pretty late?" Tybalt asked.

Franciscus considered responding in his native tongue and pretending he didn't understand, but unfortunately Tybalt had been around long enough to know better. "I always am."

"Florindel keeps you busy," Tybalt leaned forward and rested his elbows against the table as he pressed his cup to his forehead. "I was away until some ungodly hour, myself."

"Mm." Franciscus was not interested.

The Calvarian noticed as Tybalt's gaze shifted briefly toward the end of the table as one of the boys sat down. It was Tarquin, one of the Gilded Lily's more precocious creatures. The two exchanged a look, Tybalt's expression remaining immutable, while Tarquin's face shifted from agitated to something more pleasing, the sort of expression he usually donned for clients. Franciscus did not care for the exchange, as he was fond of Tarquin and did not need this half-sylph gadabout cocking up the natural order of things.

He considered saying something, but years by Florindel's side had taught him to keep his mouth shut. Quiet observance was worth more.

All the boys' voices rose at once in a chorus of greeting as Florindel entered the room, disrupting the mild tension and Franciscus' trail of thoughts. Florindel smiled at all of them, touching their heads and shoulders as he passed. He was a vision in loose white linen and an embroidered orange sash, which had been a gift from a traveling merchant who swore up and down that it was the finest silk from Simisola. Franciscus fought the urge to rise and kiss those beautiful hands, each one adorned with a thin gold ring. Just seeing the house master was enough to make his heart quicken and his stomach tremble.

He could tell that the man at his side felt the same, and that irked him. Franciscus tried not to dwell.

"Good morning," Florindel said, reaching the end of the table at last and resting his hands on both Franciscus and Tybalt's shoulders. "I trust that both of you slept well."

"Always, under your roof," Tybalt said, raising his cup in a salute.

"Well enough," Franciscus responded simultaneously.

"Wonderful." Florindel kept his smile but lowered his head, his voice dropping down to a whisper. "I must speak with you both in private."

Franciscus rose immediately, leaving the remnants of his meal on the table and dusting off his hands on the knees of his trousers. Tybalt followed suit, taking one last gulp of his wine before joining them both at the back door. His eyes darted toward Quin one last time, but the boy's face was obscured.

Franciscus still had one foot in the doorway when he caught Florindel's words. "Did you know that she was dead?"

The Calvarian racked his brain for information from the day before. They had been so busy, with the castle festivities and the influx of new clients. "Who is dead?"

"Queen Lystra." Florindel shook his head. "That poor woman. Not one patron coming from the castle even mentioned it?"

"No," Franciscus swore up and down. He had not been drinking *that* much wine after the boys had gone to bed. "Not a one that I can recall, and if anything was said to the boys..."

"One of your informants," Florindel nodded to Tybalt, "was trapped in the castle overnight. Encarz did not allow his guests to leave for hours, and no servant was even let out into the yard until late. Only an hour ago was this person able to slip out and bring the information back to me. They said that the funeral procession would begin this morning, and a town crier would make the announcement."

"Is it safe to assume, then, that the manner of death was not natural?" Tybalt asked. "I can see no reason why the king would bolt his doors against his own guests if it were."

"I am certain it was as natural as the death of every wife preceding her," Franciscus snorted.

Florindel thinned his lips in disapproval. "I am not here to play judge and jury for the royals," he said. "My boys are my only concern. The law says that any trade, market, or shop must lock their doors for three days in an observance of mourning. The funeral will begin its proceedings soon, and after the town crier makes his announcement, everything will be shut down by afternoon. Franciscus, I need you to check our stores and replenish anything that is low. Take Tybalt to the market with you for an extra hand."

The Calvarian glanced at the man beside him. "I believe that I am more than capable..."

"I am happy to help any way that I can," Tybalt broke in.

"It is greatly appreciated." Florindel rubbed the heels of his palms together, grateful that someone was being agreeable. "Of course, this had to happen today, when Pheseus is coming to discuss inventory."

Franciscus felt his blood run cold at the mention of the name. He knew that Florindel had been operating on his own for many years before their meeting, but that did not make him feel any better about leaving the master of the house alone with Pheseus.

"Could it possibly wait?" the Calvarian implored, fighting the urge to reach out and touch Florindel's arm. "At least until we return?"

"Possibly," Florindel said, "it depends upon when you do."

"We will go now." Franciscus cut a look at Tybalt, making it clear he would not be argued with. Tybalt cocked an eyebrow, but he opened the back door to let Franciscus through.

"It seems we are going now," Tybalt inclined his head toward Florindel. "We will be back soon."

"Be safe," Florindel warned.

"Always," Tybalt flashed him a smile and then disappeared through the doorway.

P HESEUS ERCOLE WAS A wolf who kept a tender flock. Every boy in the Gilded Lily had come from him and ran at the sight of his shadow. His visits were occasional—only written down for once or twice a year—but whenever he stooped his unnaturally tall frame through the doorway, doors slammed shut and chattering died down to whispers. He was seven feet tall with sleek black hair braided down his back. At his side, he carried a heavy dragonhide whip with a silver handle, and his eyes were pale green, always seeming a little empty and dull, like marbles cut from frosted glass. He had a disapproving frown and a steely voice that was enough to send urine running down the legs of even the strongest-willed Lily.

Florindel did not care for Pheseus very much, either, but he cared about quality. Pheseus had an eye for beauty and good temperaments. His selections were always on par with the latest trends and desires from the castle, and they always came impeccably trained and responsive to unspoken commands.

The Ercole was already in the drawing room when Florindel returned inside. He had let himself in, and he was standing a good distance from the fire despite the snow still caught on his cloak.

Florindel gestured broadly toward the fire. "Have a seat," he said, "I have mushroom tea, or ginger and lemon if you prefer."

"None for me." Pheseus shrugged off his cloak and swung it around to lay against the back of a chair. It seemed comically small next to him, and he chose not to sit. Rather he stood behind it, resting his hands on the back. "You wanted to discuss what I have on hand?"

"Josse has been ill for two months. His cough has been persistent, and now infected boils are beginning to appear under his arms and on his thighs. I fear he will not get any better. It is a shame, because he is a sweet child and a personal favorite of many regulars. There is also Vauquelin, who is not performing well with the patrons. The other boys do not like him, and he has started talking back to me in ways I do not care for. No amount of discipline has made a difference. He seems far better suited for a blacksmith's shop than for my establishment."

Pheseus nodded. "Vauquelin I will take back. I will check my records for his sale record."

"He has been with me for two years," Florindel stated, "longer than some."

"I will check my records, all the same," Pheseus said. "I must ensure that the proper evaluations are made to restore a boy of equal value to you. You know my procedure."

"Of course." Despite the Ercole's condescending tone, Florindel did not allow his expression to change.

Pheseus continued, "I have a recent acquisition that might interest you. He is pure sylphestine, as close to a wild fey as you might get."

Florindel's interest was piqued, though he tried not to show it. "You have vetted his pedigree?" Wild fey were rare; any full-blooded fey would be too inhuman and fragile for structure or society. Sylphestine, as Florindel was, were descendants of wild fey, with more elf in them these days than anything.

Regardless, any sylphestine bloodline was highly desirable for cleverness and beauty. And the closer to wild fey any boy was, the more beautiful and compelling he was bound to be.

"He had no family to ask. I know wild fey when I see them." Pheseus had the grace to not sound insulted, but his voice dropped an octave.

"Of course." Florindel held his gaze. "Although you must be willing to understand that I do not intend to pay the price of a near-wild fey's contract on a hunch. A courtier who does not know the difference might give you more."

"Doubtful," Pheseus said. "Once you see him, I believe you will pay my asking price and more. There is another."

"One with papers, I hope."

"Full papers, twenty-one with a sylphestine mother and a half-sylph father. Enough human blood to add some interest. The mother claimed celestial as well, and while I would never doubt the word of a woman desperate enough to sell her own son for money, I did not add it to his record, nor did I offer more for the information." The sarcasm colored his voice more than usual.

"I see," Florindel said. "You have done well enough by me in the past that I am willing to trust your judgment on both counts, and I am interested in reviewing both."

"All right," Pheseus said, "I will bring them at the end of the week when this country has finished its mourning."

"That would be best." Florindel moved to escort him toward the entrance. "Take Vauquelin with you when you go. I will fetch his papers from Franciscus' office."

"You will lose him and Josse before their replacements are guaranteed?" Pheseus did not sound overly disturbed even as he asked.

"My rotation will suffer more for them than without them." Florindel paused at the door. He curled his fingers around the edge of the frame, his knuckles turning pale, but he was only still for a moment before breaking free of the spell. "If you would be so kind as to wait. I will send Vauquelin down."

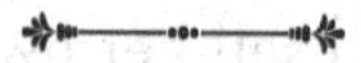

VENDORS AT THE MARKET were already beginning to break down their tents, although no one seemed eager to leave, as there were still barrels and crates of fruits, vegetables, and salted meats, along with fresh meat hanging from hooks, furs and fabrics freshly treated and dyed, baskets of bread, casks of mead and ale, and a number of other goods that Tybalt was overlooking in favor of Florindel's simple list. Franciscus followed behind him, carrying a basket in the crook of his arm. The already-thinning crowd gave the olive-green Calvarian a wide berth, which made it easier for the pair to slip through and grab what they needed.

"It seems the news got here before we did," Tybalt said, putting bundles of fresh rosemary, sage, and mint into Franciscus' basket.

"Fewer people than I was expecting," Franciscus agreed as he handed the payment over to the vendor.

Tybalt did not like it. He did not like how few people there were and how exposed he felt. He noticed that several people were shooting him odd looks, and he could not tell if it was because he had done something embarrassing, like put his shirt on inside out, or if there was another reason. No matter what, it was making him increasingly uncomfortable.

Fransiscus caught his eye. "We are nearly done, I believe."

"I do not like some of the looks I am getting," Tybalt frowned, rubbing at his chin so that the prickly black hairs scraped across his palm.

"Well, you do look like we found you in a well." Franciscus ushered him on toward the next stand, selecting a measure of apples that he knew Florindel would want to make tarts or cider.

"So maybe I did not brush my hair. That is not an excuse." Tybalt felt his paranoia growing, bringing a familiar tightness to his chest. He picked through a basket of walnuts, ignoring the vendor's disapproving scowl as he locked eyes with another stranger who was giving him a hard look from a few feet away. Tybalt snarled, his lip curling back over his teeth, and the stranger averted their gaze.

"I do not think they are looking at you." Fransiscus added some figs to the basket before moving on to the next stall.

"I am willing to entertain the possibility that you are more of a spectacle than I—" before the words even finished leaving Tybalt's mouth, he heard a strangled yell.

From the corner of his eye, he saw someone go down. He was spinning to face that direction within seconds, just in time to see a larger man descend on top of a smaller one. Tybalt sprang across the stall, nearly knocking the basket of apples over as he did so. He heard Franciscus shout something, but he could not hear it over the rush of blood in his ears.

Two more men came out of nowhere. They were shouting, angry, but he could not make out the words at first. He saw fists fly and he heard the sound of flesh making contact, heavy and relentless as they beat their quarry to the stone.

"Djrinksa!" He kept hearing it again and again as he got closer, a slur for Avralaenians that he was all too familiar with. Tybalt flicked his wrist, the flex of his fingers tugging on a string that pulled a small dagger, concealed in a forearm sheathe, and slid it into his palm. He gripped the handle tight and swung it around, digging the blade into the back of one of the larger men's thighs. The man howled and swung around, but Tybalt dodged his fist, ducking and then jabbing another attacker in the side and slicing through his jerkin.

Tybalt's focus was not even on the brutes. He was more interested in getting their victim to safety. He dodged another blow, still gripping his dagger. He was prepared to stab them as many times as necessary. He saw a hand coming for him, and he raised his arm to block the blow. It never landed. All three attackers turned tail and ran, one of them still bleeding enough to be worrisome. Tybalt tried to catch a glimpse of his savior, but all he saw was Franciscus, whose tall horns and long shadow had been enough to send off three hot-blooded fools.

Tybalt muttered something close to a thanks but did not drop his dagger, immediately kneeling beside the man on the ground. There was blood eking from the man's ear, and his face was already swollen with blood rapidly pooling into bruises. A quick inspection yielded no visibly broken bones, although a few cracked ribs were possible. Tybalt made sure there was no blood underneath his head, no visible wounds where he might have broken his skull against the cobblestone.

"Tybalt," the man's voice was ragged, his bloodied lips fighting to form the words, "I..."

Hearing his name caught him off guard. Tybalt looked up at the man's face, which was so swollen that it was forgivable he had not recognized him at first. "Do not try to talk," he said, moving back up to where he could cradle the man's head a little better. "Fione?"

"There are already rumors..." Fione struggled to push himself up onto his elbows, wincing visibly as he did so. "With Lystra's death... Avralaenian involvement."

Tybalt's brow furrowed. "From the Eastern country?" he asked. "Because I do not think that King Piotr..."

Fione tried to shrug, but he ended up dropping his head onto Tybalt's shoulder. "It does not matter. East. West. They do not know the difference here."

"I know." Tybalt rested his hand on Fione's back, rubbing it gently to try and soothe the man. He looked up at Franciscus, a dark emotion clouding his deep green eyes. "I have to get him to safety."

"We can take him back to Florindel," Fransiscus said. "If you move, I can carry him."

"I can walk..." Fione began to protest.

"I will not chance going back to the Gilded Lily," Tybalt said. "If there is even a shred of truth about the rumors being spread... I do not want Florindel to be forced to protect me. He has to take care of his boys."

Franciscus tightened his jaw. "He does," he agreed.

"Just as I need to protect my own." Which he had failed to do. Fione's condition was a prime example. Tybalt felt shame ball up in the pit of his stomach, but he could not afford to pay it any heed. It was something he would have to sit and untangle later. "We have a few safe havens outside of the city." He had to alert others of danger and get as many as he could to safety. There were members of his crew he had a responsibility to return home, and other Avralaenians in the city who he knew would need shelter. There was a possibility he was overreacting, but it was not something he could consider. He knew that Avralaenians, East or West, were already walking on eggshells in Dragolothian territory. A malicious rumor, no matter how small or how quickly it died out, would have very real and brutal consequences. Tybalt had seen it far too many times. And the truth of Lystra's death, in the end, would not matter much at all once the seed had been sown and hate had new meat to chew on.

Franciscus picked his basket back up, sliding it into the crook of his arm. "Are you sure you do not want me to carry him?"

"I will help him walk." Tybalt slid his hands underneath Fione's arms, already using his own strength and weight to help the man stand. "Go back to the Gilded Lily, keep Florindel and the boys safe. If I can get to the *Daydream*, I will see you all again in a few months."

"Sounds like a threat." Franciscus bowed his head. "Azrael be with you." He turned and walked away.

THE AFTERNOON WAS STRETCHING on. Pheseus Ercole had come and gone. Tarquin had holed himself up in his room, like many of the boys, and not willingly stuck his head out despite hearing the front door slam shut. He did not see any reason to emerge unless Florindel sent for him or it was mealtime with no patrons filling the bottom level. He could hear a few boys who had come out of their hiding as they filled the common area with their quiet chatter, lounging on the plush red couches and sipping on sweet cordial they had pinched from the kitchen stores. Josse's harsh cough was the most distracting—Tarquin could hear it all the way down the hall.

Tarquin peeked outside of his window again. This side of the bridge, there were always people out and about, people who did not necessarily give a shit about one more dead royal. Nothing was open, but that did not mean that children could not play marbles in the street because washing still had to be done, and their mothers were stringing wet clothes up on lines. The girls who sold flowers were still doing so, having switched out their usual bouquets of posies for a more appropriate white heather which grew in droves around all the poor chapel graves.

Tarquin huffed and his breath fogged up the glass. He drew a little face before it faded away.

Josse's cough sounded unbearable. He sounded like he was drowning, with every drawn breath sounding like a gargle. Tarquin could not even imagine what it was like to sleep next to him. Florindel had been keeping Josse away from the other boys since he developed boils, but Tarquin had done enough laundry to see the bloody handkerchiefs and blankets that came out of the boy's room.

He also could not imagine what it was like to sound so loud and so startling all of the time. Just listening to the sound made him squirm. He begged, in his mind, for Florindel to bring up the sherry and the honey which never quieted the cough but soothed it down to a bearable volume.

Tarquin chewed on the tip of his nail and tried to focus on other things. He watched the wispy white clouds drift across the sky. He stared at the distant mountains, wondering if he might see a dragon at the very top if he looked long enough.

Gods above. Saldon's tongue, Azrael's eyes, and Balshett's quick hands. He could not take it anymore.

Tarquin swung his legs around and slid off the side of his bed. He walked over to the door and flung it open, several blonde and gingery heads picking up when they heard the sound.

"What has got your dander up?" Kelly asked. He had lashes like snowflakes and eyes like sharp rubies on a courtier's necklace. Tarquin pursed his lips and walked right past him, reaching over and snatching up the little bottle of cherry cordial they were all sharing.

"Hey!" Christos brought his freckled legs up to tuck underneath his soft pink robe. A client had bought it for him almost a year back, and he wore it nearly every day despite it being too long. "What is the matter, Tarquin? Are you angry that Franciscus came back and did not bring the Avralaenian with him?"

Tarquin paused. "Tybalt did not come back?"

Kelly and Christos shook their heads.

"Franciscus came back and was talking to Master Florindel," Kelly said, "but I could not hear what either of them were saying. They went into the office."

Tarquin felt sick. "Do you think he is hurt?"

"Maybe he had other things to do." Kelly brought his nails up to inspect them, digging at the sides. "None of us know what you see in him. He is so hairy, and he smells."

"I do not know either some days," Tarquin snipped back. "Although I would bet he is a better lover than your prissy Count, Kelly."

"Aristeidis shaves, and he wears perfume. He smells like juniper and cloves when he makes love to me." Kelly smirked and stretched out across his seat, putting his arms above his head in a pose that would have inspired any painter. "Does Tybalt come to bed smelling like a horse? Do you have something to tell us about your own fantasies?"

"I am sure he dabs something behind his ears," Christos giggled. "A little bit of saddle oil, maybe."

"Sweat and saddle oil!" Kelly almost screeched. "Quite the *stallion* of a man!"

Tarquin wanted to smack both of them, but he knew doing so would land him several mornings of scrubbing pots. A few other boys who were sitting nearby tittered, but none of them added to the ridicule.

Rather than exact retribution, Tarquin held up the bottle of sherry with his finger through the looped glass handle. "I am taking this to Josse," he said. "I have had enough of his hacking."

"Master Florindel said to leave him alone, and that he would take care of it," Christos said. "Have you seen the boils that are under his arms? They are purple! And what is inside of them is even worse."

"Boils do not bother me," Tarquin said. "I want a nap. And I cannot rest with that sound."

Kelly and Christos shot him odd looks, but neither did anything to stop him. Tarquin continued down the hall, stopping at Josse's door, thinking only when he arrived that it might be locked. It was not, so he let himself in.

Josse was laying on his bed. His blankets were a mess, as if he had been fighting a constant state of piling them on top of himself and then shoving them back off again. The curtains were drawn over his window, so Tarquin could not otherwise seem him very well. He did not shut the door entirely behind him, leaving it cracked as he walked over to the boy's bedside. Josse shot upright when he saw someone coming, startled, and tried to say something—but could not speak before he was coughing again.

Tarquin made a face and went over to the bedside table, grabbing a dry cup with crusted edges and pulling the glass stopper out of his bottle. "I brought you some sherry," he said. "It is going to help your cough. Drink it all."

"Nothing... helps..." Josse struggled to speak, each word coming on the tail end of another hacking, horrible exhale. Tarquin felt the urge to hold his own breath; the stink of piss, rancid body odor, and looming death was enough to make him dizzy.

"It will help a little," he insisted, turning around and offering the cup to Josse. It was full nearly to the brim, but it was a small cup.

Josse looked up at him in despair with red, watery eyes. He reached out, hands shaking as he wrapped his fingers around the cup. He held it in both hands and brought it to his lips, sipping from the rim. He was able to swallow once, only a little dripping from his mouth, and it encouraged him to take a bigger drink.

He could not get it down the second time. A cough cut off his attempt, and he sprayed sherry from his mouth, dropping the cup at the same time. The drink spilled down the front of his shirt and soaked the thin blanket over his legs. Josse coughed up the rest until there was only blood, and the red spatters were all over his hands.

Tarquin recoiled, taking several steps back from the bed. Josse looked like he was crying, but from a good foot away, Tarquin could not really tell.

"I... 'm sorry..." Josse coughed again and rubbed at his face, trying to clear up snot and bile and only smearing it around with the blood from his mouth and hand. "It's... been... like this..."

"I know," Tarquin tried to sound sympathetic. He just wanted to leave, but he felt frozen to his spot. "I will get Master Florindel..."

Josse shook his head. He wanted to protest, but he did not want to cough again. He made a miserable sound, setting his hand against his chest and doubling over in the bed. He whined and rested his head against his knees, every breath rattling in his chest.

"I am here, Tarquin." Florindel appeared in the doorway, fairer than an angel, wreathed in light from the hall. Tarquin had not even heard him come up. He felt heat rush to his face as shame and fear took over, and he lowered his head.

"I am sorry, Master Florindel," Tarquin said meekly. "I was only trying to help."

"I know." Florindel drifted in, setting a small lamp down on the table beside Josse and a fine bone cup with steam rising off the surface. "You may go." He did not even look up as he rearranged the sick boy's pillows enough so that they could support him before helping him uncurl and leaning him back. Tarquin opened his mouth, not sure whether he wanted to protest or say something else. He knew he should not, and that he should do as he was told. Florindel gave him a gentle, yet firm look and that was enough to break the spell. Tarquin bit his bottom lip and slipped out toward the door.

"Th... Thank you... 'Quin..." Josse said from his place in the bed. Tarquin felt like he was going to throw up.

Tarquin grabbed the handle to draw the door closed behind him, but something made him stop. He left it cracked, as he had before, and knelt down at the base so that he could not be seen. He could still glimpse inside, but he could not see onto the bed as well anymore. He heard Florindel speaking softly, and more of Josse's hacking cough.

"Sorry... m-master..." Josse wheezed pathetically.

"Shh," Florindel soothed him. "I brought you some medicated tea."

"I c-c-cannot..."

"Shh, just try." Florindel picked up the teacup and handed it to him, sitting down on the side of the bed to be closer and support him with his free hand. "I bet it will help you sleep."

Josse made another sad sound. He raised a hand to support the teacup, but Florindel was still the one holding it. The boy was able to take a few sips before his cough returned, although it was already not as violent as it had been before.

"That is better, is it not? There is also honey. Drink some more." Florindel prompted. Josse took a few more sips, eager to drink as much as he could. There were a few quiet moments before Florindel was satisfied and set the teacup back down.

"Let me clean you up." Florindel took a folded rag from the side of the bed and began wiping at Josse's face, tenderly cleaning up the fluids he had spread. Josse was quiet while he did this, although it only took a few minutes before he was making another wretched sound.

"M-Master..." Josse paused, and Tarquin braced himself to hear another torrent of coughing. Florindel did not say anything. He started humming softly, continuing to clean up Josse's face, folding the rag for a clean spot every time a new section was soiled.

"M-Master... please..." Josse stopped again, and there was a horrible silence. Tarquin could have heard a pin drop.

Then there was a torrent of frothy vomit. It splattered onto the floor, gushing over Florindel's hand. The sound that came out of Josse's throat was something that Tarquin had never heard before—something ugly like a gargoyle's snarl. More foam and bile. From what Tarquin could see it was almost black in color. Josse heaved one final time and then collapsed back onto Florindel, his arm rolling away from his chest and dangling lifelessly at his side.

Florindel stopped humming. He laid Josse back down onto the bed and arranged him more appropriately, crossing his arms over his chest and closing his eyelids. Tarquin did not even fully comprehend, until the sheet was being pulled over the boy's head, the full horror of what he had witnessed.

Tarquin looked over his shoulder. Down the hall, he could see the other boys looking back at him, and he wondered if their expressions mirrored the fear on his.

He heard Florindel's footsteps. Tarquin stood and bolted back down the hall. His legs felt too weak to carry him, his knees trembling, but he could not stop. He did not turn his head until he made it back to his room, slamming the door behind him. He heard other doors shutting, one after the other, and he knew the other boys had similarly fled.

Though Tarquin had never seen it, he knew that some of the boys who had been here for years called Florindel *fadir morcanheim.* Father Death. He had never paid it much mind; no boys had died in almost a year.

Tarquin waited for the sound of footsteps; he waited for it to be his turn. No one came, there was not even a knock on the door. Relieved and overwhelmed, Tarquin pressed his back against the wood and slid down to the floor. Bringing his knees up to his chest, he wrapped his arms around them and cried.

8

PHARUN

THE SIMPLE EXPRESSION OF SORROW AS LOVE

THE PATH FROM THE castle to the Temple of Azrael was a familiar one. Nothing much had changed. The same buildings stood along the street, the same blacksmith shop, the same cobbler, and the same butcher. The same tenements, some of them a dangerous three-stories high and ready to topple. All of it was etched into Pharun's memory, down to the townhouses in the distance standing behind tall iron gates where the wealthy preferred to reside.

The undertaker walked beside him. Pharun, for his part, was mounted on a beautiful blood bay gelding, as the shoes of a Crowned Priest would ideally never touch the filthy cobblestones of a common street. He had lost track of the procession order otherwise. He knew that Felix was walking on his other side, and that was all he cared about. Encarz was riding his destrier somewhere further back.

A throng of common people had clustered along the sidelines, gaping at the processional with wide eyes and closed mouths, hats swept away from their heads while their hands rested on the shoulders of quiet children who had no understanding of the events and no desire to bear witness, but who also knew better than to squirm away and get in the path of a royal. Pharun kept his gaze fixed on the road, eliminating his chance of making eye contact with any one of them. He tried not to wonder about how many of them had been standing in those same spots years ago, watching him ride close to the horn of Malhii's saddle. Back then, his young mind had such little control. He could hear every single one of their thoughts, a cacophony of voices like a storm of feasting crows. They all thought he was going to die. They all hosted vulgar opinions on High Priest Malhii and his perversions. The only thing that had given Pharun comfort during that time was knowing that they could feel him push his way into their brains, whether he wanted to or not, and that it hurt them every time.

"Your eminence," the undertaker's voice snapped him out of his thoughts, "we are nearly there."

Pharun blinked slowly and brought his attention back to the present. The Temple of Azrael loomed before them—a marvel of ancient architecture, a lavish display of national devotion and wealth in fluted marble columns and intricately carved dark wood. A steep tiered staircase, as wide as the face of the building itself, led up to the mouth of the beast which came in the form of two immense doors, each inlaid with obsidian and gold. The doors were propped open with stones, belching smoke and heat from incense and wood-burning fires. Icons of Azrael and his angels kept watch from their perches along the roof, claws unsheathed, wings spread, and long tongues lolling over their bared teeth.

Pharun's next breath was a little shakier, but he held his head high as a young cleric came to take his reins. He waited for another to put a pillow down for his feet. There were a few barren steps between his mount and the temple stairs, but it was more the ritual of the gesture than anything.

High Priest Malhii was waiting on the landing of the lowest tier. His elbows were at his side, but his hands were open and spread. His ceremonial robes were the colors of blood and rust with enough heavy black velvet to keep it appropriately somber. His fingers and wrists were weighed down with jewelry, endless rings and bracelets that made every gesture seem like a chore. He wore an array of necklaces as well, each one bearing a pendant or a jewel (sometimes several). There were gold hoops and bars in each ear and rings through every braid. When Pharun looked at him, he saw more of himself than he ever did looking at Encarz, and that made him sick to his stomach.

Pharun started up the stairs, salt and thin shards of ice crunching underneath his shoes. His heart moved at a faster pace, racing in his chest, willing to tear itself out at any minute. Malhii kept his eyes steady, his gaze fixed as the prince moved closer. The long train of Pharun's ceremonial cape dragged behind him, pulling on the shoulders of his coat and making him feel like he was being strangled.

Finally, he came to a stop. One shoe came to rest on the step just below where Malhii was standing, while the other stayed just one step back. He was cold, but he would not let the high priest see him shiver. They held each other's gazes for a long minute before Pharun finally extended his hand.

Malhii scooped it up in his own, indulging himself in a single caress, running his thumb over the back of Pharun's hand before bowing his head and kissing the *Kren Veisten's* ring.

Pharun exhaled, relief somewhat soothing the sick feeling, although not banishing it altogether. He pulled his hand back and Malhii turned to face the temple doors. Together, they walked side-by-side into the belly of the waiting beast.

"It is a somber first day," Malhii spoke as they walked, keeping his voice lowered for the sake of respect, "for you to assume the full duties of *Kren Veisten.*"

"It is," Pharun agreed, not turning his head to look at the man. "I intend to invoke my right as a mourner. I will not be speaking today."

Malhii nearly stopped, but he kept going. "It is your right, honor, and privilege to speak for the royal family."

"My rights and privileges have never mattered so much before," Pharun said, "I do not see why they would today."

"It is not the day for such pettiness from you." A little more of Malhii was coming out. The strict teacher. The venomous authority. "All of that is past. You are the highest authority of Azrael, and you will speak for the queen's soul."

Pharun narrowed his eyes. "If I am Azrael's highest authority, I will be heeded."

"You are a brat," Malhii's voice was now barely above a whisper. "You have always been overindulged, and now you have acolytes laying pillows down for your feet. You may get away with embarrassing your father, but you will not humiliate me or the teachings of my temple."

Pharun set his teeth, but he did not respond.

"And make no mistake," Malhii continued even as they approached the doors, "no matter your title, Azrael speaks first to *me*. I love Him as you never learned. And I serve Him—as you were never willing."

"Funny to me," Pharun began to snap, still not turning his head to look at the high priest, "that I should have been expected to give Azrael my full devotion, when it was Saldon who sired me."

"Funny, also, that you were not a better servant. When this temple taught you how to control the powers that your celestial father gave you before leaving you to your own devices." Malhii's sneer was in his voice, even if it was not fully present on his face. "No one wanted you, child, except for me. And you are just as unbearable, and ungrateful, now as you were then."

Pharun wanted to kill him. He had it within his power. If he willed it, he could unwrap one of those carefully crafted barriers from around his mind and strike the high priest to the floor with a thought.

He did not do it. But he could have. They turned to face each other when they reached the doors.

"The flames from the pyre will bear Lystra's soul to Balam," Pharun said, his voice flat.

"Azrael will walk with her. And you will pray for her safe passage." Malhii bowed again, gesturing for Pharun to enter the temple first. Fury tightened the prince's throat, and his cape flared behind him as he turned and made his entrance.

THE FUNERAL WAS HELD in the temple atrium. Clerics clad in simple black transported the queen's bier through the cloisters, removing the glass dome from the top and then surrounding her so that they could all place their hands underneath her body and move her as carefully as possible to rest on top of the pyre. Once they set her down, they made certain that the ivory mask was still covering her face. They took the materials that had been draped around her body and tucked them underneath so that her body was completely wrapped, and nothing was hanging over the sides. Once they had done their part, the clerics stepped back, and Malhii stepped forward holding an oilskin.

Pharun was not even listening to the words the high priest was saying. He kept his eyes on everyone else present. He noted Encarz standing with Shrukian by his side, and Shrukian looked abjectly miserable. He kept his back straight and his hands in front of him, one crossed over the other like a good soldier. Encarz's posture was similar, and it had never struck Pharun before how much the two of them looked alike. Encarz had more gray in his hair, of course, and his years had left their signature in deep lines on his face. Shrukian had Lystra's curls, and he was a little taller than his father, but it was the way they set their mouths, the way they held their heads up with their shoulders thrown back, the way they puffed up their chests and the way they both clenched their hands around their rings. Shrukian had Encarz's purple eyes, his stern brow, his handsome face. It was uncanny. Pharun felt hatred flare up, burning hotter than maybe it ever had before.

He turned his head just in time to catch Malhii's summoning fingers. Pharun stepped further into the atrium, reaching out with red leather gloves to accept the oilskin. He knew every funerary prayer by memory. The ritual for Azrael especially was ingrained so deep, he was not certain he could ever forget it. The words came to him easily; he did not even have to think about them as he uttered a few stanzas before squeezing the oilskin, holding it high enough that the stream landed where it was meant. He walked around the pyre and uttered a few more lines, squeezing the oilskin again. And so it went. There were no parameters for how long a prayer should last; it could last as long as his willingness to repeat himself, or until the oil ran out.

The wood was well-soaked by the time he finally came to a stop. He turned his back to the scene and handed off the skin, not really caring who took it from his hands. Malhii spoke some final words, and torches sputtered as they were brought down to light the pyre.

Pharun retreated into the cloisters. Felix was standing there beside a pillar, his face half-shaded by the stone arch over his head. His dark blue robes brought out the beautiful golden quality of his skin, the pale fairness of his hair. He was sunlight in the frigid grey morning, and he looked up when Pharun approached, his soft blue eyes filled with melancholy and compassion.

He extended his hand. Pharun looked at it for a long moment. The pyre was starting to burn behind him, and he had no more words to say.

"Your gloves are stained," Felix said softly. He kept his hand out, inviting, unwavering.

Pharun glanced down at his hands. The oil had soaked through the red leather in spots and stained it. Parts of his gloves were still slick, and they smelled. He made a face and peeled them off, dropping them onto the ground without caring where they fell.

He felt like he could still smell the oil, but his hands were dry. Pharun reached out and accepted Felix's hand, wrapping his grey fingers around it. Felix's hand was so cold, and yet it felt comforting. The younger priest sat his other hand on top of the prince's, holding him gently and tugging, bidding him closer. Pharun had to try hard to pull in a breath, afraid that tears would come if he allowed himself a moment more of tenderness.

He pulled his hand away. Felix looked a little disappointed, but he let him go. Pharun moved to stand beside him instead, busying himself by straightening the clips pins that held his cloak in place.

"I am ready to cast this off," he muttered. Felix nodded his sympathies.

"It is nearly over," he said. "I do not believe that His Majesty will stand here the entire six hours it may take for her to burn."

"A half hour or so, an hour at most." Pharun scoffed as he crossed his arms over his chest.

He watched Shrukian's face the entire time to see if his half-brother would dare to shed another tear. He eventually allowed his hands to drop back down to his sides and felt Felix's fingers test the waters once more, curling around his inquisitively, then sliding up cautiously to see if they would be stopped.

Pharun did not stop him this time.

BEFORE THE TORCHES DESCENDED, Shrukian experienced a moment of panic.

He could not move. He could barely breathe. Though the atrium was out in the open, surrounded by stone pillars and the barest winter garden, all he could taste was smoke at the back of his throat. All he could smell was incense and oil, and all he could see was his mother's dark hair, the only visible part of her underneath the mask. He had been hanging on every word of Pharun's prayers, about the River Balam and about Azrael taking His daughter's soul by the hand and leading her through the uncertain darkness. He watched his elder brother pour oil onto her body, and still it was not registering. There was still some part of him that could not believe it was actually happening.

Then he caught sight of the torches. That was when he felt panic seize his chest. He felt frozen, but he wanted to scream, *"That is my mother, you cannot do that to her, you have no right!"*

It felt caught in his throat, like he could choke on it, *"She is your queen! That is my mother!"*

Even the terror did not feel real. He doubted whether he was truly thinking it, or if he truly felt that way, because if he was, then he should do something to stop it, should he not? He should pull the clerics away and stomp out the torches. He knew that stopping them would accomplish nothing. He knew his mother would not rise from the bier and hold out her hand, asking to be helped down. Telling himself such things over and over still did not stop his stomach from churning as the wood around her pyre started to smoke.

He stood there as long as he could. He refused to even turn his head away. When the flames began to climb, and the dark smoke started to obscure her body, he felt like he could hear her scream. He felt like he could see her thrash underneath the tight fabric wrappings, though he knew it was just waves from the heat.

The smell was overpowering. A cleric came and pressed a sachet of resin and dried flowers into his hand. Shrukian held it to his nose—myrrh and lavender—it smelled as much like death to him as burning flesh.

A gentle hand touched his arm. Shrukian looked over to see Olympia standing beside him, her sachet also pressed against her nose and her expression immutable.

He wanted to pull her into his arms, but he could not. He watched as the flames climbed ever higher.

He could have sworn he heard his mother call his name.

It was late in the afternoon by the time they returned to the castle. A meal had been prepared and set out for the royal family in the informal dining hall, with all the servants lined up solemnly, respectfully, to greet them. It was intimate space with only three or four tables at most. It was unlike the great hall that could fit half the kingdom, and instead of a balcony for music, there was a round, raised platform where the court minstrels could sit and play.

For such a somber occasion, there was no music, only the crackling of a fire and the sound of cups and bowls being moved around. Encarz took his usual place the table, while the chair next to him, Lystra's seat, was markedly empty.

Shrukian was not certain he could sit that close. He was ravenous, unsure of the last time he had eaten, but also nauseous to the point where he doubted his ability to do anything more than nibble. He grabbed a handful of figs and dropped them onto his plate next to a sliver of cheese and a single piece of bread. Even that looked monstrously unappetizing.

"You need to eat more than that," Olympia said, moving a larger piece of bread onto his plate and a cut of venison. Shrukian watched her porcelain hands move with only mild interest.

"Olympia—" he began.

She cut him off with a stern look. "You cannot grieve the rest of your life. If you allow sorrow to take one meal, then it will take the next, and so on until you are too weak to continue." She picked up his wine glass, making sure it was full. "I want to be gentle with you, but I will not watch you trod down this path of despair. That journey stops here." She sets his glass down and then pushed on the edge of his plate, sliding it back toward him. "You are a large man. Eat."

Shrukian did not present further argument. He ate a bit of venison and speared a few figs, just enough to whet his appetite and make him realize how hungry he was. He polished off what he had on his plate quickly and then reached for more. He asked a servant for ale instead of wine; Dragolothian blackberry wine had lost something of its charm since he had grown accustomed to sweet Avralaenian strawberry.

"How do you think father is doing?" Shrukian finally asked, sliding his fork over a pool of honey that had formed in the center of his little cake.

"He is father," Olympia said, "whatever he is feeling, he will not share it with any of us."

"Of anyone, I had hoped he would confide in you," Shrukian admitted. "I do not know what will happen now that mother is gone."

"Likely nothing," Olympia responded, pausing to take a sip from her glass. "He used to have a need for children and a duty to fulfill. Now, all his children are grown. If he takes another wife, I will stand amazed."

"Perhaps it is for the best that he does not," Shrukian sighed. "He will not let himself be lonely in any case."

"No, he will not. The two of you have that in common." Olympia glanced at him over her rim.

"What is that supposed to mean?" Shrukian dug his fork into his cake, not sure if he should be offended.

"I simply mean that you and father are blessed men to have never known an empty bed. Or," she turned her glass in her hands, "I suppose you have. How long were you away?"

He had been counting the hours. "Eight months."

"That is a very long time to go without."

He knew what she was asking. She did not care about how many chambermaids he took to bed. She did not keep track of the number of squires he seduced or how many young lords and ladies he charmed. She did not consider any of them to be her equal.

"Thoughts of you were enough to keep me company," he reassured her, reaching over to take her hand in his. "No Avralaenian beauty could be enough to turn my head, when all I could long for were your arms."

There he could acquit himself; he had not bedded the queen.

Olympia seemed satisfied with that. She did not press further, and Shrukian was glad. He had not thought of a way to talk about the one who *had* caught his eye. Not that it mattered now.

She laced her fingers through his and met his gaze. He was struck by her beauty, almost as if he were seeing her for the first time. He kept her portrait with him when he traveled, but no artist's brush could do justice to such sultry dark eyes, or to the beautiful curve of her full red mouth. No canvas could ever hold a deep enough color for the jet locks of hair that spilled around her shoulders, illuminated by her wintry complexion. Shrukian held her hand a little tighter, afraid she might disappear if he let go.

"You have not slept," Olympia said.

"Not at all," Shrukian replied. He felt exhaustion in every part of his body, yet still felt like he could not fall asleep if he tried.

"Finish that," Olympia said, "and then we will go up together."

Shrukian nodded and took one more bite of his cake before sliding his plate away. The promise of bed and the chance to rest with Olympia in his arms, holding her close to his broad chest and kissing her wide, beautiful shoulders, was far more appealing to him than anything at the table. He took one last long drink from his cup and then stood, extending his hand to her. Olympia took his hand and stood as well, looping her arm through his and moving close to his side. Shrukian considered bidding his father goodnight, but Encarz was engaged in conversation, and he did not want to interrupt that.

Shrukian brought Olympia's hand to his lips, kissing her knuckles three times in succession before taking her upstairs.

PHARUN SAW HIS BROTHER and sister retreat out of the corner of his eye. He was only half-listening to the conversation that his cousin Meridith was having with the king, as it was about something completely out of the realm of his interest... taxes, grain... it was unbearable. Pharun motioned for a servant to step from the shadows and refill his glass, holding it by the stem and rolling it around in his fingers.

"Well, Meridith," Pharun finally found a pause where he could slide into the conversation, "perhaps you would make a fair chancellor after all."

Meridith paused. Pharun had not spoken to him for days, and he had not expected that pattern to break anytime soon. He was not sure what he had done, but he knew when it was better to stay silent and allow for his cousin to come back to him. The turnaround this time had been far shorter than expected. "You believe so?" He placed a piece of bread into his mouth to smother the sarcasm. "I know the land where you do not."

"Yes, I have been listening," Pharun said casually, leaning back into his chair. "Land this, land that. If the wheat does not come in this Spring, what shall we do; if the taxes are any higher, there will be a revolt; if the barons do not get their share, there will be blood."

"Something to that affect." Meridith put his fingertips together. "And do we extradite the Avralaenians responsible for the queen's death?"

"If Robin Brahntaiste has any taste for peace, she will treat this as an act of sedition from her own. She will no doubt make a formal request to have the traitors sent back once they are found, because she will want to put them through her own courts. However, for the sake of good faith, she will understand that we wish to execute them ourselves."

"*If* the assassins are found," Meridith added.

"They will be," Pharun assured him. He turned his glass in his hand again and glanced over at his father. "What do you think?"

Encarz raised an eyebrow. "About Meridith acting as your chancellor? I would encourage it."

"Yes, I am certain that you would, because then I could leave the castle and fulfill my priestly duties elsewhere."

"Feeding the hungry, healing the sick... I can think of no life better suited for your bleeding heart." Encarz rolled his eyes.

"There is more to being *Kren Veisten* than that. I promised to erect High Priest Felix a temple for Morcant here in the city." Pharun held his father's gaze as he spoke. "What do you think of that?"

The visible vein throbbing underneath Encarz's eye was all too pleasing a sight. "You would have to confer with the treasury, which I believe would be your chancellor's burden."

"Extraneous details to be worked out at a later date." Pharun brushed all of that aside. There was a somber pause as he watched his father take another drink. "It would not please you if I remained here?"

Encarz gave him a look. "Why should it please me?" he asked. "I do not know what answer you are searching for."

"An honest one," Pharun said, "that is all."

"Then consider this: when you are here, do we speak out of anything more than necessity? When you are gone, do you think you cross my mind as more than a fleeting nuisance? When you were young and deep in your studies, did I ever once write to the temple to inquire after your well-being? Did I ever visit? When we were at war, and I made you a captain, it was only to protect your brother—because I knew that if you were responsible for his life, he would come home safe. You would not dare fail me, not even for a moment. And yet I thought of you more during that time than I ever had before, because I prayed to Azrael every night that you would die, and the burden of your existence would be lifted from me." He looked like he had more to say, but his throat was dry. Encarz reached down again for his cup and brought it up to his mouth. It was empty.

Pharun watched it all, expressionless. When the king waved for a servant, the prince extended his cup instead, meeting his father's gaze.

"Here, father," he said, "take mine."

Encarz sat down his empty cup and took what was offered. He placed the rim to his lips and drank deeply, the flush of too much wine already evident in his cheeks.

Pharun rested his chin against his fingers, watching. "I suppose you are correct," he said, his voice drained of all inflection. "We do not touch at any point."

"It was only Lystra," Encarz muttered, setting the glass down. His hand was shaking. "Lystra wanted to mother you."

"I had a mother," Pharun said. "You killed her."

"She—" Encarz's words were cut off. He put a hand to his throat, his larynx bobbing up and down as he tried over and over again to swallow. His brow furrowed, and dark colors rushed to his face, turning it a hideous shade of purple with splotches of blue. He tried to inhale, but all that came from his mouth was a gurgle. Spittle and foam started pouring from his open mouth, and when he looked at Pharun again, his eyes were filled with blood.

Pharun did not move. The king collapsed against the table, and several servants rushed to his side. Someone called for a physician, but it was too late.

Pharun could have healed him with a word. A thought. He knew it, and so did Encarz.

The servant who had refilled Pharun's glass was trying to slip out through the side door. Pharun caught Meridith's attention and alerted him with a signal.

Meridith was on his feet within seconds, springing toward the servant with movements lighter than a fox.

The servant yelped and cried out for pity when the baron grabbed them by the hair. They were slight and, despite their terror, not difficult to subdue.

"To think, I could have been poisoned," Pharun said without taking his eyes off the king. "I suppose it should have been me." He raised his chin. "I would not take your place now for anything. But I *will* take your place."

Encarz might have heard it. Pharun hoped that he did. There was too much chaos, too many voices. It was all over in a minute.

Pharun finally turned his head and looked at Meridith. "I suppose they should be questioned."

"No!" the servant screeched, "please, because I—!"

Pharun raised his hand. "You are right. There is no need." He brought his hand down, and Meridith drew his sword.

Meridith forced the servant to their knees. Their babbling was over in a second. He sliced their head from their neck, and it hit the ground with a sickening thump.

"The king is dead," another servant whispered in despair.

Pharun put his fingertips together, and his words were almost too quiet to hear, "Long live the king."

9

TYBALT

The Dire Consequences of Extra-Marital Dalliance

THE THICK ROSE-RED CANDLE was burning down. A deep pool had formed at the base of the tall candlestick, with wax stalactites—sharper than dragon teeth—dripping from the sides. Marcellus had long lost track of the hour without any sense of whether there was even daylight left. There was only one window in his office, and he had drawn the curtains early that morning in order to fully concentrate. Now between the spell books, maps, and ink-stained journal pages, his eyes felt bleary, and his head was throbbing.

Marcellus stood, his neck and shoulders screaming in protest. He placed a hand on the back of his neck to try and work out the kinks as he walked around the side of his desk for some reprieve. Her majesty had been very adamant about what she wanted. The rebel mages had driven themselves farther south from their last known position and seemed to be heading for the border of West Avralaen. That was Marcellus' best guess, as he had not been able to find them again since Elzbet had strengthened their protections. He knew she could not last. As powerful as she was, she could not shoulder the burden of so much magic without rest. However, if they managed to reach the border and get lost in the Red Spine, that would make his job infinitely more difficult.

If they came out the other side, it would be another story. His connections in West Avralaen ran far deeper.

"It would be far easier if I could walk around her dreams," Amnas' voice came from the corner and startled the wizard. Marcellus put a hand on his chest and took a deep breath.

"I should be used to you coming and going," Marcellus said, turning to face the dreamweaver. Amnas smiled and stretched one leg out across the cushioned window seat.

"She takes a potion," Amnas said, "so that she does not dream when she sleeps. And sleeps so little that it has lasted her this long."

"It is bound to run out," Marcellus said. "All others in her company seem to have their dreams protected by her wards. And even if she does not, with so little rest, she will make a mistake. She has made them before."

"And yet." Amnas yawned against the back of his hand. "I thought you taught her everything she knows."

"It is not so simple," Marcellus dismissed.

"Your academy, then. The one you worked so hard to prove yourself worthy of. And your peers."

"They are all dead now."

"Except for you. And is it because Elzbet is not powerful enough to kill you, or is it that you are simply lucky?"

Marcellus turned and gave his companion a dark look. "Is there a point?"

"Something to ruminate only." Amnas' smile broadened. "When you find her, is she dead?"

"As good as." Marcellus sat back down. "I imagine that the queen will want her final word."

"And then what will be the reason for your employment with the queen?"

Marcellus shrugged. "I am not overly concerned."

"God-slaying weapons, a fair Dragolothian prince, hoarded gems along the coast... Are you certain?" Amnas sat up properly, resting his pointed chin in his hand.

Marcellus hissed through his teeth. "You are a demon."

"No," Amnas corrected him, "I am an angel. One of the few older than any god."

"Yes, I am aware. And you walk around my head, and my office, whenever you please, moving things about."

"I am not in your head as often as you may think," Amnas said. "Your dreams are not that interesting."

Marcellus tried another calming deep breath. "Is your sole purpose to upset me?"

"No, it is what I consider a bit of fun to lighten my mood." Amnas stood, taking on a more serious countenance as he moved toward Marcellus' desk. "Lystra's death in Dragoloth has caused quite a stir."

"Yes," Marcellus said, "we knew that it would."

"They are going to start a war," Amnas said.

"We knew that also." Marcellus placed his fingertips against his forehead.

"Any Avralaenian, East or West in origin, is not going to be safe on their shores." Amnas tilted his head, soft red curls rippling with every movement. "Do you worry for your weapons?"

"The gun-runner has them, and you assured me that he could be trusted."

"Well, yes, though if your gun-runner gets killed then you are back where you started."

Marcellus' head was starting to feel worse. "I need to send money, then, to ensure his safety and compliance?"

"It could not hurt. He intends to flee."

"Our people have enough safe havens in the capital city." Marcellus shook his head. "Help him find one. I will not have him taking celestial weapons on some slipshod boat never to be seen again."

"He has a slipshod boat of his own. He might be tempted," Amnas said. "Should I do anything about that?"

Marcellus waved his hand, opening a drawer in his desk and lifting a heavily burdened velvet purse out by its strings. "I trust you implicitly."

"You seem to keep making that mistake." Amnas held out his hand and Marcellus gave him the purse.

"That is more than enough silver to keep him well," the wizard said. "And if he bolts regardless, I want his hands."

"He might. He is stupid." Amnas made the purse disappear with a twist of his fingers. "I would hate for this to all be for naught."

"I am certain that you would." Marcellus set his hands down on top of the map he had been studying, smoothing it out to the corners. "Perhaps you would like to impart your thoughts on where I should look for the rebel mages as well?"

Amnas did not answer. Marcellus did not have to look up to know that the dreamweaver was already gone.

T HE SIGN FOR THE Laughing Albatross was still intact. Generously speaking, of course, as it was swaying on one hinge and the soft blue lettering had all but worn away completely. The fact that it was still standing was almost all that could be said. Tybalt had been around long enough to know that it had once been a drinking hole for pirates and mercenaries, and its reputation had gone from den of iniquity to a simple place where tired fishermen could get a good stew, until it had become nothing at all. It was as worn by the waves as the coves and rocks that surrounded it, but it bore the mark of the Black Rose Company, and that meant it was safe.

Safe *enough*. Tybalt had parted ways with Fione back in the city. There were more people to find, and Tybalt had to check on the condition of the *Daydream*. It had been months since he last brought it to harbor, and despite leaving it in the care of a retired pirate and an ex-admiral, his confidence was not soaring.

"For someone who swears by Balshett so often, you really have such little faith." Sweeney, who had once been decried as the scourge of the Darkened Sea, sat on the ship's rail with an apple in hand and watched Tybalt pace back and forth.

"Faith in a god is one thing," Tybalt said. "Faith in a siren and a naiad who walks upright is another."

"Sounds like we are a little over-qualified to sit and watch your boat, if you ask me," Sweeney said.

"And yet," Tybalt sighed. Nothing seemed amiss, except for food and some materials that needed replenishing. "Does the Laughing Albatross have any provisions?"

"We have plenty. We were not planning to venture back into the city until the ground thaws." Sweeney took another bite of his apple. "You are welcome to what you need. The sooner you are home, the better, from the sound of it."

"I do not worry about myself as much," Tybalt admitted, "but I have brought many people here with me, and I am responsible for returning them unharmed."

"And Fione is gathering them up for you, is he?"

"That is my understanding."

"Good man." Sweeney tossed his half-eaten apple overboard and jumped down from the rail, crossing his arms. "If you are finished fussing over your ship, Cahal might have supper ready by now."

It was getting a little late. The sun had all but disappeared behind the mountains on the horizon, and Tybalt was struggling to see details with only the aid of a lantern. "I should probably come look again in the morning, just to be sure."

"I highly doubt that it is going to sink halfway across the Darkened Sea just because you were not here to kiss it for two months." Sweeney put his arm around Tybalt's shoulders and steered him toward the dock. "You are welcome, by the way, and despite your ingratitude, I will not tell Cahal that you doubted him."

"I could do without the poison in my soup." Tybalt rubbed his face.

"Just enough to make you sick, I am sure."

Inside the old tavern was warm. Tybalt felt his stomach cramp as soon as he caught the scent of food. He had neglected to feed himself anything since the marketplace, and he had to wipe at the corners of his mouth to keep from salivating.

"Here." Sweeney dragged out a chair from underneath a table as he passed. "Sit down. We have mead if you want that."

"That would be fine." Tybalt rubbed his hands together to get some warmth back into his fingers as he took a seat.

Sweeney walked over to the counter, his high black ponytail bobbing up and down. The kitchen door swung open at the same time as Cahal emerged carrying two bowls of soup in his gloved hands and one in the crook of his elbow.

No matter how many years passed, Tybalt was never prepared to see Cahal. He did not know the reason, but he had never found Sweeney's coloration to be very startling. The siren's skin was a dusky blue, and his eyes were muddy green like river water. He had red spotting around his temples and the high points of his cheekbones, but it was such a deep, ruddy shade that it did not stick out incredibly. Cahal's skin was bright blue with shades of purple and green, with bright red speckles across his nose and cheeks and two red stripes cutting down the path of his right eye. His eyes were the same color, glistening like rubies from underneath sleek black brows.

"I made leek and fish stew," Cahal said, bringing the bowls over to the table and setting them down.

"It smells wonderful." Tybalt pulled a bowl closer to himself. Truly it did not, but he was not about to criticize the cooking of a man with poisonous skin.

"Mm." Sweeney sat down a mug of mead and slid it toward their guest, picking up a bowl for himself as he sat down. "His ship was fine, by the way."

"I know," Cahal said, "I checked on it this morning."

"I suppose he does not trust you." Sweeney blew the steam away from his spoon.

Tybalt choked, although he blamed it on the sudden onslaught of spices from the stew.

Cahal eyed him severely. "Do you forget that it was my ship first?"

"No." Tybalt shook his head, his voice coming out a little strained. "Not at all, Admiral."

Cahal's mouth tightened at the corners. "You have a plan, then?"

"Gather as many people as I can and sail for West Avralaen by tomorrow night," Tybalt replied.

"I do not think that this will blow over for some time," Cahal said. "It could be well over a year before you are able to return to Dragolothian shores once you leave."

"I am established enough at home to keep me stable," Tybalt said. "They have just as much need for arms and Glow." He scraped his spoon along the sides of his bowl. "It may not be so terrible, anyway... to have a reason to stay home and see Mercury."

Cahal scoffed under his breath. "To think your husband would want you back."

"As long as I do not interfere with his plants." Tybalt managed a small smile. It was painful to think about how his relationship with his husband had grown so strained over the years. It was his own fault; he was often gone for months at a time, and he could not expect time to freeze in his absence. Mercury had every right to move on, but he chose to stay. Still, he did not greet Tybalt with the smile that he used to. When they were together, they barely spoke.

Sweeney cleaned his spoon by pulling it between his lips. "One at home is worth six at the harbor, they used to say."

Tybalt rolled his eyes. "You have experience with that?"

"No. I always chose 'none' on either side." Sweeney grinned, flashing all his sharp teeth. "I will take a human heart, but only because they are delicious."

Tybalt felt a shiver run up his spine. "I think I need to go to bed."

"A sound decision." Sweeney swung his hand down and clapped Tybalt on the shoulder. "If anything exciting occurs, I will be sure to wake you."

"Please do not." Tybalt stood. "Unless the building catches fire."

"Noted." Sweeney reached into the pocket of his oversized coat and dug out a pipe. Cahal's expression did not change as he crossed his arms and leaned back in his seat.

Tybalt pushed his hand through his tight black curls and stood. His whole body protested with the sudden movement, but he was tired enough that even the bug-ridden beds of the Laughing Albatross sounded like a comfort. He started up the stairs and left the sea creatures to gossip below, although they were eerily silent as he walked, watching him with reflective red and yellow eyes.

❖ ⸻ ❖

TARQUIN KNEW WHERE THE Laughing Albatross was. Before the Gilded Lily, he had spent a deal of time there injecting Red into his veins with old hollow needles he had stolen from doctors. That was before Pheseus, before everything else. It was where he had met Tybalt—in a haze of tobacco and opium smoke.

There was no guarantee that Tybalt would be here now, and the place did not even look occupied. He just knew that he had to start somewhere, and dawn was fast approaching.

The door looked like it was one strong wind away from being ripped off its hinges. Tarquin flinched when it swung open, his hand coming up to protect his face like it was going to knock him off his feet. He recognized the siren on the other side immediately, although from the way Sweeney was looking him up and down, he could not tell if it was mutual.

"Knucklebones," Tarquin said immediately, yanking the word deep from the recesses of his brain.

Sweeney arched an eyebrow. "It has been a few years since we have even asked anyone for a password."

"I see years have not favored this place." Tarquin rubbed at the back of his neck. "It is dreadfully cold."

"You want in?" Sweeney glanced over his shoulder and stepped aside. "I can get the fire going again."

Tarquin nodded his thanks and shuffled over the threshold, dropping the modest bag he had in his possession and wrapping his hands up in his coat. He had had it for many years, and it was worn thin in some places, but it was better than nothing at all. Sweeney snapped his fingers to get the boy's attention and gestured at a chair as he moved toward the dying hearth.

"We do not have anything hot to eat," he said. "Cahal will probably make something in an hour or so." He grabbed a long iron poker and went to prod at the logs, stirring up sparks.

"I am not hungry." It was the truth. He had not been able to eat since what he had witnessed between Josse and Florindel.

Sweeney tossed another log down and poked at it some more. "What is it, then?" The siren kept a shiny pistol by his side. It was difficult to ignore. Tarquin licked his dry lips and swallowed hard.

"I came looking for..." Tybalt was well-known here, but he still felt strange asking for him by name. "I am looking for Tybalt Carideo."

Sweeney made a contemplative noise in his throat. "Sounds familiar."

"I was with him in the city..." Tarquin faltered at providing the full explanation, not wanting this creature to know exactly *who* he was running from. "I lost track of him when they announced the queen's death."

Sweeney finally pulled his murky yellow eyes from the fireplace, looking Tarquin up and down. "You are part of his crew, then?"

Tarquin tried not to fidget. "Yes," he said quickly.

Sweeney made another curious sound and then stepped away from the hearth, resting the poker against its side. "He is sleeping," he said. "He will be down eventually as well."

Tarquin let out a breath of relief. At least Tybalt was here, and he did not have to go searching for him elsewhere and risk getting caught.

"Funny," Sweeney said, sitting down and bringing one leg up to rest on top of his opposite knee. "I did not think Tybalt kept any slaves."

Tarquin gasped, but he kept his hands firmly shoved between his thighs. "What do you mean?" Then he said with confidence, "He does not."

"Oh?" Sweeney tapped at his throat. Tarquin finally reached up and touched the thin silver circlet that was welded around his neck. He had tried so hard to hide it, but the scarf had slipped.

"He..." Tarquin bit at the dry skin on his bottom lip until it bled. "Would you think less of him if he did?"

"A little," Sweeney said, "considering I find it abhorrent."

"It is a touch more complicated than that," Tarquin said.

"Only a touch?" Sweeney drummed his fingers against his leg. "I have tools somewhere around here for cutting those off."

"That is—" Tarquin started without thinking.

"Illegal?" Sweeney cut him off. "I thought you had been here before."

Tarquin touched the circlet again, stroking the cold metal with his fingertips. "In exchange for what?"

"We can start with where you actually came from," Sweeney said.

"The Gilded Lily." His heart quickened even uttering the words.

"Ah." The pieces started falling together for the siren. "So you are running from Florindel Nazaire."

His words rang out like a condemnation. For Tarquin, coming from another mouth, they certainly could have been. There were plenty who loved Florindel, and there were just as many who feared him or owed him something in some way. Tarquin did not know enough about the house master's affairs to guess where Sweeney's view might fall.

"I saw…" Tarquin was not even sure he should speak about what he had witnessed. It felt forbidden, yet keeping the truth under his tongue would not serve him. "I saw another boy die. He was poisoned." He felt pressure in his chest.

Sweeney cocked his head. "There have always been rumors," he said.

"I know." The pressure was building, and Tarquin felt like he could not breathe. "I tried to forget it happened. I hid in my room for hours. Then supper came, and I could not eat. All I could think about was how I had to leave."

"It was both brave and reckless." Sweeney tried to sound reassuring. He stood again, gesturing for Tarquin to remain seated as he moved behind the bar to dig around. "As for why you chose to follow Tybalt, that is a little more puzzling. I imagine it is because he has a ship, which is useful."

"Yes," Tarquin's voice faltered a bit as he stared into the fire, "very useful."

Sweeney did not say anything else for a few minutes. When he emerged from behind the bar once more, he had a small hacksaw, the length of the entire instrument being not much more than his hand.

Tarquin's eyes widened. The siren's grin was all too large.

"Do you trust me?" Sweeney asked.

"Only just." Tarquin could not keep his nerves out of his voice.

"Well." Sweeney dropped to one knee beside him, slipping his fingers underneath the delicate circlet. "There is steel inside, is there not?"

"I believe so," Tarquin nodded.

"Do not move," Sweeney said, resting the blade's teeth against the edge of the silver and gripping the collar tight in the other hand. "I could easily slice open your throat."

"Nothing to worry about, then," Tarquin muttered. "Have you cut through many of these?"

"A handful," Sweeney said. The hacksaw blade made an awful sound as its jagged teeth ground against the metal. Tarquin tried to keep his eyes fixed straight ahead, finding a window to focus on rather than the perilous sawing. Through the dirty glass, he could see the beginnings of dawn—not quite color, but enough light to take the sky from a deep midnight black to a dusky dark blue.

The *Daydream* was out there. He could just see the tall, skinny black silhouette of the mast. He had never been on a ship before, but it had been easy to dream of following Tybalt onto one. He had never been to West Avralaen either, but he had heard enough tales that he had been able to construct a picture in his mind of what he thought it might be like. He imagined bright, warm sunlight soaking the ground. He imagined bustling marketplaces, festivals, and a range of mountains so tall that not even a high-flying dragon could crest the peaks.

Orange was starting to break up the monotony of blue. Tarquin held back a sigh, his neck already cramping from the uncomfortable angle. He did not dare move, but the rest of his body was beginning to twinge in protest.

He tried to keep his focus on the window, except something did not look right. He had expected sunrise to spread across the sky, but all of the color was staying in one spot. The streaks of orange were flickering, moving as if alive, and then he noticed sparks—and a plume of black smoke chasing them upward.

"Sweeney," he said, trying to convey his alarm without startling the creature holding a saw, "Sweeney, something is burning."

"Cahal might be in the kitchen already," Sweeney started.

"No." Tarquin's whole body was so tense that he felt like he was going to vomit. "Not the kitchen. *Look.*" He tilted his chin toward the window.

Sweeney pulled the hacksaw away, abandoning his project to stand and go see for himself. When he got to the window, he swore, making the symbol of the water god and spitting onto the floor.

"The ship is on fire," he said with a stunning amount of vitriol.

Tarquin choked on his own panic. "What can we do?" He barely had a chance to ask before the siren was tearing out the door, heading for the dock. Tarquin followed him out, running as quickly as his thin legs could carry him. Outside, the fire roared like a beast in pain. Black smoke was pouring onto the beach and made Tarquin's eyes sting, while the heat from the flames made it nearly impossible to breathe. Tarquin pulled his sleeve down over his knuckles and wiped at his eyes, trying to clear them enough to see. When he could finally focus, he saw Sweeney cutting the lines from the dock, which sent the burning mass out toward the ocean.

"We cannot save it?" Tarquin coughed into his hand. His lungs burned from the smoke.

"No," Sweeney said. "I could only save us. I did not want that to spread up here." He stood on the beach with his arms folded across his chest, watching as the ship started to lean. "Cahal is going to be so pissed."

10

PHARUN

THE DIVINE BURDEN OF A DUTIFUL CHILD

THE GREAT ARCHED WINDOW was, in Pharun's opinion, far too enormous for such a narrow hall. He did not know if the architect had ever considered that a king might wish for somewhere to sit quietly without fear of being disturbed, and if so, perhaps that was the reasoning. The velvet window seat was worn from frequent use, and there were traces of ash around the sill from where a pipe had been, perhaps once too frequently, passed back and forth.

He did not know how many nights Encarz had spent in that very window gazing out across the courtyard and into the distance, looking past the prodigious mountains that formed The Dragon's

Teeth and toward the horizon beyond where Simisola lay. Encarz had always kept his eyes forward, fixed on conquest. For Pharun, the mountains had always been stern sentinels acting as just one more barrier to keep him imprisoned.

Pressure being added to the window seat was enough to pull him from his thoughts. From the corner of his eye, Pharun caught a glimpse of Felix resting his knee against the cushion. The blond priest looked a little uncertain and glanced at Pharun as if asking for permission. In the soft light of near-dawn, his eyes looked bluer and clearer than they ever had before. His dirty blond hair was pulled back into a bun, but a few errant strays still managed to sweep into his face and mingle with his beard. He looked tired—exhausted, in all truth. Pharun moved his propped-up leg and drew it closer to his frame as an invitation. Felix took his place on the other side of the window seat, leaning his shoulders against the frame to keep as much distance between them as was proper.

"How are you?" Felix asked softly. His voice carried just far enough.

"Waiting is not my strong suit," Pharun replied, wrapping his arms loosely around his knee. "The royal physician confirmed father's death. His body is still in the infirmary, I think. They are going to start preparing it soon. His funeral is going to be far more of an affair than Lystra's."

Felix nodded. "When a queen dies, a nation mourns. When the king dies, it closes ranks."

"We have to be prepared for anything. His death may embolden our enemies. It may break any weak alliances. Everything is being held together by a thread right now."

They sat in silence for a moment before Felix spoke again. "I have not been able to sleep, thinking about how it could have been you."

A cryptic expression crossed Pharun's face. "It could have been, yes."

"I am glad that it was not," Felix said so quietly that it could barely be heard.

A somewhat bitter smile played over Pharun's lips. "Where would you be without your Crowned Priest?" He swept his tongue over his teeth and glanced out the window again. "My father's council will meet in a few hours. They will want to discuss his heir."

"Your brother?" Felix guessed. He was not prepared for the venom in Pharun's look.

"I…" Felix quickly tried to explain himself. "Only because he… You are Crowned Priest. The Trine Nation Clerical Law states—"

"I know what it says," Pharun clipped. "Believe you me when I say that my father only allowed me to take this path because he knew it would nullify any legal hope I had of becoming king."

Felix nodded, his heart pounding. "And you...?"

"I have not come this far," Pharun said, "to continue bowing to my brother's shadow."

Felix did not know what to say. He did not want to upset Pharun further and wished to all the gods that he could read the other man better. Pharun's body language was relaxed, but Felix could tell from his words that he was as tense as a wire. Felix did not know enough about courts to know who would be sitting on the king's council and who Pharun would have to contend with.

He wanted to reach out and take Pharun's hand as he had at the queen's funeral. He understood that it had been different then, that a degree of familiarity could be permitted between two priests in a holy place, one of whom was suffering a great deal of loss and pain. This place was not holy. It was intimate. He felt he had already revealed too much of himself, and that what little rectitude remained between them would be soon compromised. Before coming to Dragoloth, he had never seen this side of Pharun—severe, calculating, fighting to survive;

he had never thought of the prince as someone who needed to fight for anything. In East Avralaen, everything seemed to fall into his lap with ease. He was always arrogant, confident, never once did he bow his head or step back to think twice before he moved.

It was all a different world now, and East Avralaen felt as distant as a dream. So much had happened in such a short time, and the dark mountains and deep snowdrifts felt cold and suffocating.

From the end of the hall, they heard something drop. Both men glanced up simultaneously to see a red glass marble rolling past, finally coming to a stop when it hit the side of Pharun's boot. Nkiru emerged into view at the same instant, the shadows parting for her like a veil only to seamlessly fall back into place in her wake.

"Thank you for announcing your presence," Pharun said in reference to the marble.

"I did what I could." Nkiru made no sound at all as she came to stand before them. A twist of her long fingers brought the marble rising up from the floor as if suspended on a wire and back into her palm. "You have Queen Efemena's condolences."

"She is gracious," Pharun replied.

"You do not have mine," Nkiru said immediately. "You could have mentioned that this was part of the plan."

Pharun shrugged. "Nothing has changed. There will be war with East Avralaen now for certain. It is only a matter of when."

"The certainty of war with East Avralaen does not guarantee there will be no war against Simisola," Nkiru said. "And to think that I came here with good news."

"Which is?"

"I looked through the documents you shared with me, and I did a little digging of my own," the spider told him. "What it all amounts to is that I have found a neck for your noose."

"That *is* good news," Pharun agreed.

"He has many ties, however," Nkiru cautioned. "And his roots run deep. If I were to bring him here, his benefactors might not be willing to cut him loose without a fight."

"Are you telling me," Pharun began, "that you uncovered an actual Avralaenian countermine?"

Nkiru rolled the marble around in her palm. "I am not certain yet. I only wanted to caution you."

"I appreciate your intelligence, of course," Pharun said. "I want him brought here. Do what you must to see it through."

"As you say." The marble vanished from Nkiru's hand as she slipped it into her clothing.

"I meet with the king's council in only a few hours," Pharun said.

"Ambassador Arendse will wish an audience as well," Nkiru told him. "She will want to discuss the position of Simisolan garrisons along the border."

"Of course. If all goes well, I will happily meet with your ambassador," Pharun said, straightening his posture in the window seat. "We can discuss Simisolan troops all she likes, as well as how they might wish to aid Dragoloth in the near future."

"If all goes well," Nkiru echoed back his words. "Simisola has no quarrel with the Dragon. Your brother is your problem."

"Ah," Pharun's contempt saturated his voice, "my brother."

A COLD GUST OF air was enough to make Shrukian stir. Up until that point, he had been sleeping heavily underneath a pile of fur blankets with Olympia curled up by his side. Exhaustion had taken over almost immediately, and it had not been as difficult as he feared falling asleep once his head hit the pillow. Between the furs, the heat of Olympia's skin, and the fire roaring steadily in the hearth, he had been quite comfortable.

Even now, the cold was not enough to wake him entirely. Somewhere in the depths of his groggy brain, he reasoned that it had to be a servant slipping in to stoke the fire. His solution was to bury his arm further underneath the covers and wrap it around Olympia's waist to drag her closer. Traces of perfume still clung to her skin, and the intoxicating scent was comforting enough to lull him back to sleep.

"Shrukian." By the time he realized that his name was being called, the voice sounded a little irked. "*Shrukian.*"

"Mm?" He cracked open his eyes just enough to take in the shape beside his bed. That voice he would have recognized anywhere. "Meridith?"

His cousin was standing close, although not close enough to be within stabbing distance. Shrukian kept a dagger under his pillow for unwanted visitors, which made that a fair precaution.

"I need your attention," Meridith said. "It is important. Olympia, too. She needs to be awake."

Shrukian furrowed his brow, sitting up and freeing his arms from the mountain of covers. He reached down and rested his hand on Olympia's shoulder, stroking his thumb over the curve as he tried to shake her awake as gently as he could.

"Olympia," he murmured, reaching over to kiss her on the ear as he spoke. "Meridith is here."

"Tell him to leave," she muttered back. Shrukian had to fight back a tired smile.

"He says it is important." Shrukian straightened back up as Olympia finally stirred, sweeping his thick mass of black curls away from his face to try and pull himself together. He did not even know the hour; every curtain in the room was drawn. He looked at his cousin, whose countenance was unusually solemn.

"I am awake," Olympia said, concealing a yawn as she sat up. Neither of them had gone to bed clothed, and while Shrukian thought she looked like a vision, he was not keen on sharing that with his cousin. He pulled one of the blankets up to cover her chest, tucking it around her so that she could still lean against him comfortably while being concealed.

"Go on," Shrukian finally nodded in Meridith's direction. "What is it you have to say?"

Meridith crossed his hands in front of him. "I regret that I must be the one to bring you such grim tidings as these, cousins. Yet there is never a good way. Your father, the king, has died."

Shrukian felt cold. He looked at Meridith as if he had not heard him correctly. "My father...?"

"He was assassinated," Meridith told them. "It happened barely an hour ago. I killed the one responsible myself immediately, though that does not change anything."

Shrukian put his arm around Olympia's shoulders and held her tight. Her body was rigid, and he could only imagine the storm of grief that was overtaking her mind. She was too strong to weep in the moment, but he knew that it would come. As for himself, he was not sure how he felt. Lystra's death had felt like a physical blow, while this announcement made him feel still. Perhaps it was that fresh grief had no room where existing grief was still healing, or perhaps it was that it simply did not feel real.

Nevertheless, sorrow would have to wait. More immediate matters were going to require his attention. Encarz's death meant that the world was going to change very quickly, and Shrukian was going to bear the lion's share of the burden in putting it all back in order.

Dragoloth was in need of a king, and he knew where his responsibilities lay.

As much as he wanted to, he could not stay and comfort Olympia, and he could not fall back asleep and pretend he had never been disturbed. Shrukian pulled the rest of his covers away, moving quickly to get out of bed. His clothes from the night previous were still crumpled on the floor, and no servant had been by to lay out something fresh for him to wear. He reasoned that it must not quite be morning. His wardrobe was nearby, and he pulled out the first robe he found. "Has father's council yet met?"

"No," Meridith said. "They are waiting for you." He paused, unable to express all he wanted to say. "I am sorry."

Shrukian turned. He reached out and placed his hands on Meridith's shoulders, looking his cousin in the eye. "I remember when your father died. I was there to comfort you then."

"I will be here for you now," Meridith said, looking at Olympia as well. "Both of you."

Olympia nodded, less willing to waste time on sentiment. "I will follow you, Shrukian," she said. "Go to the council. I will dress and be there quickly. Go with him," she told Meridith. "And go now. Do not let Pharun get there first."

Shrukian's heart sank. "Pharun will not oppose me on this," he said.

"Every step of the way," Olympia said. "Now *go*."

THE COUNCIL CHAMBER WAS in the king's apartment right beside his bedchamber. It faced a beautiful courtyard that had been cleared of snow, just enough so that the king could admire the elegant marble structures and tall fountains that had been erected. The curtains were still drawn to keep out the bitter morning chill, and despite the efforts of several bright oil lamps, it felt as though it should have been midnight.

Shrukian had taken a seat at the council's table many times. Though he rarely spoke up during their discussions, he had studied them all closely—studied his father—hoping that when the time came, he would be prepared to take the reins as readily as Encarz. Now he was faced with the realization that nothing could have prepared him for the burden of a crown, nor for the death of the man he revered. Assassination was a tangled maze. The lords and barons would have opinions, he was certain, but before any matters of state were handled, justice would have to be served. If war came of this, he was prepared to lead the charge.

The chamber was empty; he was the first to arrive. He had asked Meridith to give him a moment alone and left him standing outside of the door. The chair that headed the king's table waited just out the light's reach, half-shrouded in shadow. A carved wooden dragon curled around the frame and seemed to regard him with contempt, the deep pits of its eye sockets catching just enough light to look alive.

A grey hand came out of the darkness, resting against the dragon's back and following the ridges of its spine all the way down to its tail. Shrukian caught his breath, following the path of his brother's fingers, which now seemed to be the only things capable of motion in the sudden stillness.

"Brother," Shrukian finally said, the word escaping on a hushed breath.

"Shrukian," Pharun said in return, meeting his gaze.

Shrukian did not know where to begin. "How are you?" It came out as a plea, with all his self-righteous determination being sapped out at the sight of his elder brother. "Talk to me."

"What is there to say?" Pharun asked. "Your father is dead."

"*Our* father," Shrukian corrected. "He loved you too."

The dragon underneath Pharun's hand cracked, even though he did not tighten his grip. "You cannot be king and an idiot," Pharun said. "You have to pick one. There is not a drop of his blood in my veins. He made that abundantly clear."

Shrukian drew in a careful breath. "I am not here to argue," he said. "No matter what, it is all past."

"Yes," Pharun said as the crack in the chair deepened, making a wide split down the back, though the cushion kept it from breaking entirely apart. "It is all past."

"And I have always had love for you," Shrukian said.

"As a drunkard loves his wine." Pharun's countenance held all the scorn his voice did not convey.

That hurt. Shrukian buried it as deep as he could for the moment. "We cannot be divided when the council comes together. You speak for the gods, and I am the head of state. We must work in accordance and punish those responsible for his downfall."

"Ah," Pharun said, "that is actually something that I wanted to discuss with you." He moved his hand, and the king's chair pulled away from the table on its own, allowing him to take a seat. "We have very good information that points toward East Avralaen's involvement. What do you know of that?"

"Nothing," Shrukian snapped immediately. He did not believe it for a moment. Such a conspiracy would unravel everything he had spent months negotiating. Queen Robin was their strongest ally with good reasons to support Dragolothian soldiers at Simisolan borders. War with Dragoloth would cost her more than it was worth.

"Are you so certain?" Pharun pressed his fingertips together. "You were on Avralaenian soil for the better part of a year, wooing their queen."

"Securing ships. Strengthening an alliance," Shrukian said through his teeth.

"Of course. I simply believe that you should consider how this looks. You disappear for months, you court the Avralaenian queen. You are sent to woo her for ships, but perhaps you charm her for a little more. During this time, your mother is senselessly murdered. Avralaenian involvement is suspected, but nothing can be immediately proved. You return home quickly—far quicker than a ship can bear you. Which leaves two possibilities: you were either on your way back already, without writing the king that you were returning, or you used a spell. And since you are not a caster and have no magic at your disposal, that would mean that you were rather close to someone who had a great deal of power to waste."

"My mother was dead," Shrukian cut him off. "How is that a waste?"

"And *then*," Pharun hammered on, "the night of your mother's funeral, the king is assassinated as well. Although this time, Avralaenian involvement cannot be hidden. And you, his favored son, are already in the castle ready to rise to the occasion and assume the burden of the crown. It does seem timely, does it not?"

"The things you are implying," Shrukian snarled, "are base and revolting. I would never stoop to such lows. They were my mother and father."

"Listen, dear." Pharun rested his hand against his own chest. "I believe you. I, personally, do not believe that you are capable of such things—at least not of your own accord. Being manipulated by a pretty face, however, is certainly within your nature. And whatever the case," he added before Shrukian could speak again, "it is not me that you must convince. It is the entire king's council. And once this information is brought to light, they will undoubtedly be incensed. They may not give you the chance to explain yourself."

Shrukian's mouth felt dry. "They are good men. I know them all. They served my father faithfully as Azrael; they will not believe a poisonous word against me."

"You may be right," Pharun said, "and you have a point. Of course, I have one too. I intend to contest your right to the throne, and I have a fair chance at success."

Shrukian felt his spine stiffen. "You will abdicate your position as *Kren Veisten?*"

"No," Pharun said. "I intend to wear both titles. I will drag this process through the courts where every priest and judge will be on my side. Your lords and barons cannot stack up against divine will, nor will they try when they discover how you seduced Queen Robin and attempted to merge the two countries, infesting us with Avralaenian influence."

Shrukian's hands were trembling with rage. It was becoming difficult to breathe. He wanted to grab his brother by the throat and tear out his lying, viperous tongue. He had never been so angry, certainly never with Pharun, and yet it was all he could do to stop himself. He forced himself to stay rooted to one spot, afraid of what might happen if he even budged a centimeter.

"You cannot threaten me," Shrukian finally managed to say, "when you do not have a shred of evidence, only whispers."

"Your greatest mistake," Pharun said, "would be to underestimate me."

Shrukian drew in another ragged breath. "You want war, and you do not care who is at the end of your blade."

"I want you to formally renounce your claim," Pharun told him. "I think that would clear a few things up nicely and take a great deal of pressure away from you."

"And if I were to take my chances with the barons instead?" Shrukian asked.

Pharun rolled that around in his head for a moment, giving Shrukian plenty of time to ruminate on the possibilities. "I am not the one in danger," he said at last. "You, on the other hand, stand a fair chance of being banished if not worse. So, by all means, speak to the council. I will as well. Let them decide how to proceed."

The anger rumbling in Shrukian's gut was turning into sour hatred. He watched as Pharun stood and rested his hand again on the back of the king's chair, sliding his fingertips into the yawning divide that he had created.

"As little faith as I have in your intellect," Pharun said, "I think you can be trusted to make one decent choice." As he spoke, the cushion ripped itself in two, following the split in the wood frame all the way down. The king's chair collapsed in two pieces as Pharun pulled his hand back.

Shrukian took an instinctive step back. He could hear voices and footsteps in the hallway—servants or lords, he could not make out enough to determine. His head was spinning, and it was getting harder to untangle Pharun's words from what was absolute truth even in his own skull. And what if every lord and baron was not for him, as he believed? It only took one or two to bend the ears of the rest.

He had to leave the room. He needed to be able to think, and he was suddenly overcome by paranoia that Pharun could look into his brain and see every single one of his thoughts.

Shrukian took another step back, followed by another. He looked at Pharun one more time, as if holding onto a thread of hope that this was all a charade or a nightmare.

His brother did not say anything. Shrukian turned quickly on his heel and left.

Meridith was waiting outside the door. Olympia had joined him, and the two were speaking in low voices as they waited to be welcomed inside. Shrukian did not stop to address them. He heard Olympia call out to him, but his tongue felt too heavy to speak.

Time was what he did not have, but it was what he desperately needed. A moment or two alone, that was all he wanted.

Of course, the bitter irony was that he was more alone now than he had ever been before.

11

FELIX

WHILE THE PRIEST MAKES HIS CONFESSION...

T HE TEMPLE OF AZRAEL was welcoming to all, so they claimed.

There was nothing Felix longed for more so than his home. He missed East Avralaen's green hills and gentle, warm breezes. He missed the sun on his cheeks and feeling like its golden warmth had more beauty and purpose than simply existing to keep the plants from dying out. He missed being able to breathe freely without every dry inhale making his nose burn. Above all, he missed his temple—Morcant's temple. It felt like an age since he had walked through the halls where he was raised, or since he had been able to kneel in front of the colossal icon wrought in painted bronze. Every pillar, every wall was concrete and marble. The Temple of Morcant was unparalleled in artistry and affluence, and its clergy sheltered all who stepped through its doors.

Azrael's temple was as old as the nation itself, with every king since its inception pouring generous amounts of wealth into improvements. There were more gold icons in the main prayer chamber than Felix could count. The cups and offering bowls on the alter were gold and ivory, most of them studded with jewels.

He had lost track of the countless murals and intricate stained-glass windows, always depicting Azrael as either the warrior king felling enemies with his great sword or as the chaotic trickster, tearing his way free from the seven hells and emerging in a frenzy. Azrael had worn so many faces over the centuries that it was difficult for Felix to grasp. Morcant was an immutable god. He never changed his face or his mind. He had engraved his laws in stone when the world began, and they remained untouched thousands of years later. His priests followed his example, remaining constant, steadfast, and humble even through the most harrowing trials.

And this, Felix could not help but think, had to be one of the most harrowing catechisms of his life. If there had been anywhere else he could go to feel closer to his god, he would have turned on his heel and fled. All this had little to do with the temple itself, though he would not deny an icy dread that trickled down his spine as he walked up the wide, steep staircase. He filed it away as homesickness and tried not to think about the priests who lurked inside. He hoped, above all, that he would not encounter High Priest Malhii, and that he might be able to say his prayers in peace and leave quickly.

The Temple of Azrael had a special chamber available for visitors of other faiths to attend to their prayers. Where someone else may have found offense in being turned away from the main temple, Felix found it a relief. The chamber was attached to one of the oldest sections of the building that had not been incredibly well-kept, although it still maintained a kind of worn dignity that he found comforting. Dragon's blood resin emanated a thick plume of smoke from a bowl of burning black charcoals. The smell and the heat overwhelmed the modest space. Felix felt a little dizzy as he walked up to the altar and knelt on one of the flattened pillows, quickly making the sign of Morcant over his face and chest. Even in a strange temple, he never felt far from his god. Morcant's presence was nearly instant, showing itself as a flutter in Felix's chest and pressure at the top of his skull. The high priest closed his eyes, bowing his head and stroking the pendant hanging around his neck. He did not know where to begin—and it had been so long since he had attended to his prayers properly. He felt ashamed to come here now, when he had not been consistent in his devotion.

"Morcant..." He stumbled over the words. His surroundings had already started to fade. The pressure at the top of his head increased, making the world feel like it was hurling past even though his eyes were closed. Felix doubled over on his knees, bowing deeply so that his forehead nearly touched the floor. "I need help." His words sounded strange to his own ears. He was not so sure that he had spoken aloud the second time.

His head was still spinning; now he felt like he was falling. The flutter in his chest became more pressure that made him feel like his ribs were being squeezed. He tried to breathe past it, but his lungs were on fire from the smoke, and he started coughing hard enough that he thought he was going to retch.

"Please, speak to me," Felix pleaded. "I have been having dreams, such dreams… and I do not know where to go from here."

Past the roar of blood in his ears, he heard movement. Felix glanced up, one hand still gripping his pendant while the other braced him against the floor. He saw the tops of gleaming black boots and the embroidered hem of a luxurious silk garment. On the hem were white roses and erica flowers, accentuated by pearls and framed by curling vines. Felix took another deep breath, finding it easier this time around. He could no longer smell the dragon's blood. He straightened a little on his knees, resting his hands on his lap and daring to raise his head. He knew better than to look a god in the eyes, but as high priest, he could claim the privilege of looking one in the face.

"It has been some time since we spoke." Morcant's voice was as deep as a tomb and echoed like the chambers of a mausoleum.

"Some time," Felix agreed. Shame made his face hot. It rushed all the way down his neck, and he felt the urge to double over once again. "The days are getting darker."

"You have not been home for some time." Morcant's black, withered hand crossed over His fleshier one, long, jagged nails scraping over the supple skin. "That is what plagues you."

"Among other things," Felix said helplessly. "My dreams are filled with horrors, and I cannot sleep for fear that they might be real. I am no stranger to night terrors, but when I am asleep, I can feel…" He tried to compose himself. "I can feel the flames, I can smell the smoke and burning flesh. I can hear acolytes screaming as they are tortured and beaten. And when I walk down the temple steps, I slip in blood and brains that are scattered like spilled mash."

"Usually if a priest dreams that his temple is burning, it means that there is something for which he has to atone," Morcant said simply.

Felix shook his head before he could stop himself. "I have been remiss in my prayers," he said, "but I have served faithfully in every other aspect. I have not given myself over to one temptation abroad."

"Perhaps," Morcant tilted His head, "or perhaps not."

Felix flinched as if he had been struck. "I made a mistake," he admitted. "I should not have followed the Crowned Priest so far."

"And why not?" Morcant asked. "Is it the physical distance between you and your flock that is causing such a divide in your heart?"

Felix worried his bottom lip. "Perhaps I fear for them because I am not with them. If the temple was burning, or if they were otherwise under attack, I could do nothing. I would not even know."

"Perhaps you fear for yourself," Morcant presented. "The fire that consumes your sanctuary may be one ignited deeper in your flesh."

Felix did not have a response. His mouth fell open as he tried to form one, but no words came out as he choked. He kept his eyes on Morcant, although the god's avatar stood perfectly still. Silence engulfed them for a moment until it became hard for Felix to breathe again.

"I would never abandon my vows," he said finally.

"You trouble yourself too deeply," the god replied. "Be gracious to your tender heart; it is human and can only bear so much." The avatar was starting to fade. Felix felt a miserable pull—he did not want the god to leave, and he did not want to go back to feeling so alone. Before he could stop them, tears welled up to his eyes and rolled down his cheeks hot and fast, vanishing into his beard.

"There, now," Morcant's voice still echoed strongly. "You must have some resolve. The city of Seravell is not safe for you. Return to the castle quickly."

"It is not safe?" Felix fought to compose himself, dashing his sleeve across his eyes. "Even for a priest?"

"Not for a priest of mine." Morcant had almost entirely faded from view. "Leave." His voice was gone as well.

Everything came back at once. The incense, the flickering candles, the thin pillow beneath his knees, and the birds flitting through the domed ceiling rafters. Felix felt like he was going to be sick, although he was familiar enough with that sensation to suppress it. Any encounter with the divine was going to end feeling like someone was trying to pull your stomach through your kneecaps.

Morcant's response had been unexpected. Felix thought he would come out of prayer properly chastised, and instead he felt more lost than before. His dreams about the burning temple had been too realistic to ignore, but Morcant had made it clear that the problem was less literal and more of a buried moral failing. Felix was so disgusted with himself that it left a bad taste in his mouth.

He finally rose. The chamber was starting to fill with new bodies who were seeking prayer and solace. He wondered how many of them felt cut adrift. He wondered if any of them were bringing candles or coins for Morcant.

Felix started walking down the middle aisle, keeping his chin tilted downward so as not to attract any unwanted attention. He twisted his bronze ring around his finger, mulling over everything that Morcant had said, almost wishing he had not asked.

A throng of people was making its way up the main temple steps. Felix skirted them all, moving down the side and turning sharply when he reached the bottom step. He had taken a carriage here, but he could not see it now. He reasoned that he was on the wrong side of the crowd and just had to wait for it to pass. He kept turning the ring, moving it up and down his finger.

Something pricked him through his robes. Felix froze, waiting to see if he felt it again. It pressed forward, a little harsher the second time, centered in the lowest part of his back. Felix stayed as still as he could, not moving even as a hand came around and grasped his wrist.

"*Dormez Salvut*," he said in good faith.

"Either your accent is too thick or your skull is. Either way, it never sounds right coming out of an Avralaenian mouth," the voice coming from behind him spat.

"My apologies," Felix said dryly. "Would you prefer *Keirleigh Soelenmbaum?* I seldom meet a Dragolothian who can comprehend a language outside of their own."

The blade got close enough to break the skin. Felix gritted his teeth against the flash of pain and tried to ignore the blood trickling down his spine. "You are bold to attack a priest."

"Bolder than a queen who sends assassins to do her dirty work," the voice said.

"Yet not enough to show your face?"

The assailant grabbed his shoulder. Felix moved to push it away, but the person behind him had the advantage of being both stronger and armed. The blade swiped at his face, although it just barely grazed his cheek. A blow to the stomach sent him reeling backward, pain shooting down his legs and making them tremble.

"You can look at me now," his attacker said, advancing quickly and raising their dagger. "Give me your ring, or I will take the whole finger."

Felix clenched his jaw. "You will have to," he said, "if you want it so badly."

His attacker pivoted on one foot, slamming a fist into his mouth. He could have sworn that he felt metal, but it made no difference to the blood that welled up from his bitten tongue. He was able to stop the next blow, catching the thief's fist, but the dagger swooped down in the same motion and sliced through his necklace. His pendant dropped to the street, and the thief kicked it out of the way, twisting their hand out of his grip and leaping out of range, keeping their eyes locked on him as they crouched further down to pick up the broken necklace.

"Priest or no priest," they said hardly panting, "you are not welcome here." They tucked the pendant away even as they disappeared, melting back into the busy street. Felix could not have followed them if he wanted to. His vision was blurred from the blows, and his knees were shaking too violently for him to stay upright. He grabbed onto a pillar where he could lean heavily, spitting more blood and vomiting bile onto the cobblestone.

"Your eminence?" he heard a gentle voice ask. He closed his eyes and pressed his cheek against the cool marble, trying to chase away the heat from his face.

"Hm?" It was all he could manage. He heard someone approaching him, and he could only pray that it was not another rogue with a chip on their shoulder. A hand touched his face, and he flinched, opening his eyes just a fraction.

The face in front of his looked youthful. His first thought was that he had never seen anyone so beautiful. Hooded almond-shaped eyes as green as spring grass seemed to be evaluating the damage. He caught hints of long blond hair, although most of it was tied up in a scarf, and delicately pointed ears were lined with gold and silver hoops and chains. Felix opened his eyes all the way and did not move even when the stunning creature touched his face again and turned it slightly to the side. From the ears, he could hazard sylph or elf, although he did not like to make assumptions.

"Nothing is broken," the beauty in front of him said. "I can get you some salve."

"I am all right," Felix said, even though he could feel his jaw swelling. "It is not my first time."

The beauty raised an eyebrow and then took a step back, just enough to give Felix some space. "Are you the sort of priest that does not fight back?"

"We are supposed to keep the peace," Felix said, "no matter the cost."

"Hm." They rested one hand on their hip. "Even if it is your life? That seems a steep price for piety." They shook their head. "Come back with me. I will clean those cuts and feed you."

"You are far too generous." Felix had no desire other than to follow them, but he could only imagine what Pharun would do if he was gone for too long. "Besides, I do not wish to put you in any danger."

"I am in no danger here." It was only when they switched to speaking Dragolothian that Felix realized they had been communicating with him in his own tongue; they spoke Avralaenian so naturally. "I could probably teach you a thing or two."

"I have no doubt." He gave them a genuine smile, hoping that there was not too much blood on his teeth. "You are incredible."

They gave him a soft smile in return, the expression of someone who was used to being showered with compliments. "I will not allow you to walk alone. Where are you going?"

"I have safe transportation," he reassured them, straightening a little. "I will not walk... I do not know if I could, even if I wanted to defy you—which I do not."

The beauty inclined their head, and Felix thought he caught a glimpse of gossamer wings peeking out from the low back of their robe. "You seem to have your wits about you. I wish you a safe ride back and a peaceful recovery."

"My name is Felix," he stammered before they could turn away fully. "Felix d'Artion, High Priest of Morcant."

The sylph—and he was certain they were a sylph, for when they turned, he saw their wings in full—paused and regarded him once more. He could not take his eyes away from the wings, which shimmered with iridescent tones of soft pink, yellow, and blue in the sunlight. It was difficult not to stare, even though he knew that it was rude.

"Florindel Nazaire," they said, inclining their head. "It is my honor, your eminence."

"Florindel," he said, slightly awed, "the honor is my own. I will remember to repay your kindness."

"*Slaan*," the Avralaenian farewell rolled off Florindel's tongue as he turned again and walked away.

T HE *DAYDREAM* WAS LOST. Tybalt felt like his heart was resting with it at the bottom of the ocean.

If Cahal was taking it worse than him, he could not tell. The former admiral was standing on the beach, arms crossed as he watched Sweeney swim back and forth. The siren had taken it upon himself to dive and see what could be recovered from the wreckage—which was, of course, not much. He seemed to have given up on the process and was now enjoying the water, lurking almost fully submerged with only his eyes above the surface.

"You must be freezing," Cahal said without turning his head. Tybalt rubbed at his bare arms. He had been sleeping completely in the buff and had barely paused long enough to put on a pair of pants before running out.

"I am cold," he admitted. "I suppose there is nothing for me to do out here. I may go back inside."

"Sweeney stuck that boy of yours by the fire and told him to wait," Cahal said. "That is something I would handle sooner rather than later."

Tybalt nodded tiredly, rubbing his face with both of his hands. "I do not know how Quin found me," he said. "I do not know why he left the Gilded Lily… or if he even realizes how foolhardy that was."

"I have never known Florindel to be vengeful," Cahal spared him a glance, "if that helps."

"I have." Tybalt tried not to sound too despairing. He was not wearing any shoes, either, and the rocks and shells on the beach were not merciful to his soles. "There is nothing more I can do?"

"No," Cahal said. "Go back inside."

Tybalt did not need to be told again. He turned and started walking back toward the Laughing Albatross.

He could still smell smoke the whole way up, and it made him bitter.

The fireplace had been abandoned by the time Tybalt got there. The back tavern door swung shut behind him and banged against the frame to announce his presence, causing a downy grey head to pop up and disappear again. Tybalt inhaled sharply, trying to summon something forceful and stern to say as he watched Quin's wiry body weave its way through the legs of several tables and then spring up again when he was a little closer.

"Tybalt!" Tarquin greeted breathlessly. He grabbed onto the edge of a table and hopped up, leaning back on his hands and splaying his thighs apart. He smiled brightly at the half-sylph and tilted his head so that his ashen curls could tumble in the way of his glistening hazel eyes.

"Do not be charming with me," Tybalt admonished him, moving closer and grabbing at the tops of Tarquin's knees. "You have always been very clever, and I never thought that I would have to give you a lecture. Let alone that I would have to tell you how stupid it is to run from Florindel Nazaire of all people—not to mention coming here on a hunch all by yourself when anything could have happened to you...!"

"I could not stay!" Tarquin said through gritted teeth. "You do not understand!"

"No, I do not."

"And I know this city as well as you do, mind! If not better."

"Why could you not stay?" Tybalt felt like his chest was heaving… anger, worry, and fear all sitting on top of one another and making it hard to breathe.

"Josse died," Tarquin lowered his voice to a hushed tone. "Florindel killed him. You may not believe me, but I saw it happen!"

"I believe you." Tybalt squeezed the young sylph's knees even harder. "But think. What if something had happened to you? I never would have known. I would have gone back to the Gilded Lily one day and found out you were missing, and no one would be able to tell me why."

"No, you would not have," Tarquin bit back. "You were never going to come back."

"There is a lot going on in Seravell right now. It is more dangerous for me to stay. And I did not want to bring trouble to Florindel's door—to *your* door."

"I would have been dead anyway," Tarquin said bitterly. "You would have gone to the Gilded Lily, and I would be dead or missing—and it would be because Master Florindel dropped poison in my tea."

"I do not know," Tybalt said, opening his arms at last. Tarquin leaned into them, burying his face against Tybalt's hairy chest.

"He does not love us as he says," Tarquin choked back a sob. "He does not protect us. He is not our master or our father; he is an angel of death."

Tybalt rubbed the boy's back, hoping the steady motion would calm him down. "He does love you," he said softly. "His heart breaks to see any one of you suffering. And I know that Josse was dreadfully sick."

Tarquin made a miserable sound, although he still did not pull away from Tybalt's chest. "I will not go back."

"I am not going to make you, Quin," Tybalt sighed, resting his hand on those soft grey locks and dropping his chin to kiss Tarquin's forehead. "Although now my ship is resting at the bottom of the ocean... and I do not know how we are going to get back to West Avralaen."

"Sweeney said that he would steal another," Tarquin said, sitting up a little and wiping at his face. "He said that it would not be that hard."

"Mm," Tybalt shifted his jaw. "He would say something like that."

"Will you take me to your home when we get there?" Tarquin took in another trembling breath. Tybalt opened his mouth and then closed it again, unsure of how he should answer and turning every possibility over rapidly in his head.

"I will make sure you are safe," he said finally. "I will protect you." It was all he could really promise.

Tarquin pressed his lips together in an unhappy line. Tybalt knew that he wanted a better answer, but it was a discussion they could have when things were back on course. At the moment, all Tybalt could think about was how they were going to get another ship and why no one else from his crew had come to meet him.

He pulled away from Tarquin, but not before pressing his lips against the boy's forehead one more time. "You really are—I am glad to see you," he said, as if that was any consolation. "I am glad that you are safe."

Tarquin turned his head slightly and nodded, his fingers curling unhappily and dragging his nails over the table surface. "I want to lie down."

"Yes," Tybalt agreed. "You need your rest."

Tarquin slid down from his perch and stretched. Tybalt tried not to pay attention to the rising hem of his soft linen shirt that threatened to expose his belly. Quin cast him one last look, as if considering saying something more, but did not speak again before making his way upstairs.

Tybalt waited until Quin disappeared before collapsing into a chair. He groaned, hunching over and rubbing his face with his hands while grinding his fingers against the bridge of his nose. He was tired. He felt cornered. He felt responsible for Tarquin on top of his existing responsibility to get his crew home alive. He thought about Lord Marcellus' pistol—still in his possession—and wondered idly if it would hurt to take a bullet through his mouth.

Something touched his back. Tybalt was startled and tried to sit up, but he felt the round back of a shoe slide up his spine, and the sharp edge of a heel planted itself firmly between his shoulder blades.

"Good morning." He recognized Amnas' voice instantly. Tybalt did not sink back down into his position; he sat half-upright with his elbows digging into his thighs to support him. The angel had to be sitting on the table in the same spot Tarquin just vacated.

"You just come and go as you please, then?" Tybalt set his tongue between his teeth. "Does his excellency want his pistol back?"

"No," Amnas said. "He is rather invested in the idea of you keeping it, in point of fact. And surely you would not have tried to smuggle it away on a boat? He would have had your head."

"Yes, well," Tybalt grunted, "his excellency must be aware of the current situation with which I am faced."

"He is aware, and he is more than willing to support you in weathering it out." Amnas dropped a heavy coin purse onto Tybalt's back where his shoe rested. The impact hurt, and Tybalt nearly bit his tongue in half stopping a foul explosion of language.

"What good is coin when I cannot go to the marketplace without being accosted? I have people who need shelter. The price is too high. Even his excellency cannot pay it," Tybalt snarled.

"Do you not trust my lord to keep you?" Amnas' voice lilted in that condescending way. "What if I told you that some of your people were already being sheltered by the Company?"

"*Some* is not *all*, and I might call you a liar."

"Which I would not advise." Amnas ground his heel against Tybalt's spine, forcing him down an inch. "Allow me to reduce this to even simpler terms: if you do not comply with his excellency's wishes, then he will have you dismembered."

"Will he delegate that task to you? Since he likes to hand off his work." Tybalt gasped at an unexpected spike of pain that shot up to ring against the base of his skull. Amnas began humming, and Tybalt's hands started going numb.

"This is going to be the last time I instruct you nicely," the angel said. "Stay here, keep your head down. Use this money for anything you might need. You have friends still, I assume. Send them into the city instead."

Tybalt spat blood from his aching tongue onto the floor. "Stay here, keep my head down—and his excellency will relieve me of this burden... whenever he feels like it?"

"Yes." Amnas finally removed his shoe, scraping it down Tybalt's side and slicing open the skin. "That is the general idea."

Tybalt felt a little blood start to drip down his side as he sat up. He did not look for Amnas; he knew the dreamweaver was already gone. The only thing that remained was the coin purse sitting on the table next to a single embroidered white glove. Tybalt's lip curled, and he swept up both, hurling the white glove into the fireplace with particular ire.

12

SHRUKIAN

…The Prince Considers His Alliances

'YOUR EXCELLENCY…'

Shrukian did not know how to begin.

'*My Lord Andronicus…*'

He had already scratched through several lines and started over. He discarded his last attempt and started over on a new sheet of paper.

'*My Dear Marcellus…*'

He ground his knuckles against his temple. Nothing that he penned seemed proper. And he knew full well that it would take weeks or months for his letter to reach Marcellus—if it reached him at all. He was risking a great deal by even writing the Avralaenian ambassador to begin with, but he did not know what else to do.

If Pharun could turn the king's council against him, then it was only a matter of time before the castle was no longer a safe place for Shrukian to remain. He had no men to fight for him. He had bled on the battlefield with many of the king's soldiers, but he had only been a lieutenant at that time, and Pharun had been their general. They would follow Pharun if they believed he had the favor of Azrael and the power of the country's barons stacked behind him.

Shrukian needed an army. He needed wealth, force, and time to combat his brother. And if that was the way Pharun wanted everything to play out, then Shrukian was willing to leave immediately—especially if it meant mitigating the risks of anyone else he loved getting caught in the crossfire.

It pained him to think of leaving Olympia once again. He knew she would not forgive him, although he would beg that she could. She was in more danger if Pharun thought there was a chance that they could conspire together. On her own, she was a holy princess and an asset.

Shrukian noticed he was gripping his pen so tightly that it had begun to bend. He picked up on the words he had started, not caring any longer for propriety so much as getting the letter written and leaving as quickly as possible.

'My Dear Marcellus,
Please forgive the urgency of this letter.'

"Shrukian," Olympia announced her presence with a word, crossing over to the desk and moving to snatch the paper for his attention. Shrukian brought his hand down, slamming his open palm on the letter's face and looking up at his sister.

"Have you spoken to Pharun?" he asked.

Olympia shook her head.

"Meridith went," she told him. "He knows Pharun best, so I allowed it. What did Pharun say to you?"

"That he does not want me to be king." It was an insultingly concise version of events, but there was no time for a more thorough explanation. "He threatened to turn the entire council against me if I do not step down. I intend to take him at his word."

"And do what?" Olympia glanced down at the letter. Most of it was covered by his large hand, but she still understood what was happening. "If you leave now, you are a coward."

"I want to keep you alive and well," Shrukian said, lowering his voice and reaching out to take her by the wrist. "And I need an army to fight him."

"Do you think anyone will give you men and horses when they see you turn pale and run? There is no one who would take you for a leader then! And perhaps they should not. Father would be mortified."

"Father's body is not even cold," Shrukian shot back. "Pharun is not so much as giving us time to mourn."

"I thought you would have learned something of intrigue while you were in East Avralaen," Olympia said. "You stay close. You play the game his way, and then you take him down with cunning if not force. You are the *dragon,* and dragons eat peacocks. The more distance you put between yourself and this throne, the more likely you are to lose it."

"If I were to stay close and play by his rules, as you say... and you were hurt in the process, I would never forgive myself. I have a head for strategy; I can compel men to fight, but I do not have the flair for deceit and court intrigue. I am not fool enough to charge into

◆——◆——◆

IT WAS RAINING IN East Avralaen. The hood of Elzbet's cloak was not holding up very well against the downpour. Her hair was soaked through and plastered to the sides of her neck. Cold water trickled down the back of her collar just enough for the fabric to start sticking to her skin. A few sparse trees at the thin forest line offered some shelter, but pressing forward would mean crossing over into the Red Spine.

The Red Spine was a colossal mountain range that cut the continent in half, dividing East and West Avralaen and setting a firm boundary for either side. It was named for its red clay soil, which could become slick and treacherous quickly, especially under the current conditions. At the mountains' base was a dense, dark forest so thick that sunlight could not penetrate its canopy. The trees grew as wide as three men and taller than castle spires.

Entire armies had been swallowed by the Red Spine. Old wives told stories about how it was the entrance to Balam, and once you passed through, you would find yourself no longer part of the living. Many mages had disappeared into its trees chasing secrets and artifacts that were, to Elzbet, as much fable as anything else that was said to come from the cursed forest. Even now, facing it, there was a racing doubt in her mind that she could not quell. The only certainty that she had was that this was not her first choice. The only thing compelling her forward was the knowledge that her dreamless potion had run out. She had kept the bottle for the few drops clinging to the sides, but it was not enough to keep Marcellus and his dreamweaver at bay. When she succumbed to sleep, they would inevitably be found—but not even he would not be fool enough to chase her into the Red Spine.

What might be waiting for them on the other side was another worry. All she was trying to do now was buy time.

"I am giving you the last of my trust," she said, knowing that Ringo could hear her. "There will be nothing left if we do not make it through here."

"Aptly said." Ringo moved to stand beside her. "Although perhaps not for the reasons you meant."

Elzbet turned her head to look at him. "You know what I meant. You said that you could guide us through, and I am taking you at your word."

"I lived hidden by these trees," Ringo said. "I studied deep, old magic here. I know my way by heart. It is the mountains you should worry about crossing."

"Caves and narrow passes are not among my worries," she said. "Even if we lose every man to this venture, the orb needs to be maintained."

"I will worry about the men, then, and you worry about your bauble." Ringo pulled his hood down further over his face. Elzbet mimicked the gesture, making a brief sign of Morcant in the same motion.

The first step forward they took together.

NOT EVERY SEAT IN the king's council chamber had been filled. A few notable faces were missing, although Pharun was reassured multiple times that they had already been pulled away from the castle for extenuating obligations, and there was no rancor or insult meant. Most of the members who were in attendance were people he had known his entire life. High Priest Malhii had been among the first to arrive, and he had taken his seat next to Lord Thyron Resnik, the Master of Archives. There was Horus Agyris, the Secretary of the Treasury, and

Captain Sokaire Caiphus of the royal guard. On the far end of the table was the consummate shrinking violet Lord Charlemagne Vale, who had recently accepted with great reluctance the position of naval commander.

Then, of course, there was Baron Meridith Traske, bearing the weight of his father's legacy on his broad shoulders. His newly inherited title was still an ill-fitted one, though Jarian had been dead long enough that he should have been wearing it a little better. He hovered back as if he was uncertain of his place, lacking the confidence to take his seat beside Pharun while sliding his hand over the curved back of a chair.

Pharun considered approaching him, but familiarity seemed a grace that would be too generous. What further irked him was that it seemed as though Meridith was waiting for him to make some gesture, to beckon him forward or signal him with a word.

If they did not need each other so badly, Pharun would have sent him from the room without him even needing to speak up.

Instead, Pharun addressed him cordially. "Baron Traske, join us."

Meridith gave him a look even as he pulled his chair out to sit. The baron could not help but feel like all eyes were on him during his descent.

Uncharacteristically, Lord Charlemagne was the first to speak back up. "If there is to be war with East Avralaen, we do not have the ships."

"Bolstering our navy was the main objective in our negotiations with them," Captain Sokaire agreed. "Now those relations have been dissolved."

"You should exercise some restraint," High Priest Malhii said, keeping his eyes on Pharun as he spoke. "You need to suture Dragoloth's wounds first and foremost."

Pharun's lip curled. "No one is saying to launch an attack tomorrow," he said. "There are, of course, matters that must be attended to first. My father's funeral must be arranged, and my ascension needs to be solidified."

"It is your ascension," Malhii began, "over which I am stumbling." He glanced over his shoulder at Lord Thyron. "Archivist, you are the one in possession of the former king's will. Do you not also hold the documents for Pharun's naming as *Kren Veisten?*"

Before the Master of Archives could respond, Pharun cut in, "With all *due* respect, your eminence, were you not present for my briefing?"

"When you declared your brother a traitor? Yes, I have heard such tirades from you before." Malhii arrested Pharun's gaze once again, holding it without flinching. "And no matter how close you think you are to Firmament, you are no child of Azrael. The throne of Dragoloth is sacredly bonded to his bloodline. Would you rather have a traitor on the throne or a heretic?" His last words addressed the room.

The council shifted uncomfortably in their seats.

Meridith licked his lips and crossed his legs. "If the prince is, in fact, responsible for the deaths of the king and queen, he should not be rewarded with a coronation. He should be taken to trial."

"Which is an easy thing to say," Lord Thyron said, "when you stand in line to inherit after Shrukian."

"I am not motivated by lust for the throne," Meridith growled back. "My only interest lies in justice for my uncle's assassination and in wanting to see Dragoloth prosper."

Pharun's lips tightened as he dragged his tongue over his teeth. The long table in front of him began to shake, and the council turned their heads, each in time to bear witness to it splitting in half, a long crack running down the center and stopping just before it reached the end.

"I do not believe," Pharun said, "that we have reached a proper understanding."

Blood began to well up from the split like a wound. It oozed over the jagged sides, forming puddles on the table like spilled wine. Meredith moved his hand so that it would not stain his cuffs. Malhii did not pull away, even as the blood soaked his sleeve.

"I have been chosen by the gods, above all, to be their mouthpiece," Pharun said. "I preside over the clergies of Saldon, Morcant, *and* Azrael—the Most High of Firmament. My heart beats with Saldon's blood. I wield power that not one of you sitting here could comprehend."

"Are you so sure?" Malhii asked so softly he could barely be heard.

Pharun ignored him. "I am not asking for your permission or your blessing. I am here to inform you of three things. Encarz is dead. Shrukian is a traitor. And I will be king."

The blood on the table turned black. Malhii lifted his arm at last, pushing up his sleeves and wrapping the longest parts around his forearm. "And you will not tolerate opposition. You never do."

Pharun had to take a moment to breathe before responding to the high priest, "Do you oppose me, your eminence?"

"I see all of your mistakes as opportunities for instruction," Malhii responded.

"I am no longer your pupil," Pharun said venomously.

"If you are to be king, then I am to be your council," Malhii corrected him, "and that puts us more or less back where we began."

Meridith cleared his throat, trying to interrupt some of the tension that was mounting quickly in the room. "Perhaps the council should adjourn, Your Highness," he suggested, turning his eyes toward Pharun. "You have many arrangements for your father to see to."

It was a gamble, but Meridith had little doubt that Pharun would hold every one of them captive in that room until they voiced their undivided support. Meridith knew that his cousin was inevitable, like all things divine, and that he would get his way—but there was no need to take hostages and make the entire thing more difficult to swallow. The members of the council would be more amenable after breakfast.

"We will reconvene," Pharun agreed, and Meridith released a sigh of relief. Lord Thyron stood quickly, ready to leave as soon as he was dismissed.

"Your Highness," the archivist muttered, dashing his gaze toward the ground and bowing his head. His cheeks were flushed, which Meridith knew was a tell of his anger, but he had no time to delve into what part of the meeting had gotten the man's dander up so. He made a mental note to corner the Master of Archives later and speak with him. Lord Charlemagne followed at Thyron's heels. It was all very interesting.

When most of the council had dispersed, only Malhii remained in the room with the two royals. He wove his knobby fingers together and stroked one thumb over the other, his many rings clinking with the contact.

"Speak to me like that again," Pharun said, "and I will see you disrobed, beaten, and quartered."

"Who would you put in my place?" Malhii tilted his head, unbothered.

"Someone capable of showing respect," Pharun clipped.

"To you? Your search would be never-ending." Malhii raised his chin. "I give respect where it is earned."

"And I have done nothing to earn your respect over the years?" Pharun seethed.

"You wish to be regarded as a deity," Malhii said, "yet you work no wonders and you do not serve those who would worship you. You wish to be regarded as a king, and you intimidate your council and sever connections with your strongest allies. Every display of force you exert is not strength—it is an egregious abuse of power."

"You would know," Pharun said. "You are the expert."

Malhii's sinuous lips twisted into something like a smile. "You forget, I knew your grandfather. I am no stranger to Mahtrador stubbornness or temper. I have been threatened more creatively and by far more valiant kings than yourself, so you may try again."

"Perhaps I will be the one to be rid of you at last," Pharun said.

"If you wish to disrupt the temple, incite the wrath of Azrael, and turn your new subjects against you—then I would encourage you to try," Malhii said. "It would be the most brazen thing you have ever done. Although I have a feeling that the affections of the latter crowd will be the hardest won. I do not think you want to start your reign off on such a bad note."

"One thing I have always told you is to never presume to know me," Pharun said icily.

Malhii spread his hands and inclined his head. He did not seem interested in any further argument. He stood, dragging his long nails over the surface of the table.

"Just remember," Malhii said, "without me, you would not even be alive."

"Do not think I have forgiven you for that, either," Pharun said dismissively.

Malhii took his cue. He left the room, oozing into the hallway. *Like pus being drained from a boil*, was Meridith's thought. Pharun could not help but catch it. The extension of his power, even to the small degree he had exhibited, had taken down enough barriers to allow a few abilities to run unchecked. Picking up on Meridith's sullen thoughts were the least of his worries.

With Malhii gone, Pharun finally allowed himself a seat. He dropped down into the chair where Lord Thyron had been sitting, picking up a coin that had been left behind and spinning it on its side.

"So, then," Pharun said, "it is down to us."

"So it would seem," Meridith told him. Pharun spun the coin again, and Meridith watched, momentarily mesmerized by its whirl.

"Do you think Jarian would be proud of you?" Pharun asked, watching Meridith instead of the coin. His cousin blinked for a moment, pulling himself back into the present, and then he shook his head.

"My father?" He brushed his red hair back. "He would not want you to be king."

"How lucky for me that he is dead." Pharun brought one ankle up to rest against the edge of the table, reclining further in his seat. "You want me to be king, though."

"Are we to accept that as fact, or will you explain to me why?"

"In terms of the throne, according to the terms set by my father, if Shrukian is not king, then it all falls to you. Shrukian is a traitor, so this will land in your lap. Then I would be forced to take it from you. See that I am trying to save us both a lot of trouble?"

"You say that with such confidence, 'Shrukian is a traitor,'" Meridith said. "I do not know if I believe you."

"You do not think he is capable of wickedness, and I understand that. It is not about what you believe, it is about what I can prove. More to the point, it is your word against mine, and his weak defense against my evidence."

"Even when we were children, you were telling lies and getting away with them," Meridith told him. "Truth does not matter here, and both of us know it. So why do you continue to lie to me, even when we are in private?"

Pharun dragged his nail thoughtfully over his bottom lip. "The years between us," he said at last, "stretch further than you think."

"You will have to trust someone eventually," Meridith said. "And why should it not be me?"

"Hm." Pharun glanced toward the window. "Your father and mine were very close."

"They were like brothers," Meridith agreed.

"Jarian probably never called Encarz a liar to his face," Pharun said. "He was smarter than you."

"As is evident by the fact that he lived many years," Meridith scoffed under his breath.

"Do not give up hope," Pharun said flippantly. "There is life left for you to live yet."

"As long as I do not oppose you?" Meridith asked. "Or call you a liar?"

"Darling, you believe I would have you executed?" Pharun sighed. "You must not put as much faith in our childhood as you claim."

"You have changed," Meridith said. "And you will not let me in to know you again."

"As you said," Pharun reminded him, "I will have to trust someone eventually."

Meridith looked at him with uncertainty. "I never lost faith in you. I hold as much belief in you as any god. Yet I still love you, Pharun, and I will tell you when you are wrong."

"I do not need blind devotion. I need a right hand to wield my sword." Pharun slid his shoe away from the table and leaned forward, squeezing out a little more of the distance between them. "I want you to be for me what your father was for mine. And you need me, Meridith, more than you think."

He could see Meridith turning it all over in his head. He caught the flashes of doubt, desperation, and fear that were going off inside his cousin's skull. He did not even try to be polite and shut it off. He drank it all in because he liked knowing he was winning.

"I am with you," Meridith said with a touch of defeat coloring his voice. "I will always be with you."

Pharun smiled at him. "And there, you see?" He curled a strand of silver hair around his grey finger. "I feel as though I can trust you already."

13

FRANCISCUS

THE HAND THAT GIVES

AT THE TOP OF the stairs inside of the Gilded Lily, boys were crowding the banister. They all pressed together against the bars, straining to see or hear anything of the conversation that was occurring just below. Some of them could *just* see the tops of Franciscus' horns. Others thought they *might* have caught a glimpse of Florindel's hand flashing back and forth as he spoke. None of them could really see more than that. They rested on their toes, hands barely touching one another in case they were spotted and needed to scatter. No one wanted to be caught spying; there were already plenty of whispers going around about what had happened to Tarquin.

Josse's death had rattled them all, but it was Tarquin's disappearance that caused the biggest stir. Half of the boys were convinced that he had run on his own, simply vanishing in the middle of the night when everyone else was at rest. The other half were determined that it had to do with Florindel, and no one was brave enough to ask the master of the house directly.

"I cannot understand what he is saying," Christos whispered.

"And you will not, if you do not quiet down," Kelly whispered back. The white-haired sylph crouched even lower until his chin was practically touching the floor. Franciscus was shaking his head. The Calvarian's words were a little harder to understand at this height because of his clunky Northern accent. Kelly thought he heard the words *find* and *Pheseus* but he did not want to incite panic by squawking about it too soon. His heart plummeted into his stomach at the idea of his friend getting dragged back by the hair in the hand of that soulless beast.

Franciscus took a step back. The boys hunkered down further, as if that could prevent them from being seen. Franciscus was still speaking when he glanced up, blazing orange eyes lighting up in the afternoon shadow that fell over his face.

"We have been overhead, Master Florindel," Franciscus said, neither raising his voice nor shifting his tone.

Florindel stepped closer to his bookkeeper, folding his arms over his chest and glancing up at the landing. "You do not have to cluster together so tightly, lilies. You can speak to us as you wish."

Slowly, the sylphestine boys peeled away from one another. A few faded away from the banister, too embarrassed to be discovered, while a few more scattered further down the steps. Kelly stood up completely and brushed himself off, taking hold of the banister and leaning against it. He hooked his bare ankle around one of the posts despite knowing he was not supposed to.

"What happened to Tarquin?" he asked, feeling bold despite the knot in his belly. "Did he run away?"

"He is not dead, is he?" Christos asked on the heels of that, still half-hidden.

"Not that we know of," Florindel said. "Of course, we cannot know for certain. We can only hope that our Tarquin is safe and well, wherever he is."

"Is he going to come home?" Kelly pressed. "You will let him come home, won't you, *fadir?*"

Florindel's chest rose and fell with a deep breath. "Tarquin will be welcomed with open arms, should he choose to come back."

Some of the knot in Kelly's stomach eased. "I will go find him!" He leaned even further over the banister, eager. "What if he is hurt, and he needs us?"

"Kelly," Florindel said sharply, "do not lean on the banister. As much as I adore your gentle soul, you will not be leaving to look for Tarquin on your own. I do not want any of you to try. Terrible things can happen to you unaccompanied in the city."

Kelly lowered his head, chastised, and took a step back. Salty tears stung his eyes as they welled up too fast for him to fight back. He had to lift his hands and cover his eyes to keep them from flowing down his cheeks. "He could be lost," the boy's voice broke. "And what if something awful has happened to him?"

Franciscus looked at Florindel, unsure of how to read him. Kelly, Christos, and all the rest of those dear boys were breaking the Calvarian's heart. "Master Florindel," he said, keeping his voice too low and soft to be overhead, "you will show mercy to the boy when he returns?"

Florindel glanced at Franciscus and nodded. "*If* he returns," he said. "Do not make promises that you cannot keep."

"I will not make promises," Francisus said, "but I will go look for him. With your permission, of course."

Florindel considered it for a moment, his eyes wandering back up toward the banister where the boys were waiting, barely breathing, and poor Kelly could not even look up. "I suppose I do not need you much for a few days," Florindel finally said. "And no one is likely to give you trouble."

Franciscus nodded his agreement. As much as his kind was not loved, the likelihood of someone openly attacking him was very low. The most they would do is get out of his way and, at worst, be very unhelpful. "I will be back by sundown tomorrow if I do not find him," Franciscus said.

They all knew Tarquin, and he knew Seravell's streets better than most of them. If he wanted to vanish, he was more than capable. Yet Franciscus would have felt remiss if he did not at least try. He owed the boys, and Florindel, that much.

"All right," Florindel agreed. He turned his face again toward the boys, raising his voice to be better heard once again. "Dry your eyes, my loves. Kelly, pick up your head. Franciscus is going out into the city today. Tarquin may not wish to be found, but if he can be, Franciscus will bring him home."

The boys cooed their approval, several of them bursting into a fresh set of tears—whether from relief or anxiety at the uncertain, it was not clear. Kelly all but ran down the stairs, running up to Franciscus and wrapping his arms around him. Typically for a sylph, Kelly was small, and barely came up to the seven-foot tall Calvarian's waist.

"I would come with you," Kelly said, "if I could."

"I know," Francisus told him, resting his hands on the boy's shoulders and politely avoiding his wings. "I will do my best to bring him back to all of you."

Kelly gave him another squeeze. "Saldon be with you," he said softly before releasing his hold and stepping back. The boy looked at Florindel as if considering hugging him as well, but instead he dipped into a shy little bow.

Florindel smiled gently, cupping Kelly's face and stroking his cheek. He pulled the boy closer to him, resting one hand on his shoulder and using the other to comb through Kelly's white hair.

"If you are going to go, then it should be soon." Florindel said.

"You are right," Franciscus agreed. He looked up at all of the boys' faces once more, taking each one in and making a promise to himself that he was not going to fail. He could not bear to come home empty-handed after getting up their hopes. And he could only pray to Saldon, or whatever god was listening, that when he found Tarquin, it would not be too late.

⟡━━━•••━━━⟡

I T HAD BEEN A long time since Franciscus had been into the gutters of Seravell. Since coming into Florindel's service, he had been to parts of the capital city he had never been able to walk before without looking over his shoulder. Simple things, such as going to the market or praying in the temple, had never been easy or boring before, and now they were mundane daily tasks. And though the Gilded Lily existed on the 'wrong' side of the bridge, the life he lived before and the life he lived now remained so entirely separate that he did not even feel like the same person who used to steal bread just to eat.

He turned his face toward the street and tried to redirect himself. The Gilded Lily rested at the top of a small hill, and the cobblestoned street dipped just below. Behind him was the bridge which arched over the Castelmaine River, which Franciscus knew Tarquin would not have crossed. Tarquin would not have moved closer to the castle or anywhere else his likeness might be floating around with a few coins attached. If anything, he would have gone closer to the coast where marauders and dirty men collected like crusting sea foam. He liked their drugs and their piss-watered down wine.

Regardless, someone would have seen him and recognized him.

The Tipsy Green Faery was a familiar old haunt and the first place Franciscus decided to try. Roderic, the owner, would never serve him or speak with him—but that did not mean there would be no one there with good information. It smelled just like he remembered—pungent wormwood and opium barely covering up the odor of too many bodies crowded in one place. There were not many people now, but that would change as the afternoon wore on. Franciscus made himself comfortable at the bar, signaling the maid polishing glasses just behind it. She glanced at him but did not seem to be in a hurry to set down her task. That was fine. He had a little time. He did not see Roderic anywhere, which was a bit of a relief.

Franciscus looked around the room, trying to take stock of what he had to work with. A few heads had raised when he walked through the door, but almost all of them had turned away in disinterest once he settled. Calvarians in Dragoloth were not an unusual sight anymore.

One pair of eyes did not look away. Franciscus caught them with his own, noting the deep rich red before all else. The person in his sights was dressed like a Simisolan in dark blues and soft greys, although they wore no jewelry or anything else that might help distinguish them. In fact, they seemed to sit very comfortably with the hazy afternoon shadows, and the longer Franciscus looked at them, the more he doubted they were actually there.

Then they picked up their drink, and the spell was broken. Franciscus rubbed at his eyes and turned back toward the barmaid just in time for her to walk up. He asked for mead and set a few coins down on the counter, distracted by the feeling that he was still being watched from across the room.

Franciscus rubbed at the back of his head as if he could simply swat the sensation away. The barmaid came back and set a tankard of mead down in front of him, not saying anything else as she walked away. In the same instant, a red glass marble rolled across the counter, clinking softly against the side of his cup.

"Calvarian," a voice beside him spoke, "you do not see many."

The voice startled him less than the marble had, and he picked it up. "Perhaps not in Simisola," he said, holding the marble up. "Yours?"

The stranger from across the room was sitting next to him, close enough that if they both turned around, they could touch knees. He had not even heard them move.

"You are here looking for someone," they said, rather than answer. They plucked the marble from his hand anyway. "Someone special?"

"Someone lost." Franciscus was not sure why, but their presence unnerved him. Maybe it was the way that he always seemed to be looking them in the eye, even when he did not want to. "Someone I do not think you would recognize or know."

"Try me." They passed their hand over his cup, and the marble was gone. When Franciscus looked, he saw it sitting at the bottom of his tankard looking like a drop of blood in the otherwise honey-golden liquid.

"I do not think..." He needed to leave, but he was not sure he could get away. It was not like being stuck to his seat; it was a matter of getting his body to cooperate with his brain's frantic commands. "I have to go. They are not here."

"Of course they are not here, but maybe we can help each other. I am looking for someone as well."

The stranger pressed their fingertips slightly against the side of his tankard, urging it just a bit forward. "Drink." The second time they spoke, their voice filled every chamber in his head. Franciscus felt compelled to pick up his drink and did so with such rapidity that he almost poured it down his own shirtfront. A little sloshed over the edge and splashed against his chin, but he did not care. He downed as much as he could, taking three generous swallows before feeling like he could set the tankard back down. He gasped a bit, like he had been drowning and was coming up for air.

The stranger continued to watch him without twitching. "How do you feel?"

He felt warmer, better. The drink had soothed his jumbled nerves. He relaxed visibly in his seat and even leaned a bit on the counter, pushing his hand through his wavy brown hair. "It is good mead," he said. "It has been a long time since I have darkened these doors."

The stranger laughed. To Franciscus, it was the most beautiful sound in the world. He felt a rush of euphoria and instantly wanted to hear it again.

"Your past is as troubled as mine." They started to move their fingers, weaving them through and around one another. "What did you say your name was? Since I told you mine."

Franciscus stared at them, trying to remember when they had told him their name, but all he could think about was the way their fingers were moving. "Franciscus," he said. "Ah, no surname, I am afraid."

"Alone, then? No family?"

"I have family," he was quick to correct. "Just none by blood."

"Fair enough," the stranger said. "And someone you love is lost?"

"Yes." Franciscus took another drink from his tankard, although it did not taste as good as before. "One of my, our, boys... he left."

"You must be worried sick," the stranger sounded sympathetic.

"It is a dangerous city, and he is sylph." Franciscus could feel urgency tugging at his brain, but his body was being even less cooperative than before. His tongue was too loose in his head for him to have only had a little bit of mead, but he could not stop himself from speaking. "You must know how they are treated."

"I am very aware of your city's prejudices," the stranger said. "You must feel the weight of them yourself."

"Yes... sometimes."

"So where do you think Tybalt Carideo might have gone?"

Tybalt… had he said that name? He had been thinking about Tarquin, but at this point the disparity between what he was thinking and what was coming out of his mouth was tremendous. "Tybalt… no. I do not know where he is."

"Oh," the stranger said, "I thought you might, since you seem to know him so well."

His head was starting to feel like someone was holding it, invisible fingers squeezing his crown. "I… do," he gasped. "If you work in the right circles, the wrong circles, you cross paths with everyone eventually."

"I am sure. And he has crossed paths with you lately?"

Franciscus shook his head, but he could not shake the feeling. "I do not know where he is… truthfully!" The pressure was turning into pain, and even to his own ears his voice sounded like it was being wrenched from his throat. "He may have left."

"Doubtful. I hope not for your sake, let us say that." The stranger's voice was not as friendly as it had become, but their fingers did not stop moving. "I want to know where he *might* have gone. Give me names, and do not make me squeeze them out of you."

Franciscus ground his teeth against the pain. His hands were shaking to the point where he could not even grip his cup if he wanted to. "Anywhere with the black rose," he said. "It is not hard to find if you know where to look."

"*Names!*" That voice compelled him again, this time making it feel like his stomach was being filled to bursting.

"The Red Sparrow. The Five Hands. The Laughing Albatross. That is all I know!" *The Gilded Lily.* It wanted to burst from his mouth, but he swallowed it, despite feeling like he wanted to vomit.

The stranger's fingers stopped their hypnotic movement. One hand turned, their fingers curling inward in a beckoning gesture. Franciscus' stomach lurched, and his mouth fell open. He made a short, strangled sound as bile and mead surged up from his stomach and poured out of his mouth. The red glass marble shot out from his gullet and landed back in the stranger's hand.

They did not say another word. Franciscus turned away from the counter and vomited again, spewing onto his own shoes and the floor. When he was finally able to sit upright, the stranger had vanished completely, but his body was his own once more.

He was still shaking too much to try and stand. He could hear the barmaid saying something to him, and he felt a rag hit the back of his neck, but his head hurt too much to properly comprehend words.

The only thing he could think was that he had said too much. It had been out of his hands, but that did not matter now. He could only hope that Tybalt was smarter than he seemed and had already left Dragoloth. Else Franciscus hoped he would never have to lay eyes on the body.

HIS FATHER'S DESTRIER WAS a beautiful horse. In his boyhood, Shrukian had spent many hours in the stables shirking his studies just to spend time with the foal. He had watched it grow and studied the trainers' methods, hoping one day to raise his own. Seeing it again threatened to bring back the overwhelming tide of emotions that he had been trying to press down, and it was all he could do to hold up his hand and see if he could coax the stallion to greet him.

"Hesiod," he clicked his tongue invitingly, getting close to the table door. "Beautiful boy... Hello."

His heart sparked with joy when he felt a velvety nuzzle against his palm accompanied by a soft huff. Despite his misery, Shrukian could not help but smile.

"There we go," he said, giving the horse another moment with his hand before reaching up to stroke its neck. "Gorgeous boy. I have missed you." Hesiod's glossy black coat gleamed, and his mane had been braided with dark purple ribbons. Shrukian wondered if Pharun intended to ride him to their father's funeral—the thought made him sick. "Do you want to come with me?" He lowered his voice a little, as if he were in danger of being overheard. The stable was empty, but it echoed something monstrous. He did not come here for his father's horse. He had intended to tack whichever one was fresh and take off as quickly as he could. Yet the longer he lingered, the more determined he was to take Hesiod with him. He was already lifting the stall door's latch.

"Morcant be with you," a solemn voice came from the other end of the stable. Shrukian paused in his work, glancing up long enough to catch sight of the blond priest who had been following his brother around so loyally.

"I beg your pardon?" the prince asked.

"I wish you a safe journey," the priest added, stepping a little closer and spreading his hands. "I will ask that Morcant protects and guides you."

"That is kind of you," Shrukian said in return, resuming the task in front of him. "I will take any favor I can get." It was silent for a beat, and then, "I do not think we were ever properly introduced."

"We were not," Felix said. "I am Felix d'Artion, High Priest of Morcant."

Shrukian nodded. "Shrukian Mahtrador," he said, "although you knew that."

A smile touched Felix's lips. Shrukian could see discoloration just underneath the priest's mouth, and for one furious moment, he wondered what his brother had done.

"You are hard to miss," Felix said. He seemed hesitant to say whatever else was on his mind, but Shrukian was nearly finished, and the priest was running out of time.

"Are you going back to East Avralaen?" Felix finally mustered up the courage to ask. Shrukian cast a dark look his way.

"It is a bold question to ask," the prince replied, "when I do not know you or trust you well enough to give you an answer."

"Of course." Felix placed his hands together, properly rebuked. "It is my home, you understand. I miss it dearly. Should you need shelter while traveling, if you see a black rose in the window or by the door, you will be welcome there."

Shrukian pulled the saddle's strap tight. "I will mark that down." He checked once more to make sure everything was in place before taking Hesiod by the reins and leading the stallion out of its stall. "And while we are passing around words of caution, allow me to give some to you." He stopped just beside the priest, leaning over enough to be heard. "Do not get involved with my brother," he whispered. "He does not love you. He does not love anyone. And he never will. He is not capable. He will use you, and he will spit you out when he has drained you of everything you are."

Felix froze. He had no response except to clench his jaw, his tongue suddenly feeling heavier than lead.

"I say this," Shrukian hammered on, "out of care." When Felix still did not reply, he kept walking, Hesiod's heavy steps echoing off the stable walls.

"I am a priest," Felix finally managed to say, his voice coming out a little more strained than intended, "with vows to uphold."

Shrukian paused long enough to retort. "Do you believe that it matters?"

"I believe," Felix said, "in his integrity as Crowned Priest."

Shrukian raised an incredulous eyebrow. "I see," he sighed. "Please, Felix, for the love of Azrael—go back to your home."

The priest had nothing more to say. Shrukian put a leg up over his mount and pulled himself up into the saddle, Hesiod's hooves striking the ground louder than thunder as he tore out of the stable.

14
PHARUN

The Despicable Machinations of Hypocrites

THE PALACE LIBRARY KEPT many secrets. Its books were the one constant in an ever-changing court, where kings fell and were crowned one as quickly as the other, and while courtiers swirled in and out dropping heads and titles like seasonal flower petals. They were all bound in dark leather and elegantly engraved, some of them more worn by searching hands and the passage of time than others. Mahii found himself looking through familiar volumes of the philosopher Desiderius and the poet Cloephus; nothing particularly enticing, he only wanted to look busy.

There were voices coming from the sitting room adjacent to the library and connected by a door. It was cracked just enough, and the voices he recognized as Lord Thyron and Lord Charlemagne. He had never cared much for what either of them had to say. He considered Charlemagne a dilettante fop, and Thyron was just enough of a radical to be dangerous. However, in the privacy of a secluded sitting room, there was an increased possibility that one of them might say something worth overhearing.

"Neither of us want this," Charlemagne hissed through his teeth. "No one does, but we must face that it is going to happen."

"The entire monarchy is folding in on itself," Lord Thyron whispered back venomously. "And you tell me that there are no alternatives?"

"Not one," Charlemagne lowered his voice to such a whisper that Malhii had to strain to hear it. "And you are making it very difficult to associate with you in public, *my lord.* If you continue to say further untoward things in reference to treason, then I will be forced to disregard you in court."

"Neither my reputation nor my self-worth hinge on the approval of Vale," Lord Thyron snipped. "And certainly not on that of a lesser one."

"Perhaps not. But I know what *does* hinge on my approval, Lord Resnik, and I recommend you take better care of your assets."

That quieted Thyron quickly. Malhii slid the book he was holding back into place, amused, before pulling out another and opening it up from the center.

"With as much as I have put into my assets, I should think they would be secured by now," Lord Thyron whispered.

"You make many assumptions, my lord," Charlemagne said. "Perhaps the boldest of which is that you will keep your head through all of this."

The sitting room door opened the rest of the way. Malhii feigned captivated interest in the volume of poetry he was holding. One of the lords stormed out behind him—and judging by the heavy trail of perfume, it was Lord Charlemagne.

Thyron made a disgruntled sound behind him. Malhii slid his fingers down the dark crease of the book's open spine.

"Is there a storm brewing in paradise?" the high priest asked. He rotated a half turn and looked at Thyron.

The lord did not even look present as he straightened out the cuffs of his severe black coat.

"Lord Charlemagne is having a difficult morning," he said dismissively.

"The king's death rests heavily on all of our shoulders," Malhii said sympathetically, snapping his book closed and putting it back in its place. "Only Azrael can guide us through the impending cataclysm, and I pray that He will."

"'*Cataclysm*,'" Thyron scoffed. "There is no better word. If Pharun takes the throne, there will be a mass exodus or an uprising."

"Or perhaps neither. But there will be a rash of executions," Malhii cautioned, "especially of those who do not know to hold their tongue before inciting riots."

"And what would you know about holding your tongue?" Lord Thyron challenged. "You speak your own mind often enough."

"A tongue that wags in a mouth with no voice is powerless," Malhii said. "I am well aware of the neck that my head is attached to—and how my words hold weight."

Lord Thyron pressed his lips together in an unimpressed line. Before he could speak again, the library doors opened, and Meridith Traske walked in.

Malhii took the interruption with grace, evaluating Meridith's state quickly with a glance. The red-haired baron looked exhausted, and there was little wonder why. "You are alive," Malhii said as if that was not to be expected. "Pharun must not have disliked *everything* you had to say."

"Pharun and I have come to an understanding," Meridith said. It was difficult for him to be polite. Malhii had always been of the opinion that the young baron would have benefitted from spending a few years in the temple. So much for lost causes.

"And what does this understanding entail?" Lord Thyron asked. "We must all submit to his will, am I correct? Or we can be put to trial for insurrection?"

"Something of that kind," was Meridith's response. "In preparation for his father's funeral and in anticipation of his coronation, he has declared that the king's council will not be dismissed, and its attendants will not be permitted to leave castle grounds until the coronation is over."

"That could be months," Lord Thyron protested. "You are telling me we are his prisoners until then?"

Malhii took a seat, grabbing the skirt of his robe and sweeping it out of the way of his descent. "That is a little overdramatic, Lord Thyron," he said. "I would say that you are no more his prisoners than the Simisolan ambassador."

"I noticed the exclusion of yourself just now, your eminence," Lord Thyron said. "Are you not part of the king's council?"

"Yes, although I am not bound strictly by the king's law." Malhii put his fingertips together. "Particularly in the instance of coronations and funerals, over which I must be present to preside."

"I see." Lord Thyron shifted his jaw. "That is how it is going to be, then? We are all to stand by and allow him to do as he pleases without opposition?"

"You could ask him," Malhii said indifferently. "Although that seems to be exactly what he wants."

"Forgive me, your eminence, but you are far too flippant regarding this matter," Thyron said. "And I will not bend my knee to him without proper due course. I will die before I submit to tyranny."

"That is one thing on which we can agree," Malhii told him.

Lord Thyron did not have anything to say to that. He gripped the knot in his cravat and excused himself, pushing his way between Meridith and High Priest Malhii. Both men watched him exit, the young baron looking more exhausted with each passing moment.

Malhii regarded him with a minorly inquisitive tilt of his head. "Is there something more you wish to say, Baron?"

"No." Meridith shook his head after a pause. "I have nothing more to say." He turned to go, then he stopped, his fretful hands pulling at loose strings hanging from his cuffs. "If it was not Azrael's will, it could not be done. Could it?"

"When the wills of gods and kings clash, there is only ever one victor," Malhii said.

Meridith nodded, twisting a loose thread around his fingertip until it turned purple. He snapped the thread off then and rolled it around his fingertips as he went back toward the library doors, not even granting the high priest a proper goodbye.

***

"**T**HERE YOU ARE."

The sound of Pharun's voice brought Felix's head up. He felt his heart jump into his throat at the same time, slightly dizzy from the sudden rush of blood. Shrukian was long gone, and the stable was empty, but Felix found the quiet comforting. Of course it was not meant to last.

"Did I startle you?" Pharun asked before Felix could say anything. He appeared behind the high priest, barely touching the back of his neck.

Felix shivered and clutched the amulet around his neck, although he did not dare move forward to put space between them. "No," he lied out of habit. "I was thinking."

"I see," Pharun smiled, his finger getting caught up in a lock of Felix's sandy-blond hair. "And what were you thinking about, your eminence?"

"I was thinking about home," Felix told him. It was not a lie. "My heart aches for East Avralaen more so today than any other day."

"Mm," Pharun remarked. "Is it because spring is finally coming to Dragoloth? It is getting warmer, and I know you long for your beloved Avralaenian sun."

"It is partially the sunshine," Felix admitted. "It is many other things as well. Of course I miss the longer days and walking down the streets barefoot, because warmth still lingers in the cobblestones. I miss soft green grass and fresh olives."

"I do not think it is the lack of fresh olives that is bringing such sadness to your eyes," Pharun observed.

Felix drew in a trembling breath. "Above all, I miss my temple," he finally admitted. "I miss being able to pray in front of Morcant's icon and burn incense on an altar constructed just for him. The Temple of Azrael is a beautiful sanctuary, and High Priest Malhii has been more than generous in his accommodations, but I must admit... I still do not feel welcome there, not entirely. For several reasons." He could still feel a few of those reasons in the form of mottled bruises on his stomach and hips. Every time his cloth rubbed against a bruise, he winced.

"You will have your own temple soon," Pharun promised him. "And you may dedicate it to whomever you like."

Felix felt some of his resolve return at that. "I am, of course, entirely unworthy of your benevolence. And I will happily oversee the construction of a new temple here in Seravell, especially one that is dedicated to Morcant. But it is my wish to return home at the end of it all."

"Of course," Pharun said, though his inflection made him sound displeased. "I would not hold you captive abroad."

Felix closed his eyes. "I came with you of my own will," he said. "I simply wish to leave of my own will also."

"I will worry for you, of course," Pharun remarked. "If there is war with East Avralaen, I do not want to be sending you back into the mouth of the lion. Or the, ah, claws of the gryphon? To play on your national symbol."

"You do not believe I would be safe in my own home country?"

"War is a wretched thing. I have seen enough of it to know."

"It is a large continent. East Avralaen is a big country." Felix finally turned to face Pharun. "If there is war, then my acolytes will need their high priest more than ever. Would you abandon your flock in the face of such dire times? My temples are shelters. My priests are healers."

"Keeping you here, then, seems to be more to my advantage." Pharun played it off as if he was teasing, although it was clear from his tone that he was not.

Felix steeled his gaze, curling his fingers inward and trying his best not to get into a physical altercation with the Crowned Priest. Mouth of the gods or not, Pharun had no right to make horrific implications or to mock Felix about his calling.

"My vows to Morcant bind me to my flock as well as to Him," the blond priest said. "I will stay for your coronation, Your Highness, but I cannot linger beyond that—not when there are people who will need me so much."

Pharun curled his finger underneath Felix's chin, forcing it up a little higher. "You have a duty to me as well."

"Yes," Felix agreed. "And I will beg your forgiveness, but I will not ask for your permission. Not for this."

Pharun held his gaze for a long minute. He then slid his hand up to cup Felix's cheek, stroking his thumb over the coarse blond hair along the priest's jawline. "It is your conviction that I find enticing," he said at last.

Felix swallowed hard and dropped his eyes, not easy to do when Pharun's fingers were pressed into the soft part of his chin and making it impossible to lower his head. "I am simply an extension of Morcant's hand," he said humbly. "I am a servant. All I want is to be able to do my job well."

"You do many things well," Pharun said. "You make me proud." He pulled his fingers back, allowing them to linger against Felix's skin the entire way. "There is still time. I am not king yet."

"Yet," Felix said softly, resting his hand against his amulet once more. His chest hurt with how fast his heart was racing. "If I may be candid..."

"Have you not been?" Pharun sounded amused.

"I worry for you," Felix continued. "You are taking such a hard road. To maintain your title of Crowned Priest and to sit on Dragoloth's throne as well... You have even more enemies than you realize, and I fear they will stop at nothing to see you fall."

"I do. And they will not. You are correct on both points," Pharun said. "Even now, the king's council does not fully support me. My own brother thinks I have no right to the throne. I fear," he lowered his voice just a touch, "that you may be the only one who does not doubt me."

Felix felt his heart soften, and most of his anger evaporated in the face of Pharun's vulnerability. "I have always believed in you. This is your birthright, your patrimony, and you are worthy of fulfilling the role—what you were foreordained to become."

"Your devotion will not go unrewarded..." Pharun's eyes lingered, for the first time since they began talking, on the swollen discoloration around Felix's lip. He then noticed the bruises near his throat, climbing up toward his jaw, largely concealed by his blond facial hair.

"What happened?" he demanded sharply. His voice took such a sudden turn that Felix did not know how to respond.

"What do you mean?" the priest asked. Pharun grabbed his jaw again, squeezing it a little too tightly this time.

"You have bruises all over your face," Pharun said. "How did you get them?"

Felix felt sick. He shook his head. "It is not safe," he said carefully, "for an Avralaenian in the city at this time." He hoped that he did not seem obstinate or accusatory in the face of what he knew was simple concern.

"It is not," Pharun agreed, "and for good reason." He squeezed Felix's jaw a little tighter, his finger pushing into a deep bruise and making Felix wince. "You must not go out into the city unattended. Do you understand what I am saying? In fact, you should not step out at all. There is a chapel on the palace grounds; you may pray there."

Felix frowned. "It is not the same," he said. "I need the temple to feel close to Morcant."

"Morcant does not live in the walls of a temple. You should be able to feel him, my sweet Felix, if you were imprisoned in a box. If you cannot commune with Morcant properly without precious accommodations, then you are hardly suitable to be high priest." It was harsh, and he knew it, but Pharun could not stop himself. The ugly dark bruises on Felix's skin made him livid, and he was tired of the soft, timid excuses.

His words cut deep. Felix felt like he had been slapped. He reached up to take hold of Pharun's wrist and tugged his hand away. Felix turned his head then, his face flushed bright strawberry pink with anger.

"I carry Morcant with me always," he said, "but I am human, Pharun. Unlike you."

"Because I am not human, I cannot understand you?" Pharun's lip curled.

"Divine blood flows in your veins. You could speak to Saldon at supper if you desired. You need no candles or incense to entice Him to answer your prayers. You enjoy those things. You utilize them because it helps, but they are not necessary. It is all formality. I do not have that privilege. If I want to speak to Morcant, I need to make certain to pay proper obeisance. These chapels and temples that are not dedicated to His worship make it more difficult to reach him because the air is crowded with so many other voices and so many other gods. You know this—I do not have to explain it to you!"

Felix was raising his voice. He knew that he should not yell. If Pharun had struck him right then, he would have deserved it. He would have to pay penance for overstepping his authority, for dishonoring the Crowned Priest—and probably a half dozen other small protocols he had broken in this meeting alone. It was only now that he realized just how much their voices echoed in the stable, and the sound of his own exasperation made him flush with shame. He could feel his ears burning.

"I understand," Pharun said, his voice deceptively calm. "I know what it is like, better than you might think. To feel cut off from your heavenly father is devastatingly lonely. However, these are treacherous times. Tensions are mounting, quite obviously from the fact that you—from a class of people that is considered untouchable—came home to me with bruises. I would never forgive myself if something worse happened to you. I have forbidden members of the king's council from leaving until after my coronation, and I am extending that to you."

A wall of despair nearly swept Felix off his feet. He had to reach out and grasp Pharun's arm just to hold himself steady. "You do not trust me." It was all he could say.

"When it comes to your own care? Not even a little." Pharun grabbed the back of Felix's head, dragging him close and pressing his lips to the priest's forehead. "You need to trust me."

"I do," Felix said, even with doubt burying its seed in his stomach.

"Good." Pharun finally released him, twisting one of his clerical rings around his thumb. "Go back into the palace. You need rest and a warm bath. I will see that you have both."

Felix did not have anything else to say. He bowed his head to his superior, heavy as it was with self-loathing and rage.

SHRUKIAN LIKED THE TIPSY Green Faery for many reasons. It was one of the only places in the city that served absinthe—which he thought tasted a bit like soap, but he liked the way wormwood smelled. He enjoyed watching other people drink it as well. It was such a pretty color, and he was unendingly fascinated by the process of pouring it over a sugar cube, allowing it to stream through a perforated spoon just to make it enjoyable. Their ale was also some of the best he had ever tasted, and he had many fond memories of sneaking out of the palace to meet his friend Gunnar, a former royal guard lieutenant, there and drink with him.

Remembering Gunnar brought a wave of sadness, yet another thing for Shrukian to shove down as he dismounted and passed his horse off to a waiting stable boy. He gave the boy several silver coins for his trouble—more than his services were worth, but Shrukian wanted to make certain his mount was cared for.

He was greeted by the familiar scent of wormwood as soon as he walked through the door, along with the heat of a roaring fire, the smoke of which burned his lungs in a mild, pleasant way. Shrukian walked over to the bar and peeled off his riding gloves, setting them down on the countertop and gesturing to catch the barmaid's attention.

He could not linger. He did not know if Pharun was going to send anyone after him. This place was far from the palace, past the bridge, and Shrukian reasoned he could more than likely stay at least one night if he needed to. He wanted to press on, but he still did not know exactly where he was going. His current reasoning was that he needed to get to a ship, and he was on the best path for the coast.

The barmaid came over and leaned on the counter, resting her elbows on the surface and granting him a winning smile. "What can I get for you?" she asked. She was absolutely beautiful, and the more he took in of her untamed strawberry blonde hair and freckled nose, the harder he considered staying the night.

"Ale, please," he said. "I want the darkest you have." His eyes betrayed him as a royal, but if she noticed, she did not seem to think much of it. She disappeared for a minute and returned with a pint of ale so dark that he could not have shone a light through it. He expressed his gratitude with a smile and several more coins, bringing the drink to his lips and downing almost a third of it in a few gigantic gulps. He had not even realized how thirsty he was.

"When do you think the king's funeral will be?" The man who asked the question sat at the end of the bar several seats away. Shrukian thought at first that he was being addressed, but the barmaid responded before he could.

"A few days from now, or a few weeks. There is no telling with royal funerals." She refilled the patron's cup with a nice amber mead as she spoke.

"The queen's happened fairly quickly," the patron continued, curling his hand around his drink to take it.

The barmaid shrugged.

"Queens are different," she said. "I think a lot more has to be arranged when it is a king." She swiped her cloth over the countertop, clearly preoccupied. "I do not know anything about that sort of thing. You should ask someone else."

"What do you think?" The patron finally did turn to face Shrukian, but Shrukian ignored him, drinking deeply from his ale instead. Over the sound of his own swallows, he could tell that the man was still trying to speak to him, but he had no interest in engaging. The details of his father's funeral were unbeknownst even to him, and that cut too deeply to speculate.

"There may be war," he heard someone else say. Shrukian glanced up to see who he assumed to be the bar owner polishing glasses. The barmaid rolled her eyes and continued to sweep her cloth along the counter, getting further and further away from the conversation.

"Oh, there will be." The patron hiccupped. "There will be war with Simisola *and* war with East Avralaen. Mark my words. We will never have peace again."

"Simisola? I do not think so." The bar owner set the glass he was finished with down and picked up another. "I do not think we are that stupid. And East Avralaen has a bigger navy."

"Which is why we will attack Simisola first," the patron reasoned. "With all of that gold, we could build a whole new fleet."

"Hm." The owner did not seem convinced. "I think if we make it to East Avralaen's shores, it will be a miracle. Furthermore, I think if we make it to their capital city, it will be by the divine will of Azrael alone. And there is so much land. We do not have the men even if we did have the ships."

"How do you know?" the patron asked. "About all of that land and whatever else?"

The bar owner flipped over another glass and filled it. "Here," he said, "try this. I opened the cask this morning."

Shrukian could feel a headache starting to come on. In the back of his brain, he knew that eating was probably a good idea, but he could not bring himself to try. He set his eyes on the barmaid instead, finding something oddly settling about the way she went about her mundane tasks.

Eventually, she turned around and looked at him again. Her smile did not go all the way up to her dark brown eyes. "Would you like another, or do you want to try something else?" she asked.

"Another," Shrukian responded almost immediately, "please." He set some more coins down on the counter. It was all he could think to do. She swept them up without a word and refilled his pint.

"All I know," said the patron at the end, "is that our country is doomed. I do not think either prince is up to the task of picking it all up. They inherited a right mess for sure, and that is not their fault—but they will drag us all down with them."

Shrukian made a face. He tried to hide it behind his pint.

"Forget about overseas," the bar owner said. "We need to worry about the war that will happen here."

There were murmurs of agreement from the patron and the barmaid, then the tavern fell eerily silent.

Shrukian felt like the ale was turning sour in his stomach. He could not bring himself to finish it, although he downed at least half of the second pint just to be polite. The barmaid eventually came back over, leaning on the counter again to address him.

"Would you like something to eat?" she asked. "I have rabbit stew and fresh bread from this morning. I made it all myself."

Shrukian managed a small smile for her. "I do not think that I could," he said, although he hated to turn it down. "Do you have any rooms available for the night?"

"I will ask Roderic," she said, straightening up. "I will be right back." She reached over, patting the back of his hand in a familiar way before walking over to where the owner was standing.

Shrukian watched her without any real sense of impatience as he waited for a response. From the corner of his eye, he noticed someone walking up and taking a seat next to him. It was another swathe of red hair, although deeper in color and longer than that of the barmaid.

"Your Royal Highness," Amnas said. Shrukian nearly did a double take. A flood of emotions—relief being among the strongest—hit him all at once. His mouth went dry as he held out a hand, thinking to touch the celestial before thinking better of it.

"Amnas?" He was not certain if he remembered the name correctly, but something told him that it was right. Amnas nodded, his smile dazzling and unsettlingly bright.

"You remember. That is darling. Not many can—or they do not care to."

"Of course I remember. I owe you a debt," Shrukian said. The dreamweaver waved his hand.

"Yes," he said somewhat dismissively. "That is not why I am here." Amnas regarded Shrukian with his round cinnamon-colored eyes, the face of an innocent child on a swordsman's svelte body.

"May I ask, then...?" Gripped by sudden fear, he asked, "Is Marcellus all right?"

"He is fine," Amnas said, waving his hand. "I was on my way to take your letter to him, actually."

"My letter?" Shrukian furrowed his brow. "The one that I sent out with the courier? How...?"

Amnas turned his hand again. This time he plucked a sealed white letter from the air, presenting it with a flourish and displaying Marcellus' name written across the front in Shrukian's severe handwriting.

"You really should not send out such important or incriminating notes," Amnas said. "They can be so easily intercepted."

Shrukian's mouth went dry. He took another sip of ale. "How did you know?"

Amnas pulled up one narrow shoulder in a shrug.

Shrukian pressed his fingers into his temples. "All right," he accepted it. "It will get to him faster if you are the one carrying it. For that, I owe you a debt twice over."

"That will all come at another time," Amnas said. "Right now, I have a vested interest in getting you back to East Avralaen as quickly as possible."

"Why?" Shrukian asked, despite the fact that his heart started racing at the thought.

"It is within your best interests and mine; we will simply say that." Amnas smiled again. "Stay where I can find you, Prince. And stay alive."

"I had intended to do so," Shrukian said.

The barmaid came back over, setting her hand back on the counter to get Shrukian's attention. "Do you still want that room?" she asked.

Shrukian turned his head. He was vaguely aware of Amnas' movement, and there was something unsettling about the dreamweaver just coming and going as he pleased without a sound. "Please," the prince said, "I will pay as far in advance as you allow."

She smiled at him and brought him another ale, sliding it across the counter. "On the house," she said. "I will get that room ready for you."

Shrukian nodded his thanks. He would have to keep moving soon, but he felt better knowing that his letter was at least on its way—very quickly—to the right hands. He trusted Amnas. He did not know why, but he did.

Marcellus would help him. Of that, he had no doubt. Shrukian fought to conceal a small, grateful smile as he brought his pint to his lips.

This was a battle he was going to win after all.

15

TYBALT

THE LAWLESS EXPANSE OF THE OCEAN AND ITS DWELLERS

NIGHT FELL HEAVILY ON the Laughing Albatross once again. Tybalt felt like his days were all starting to bleed together. The ocean was so tranquil, he theorized that he must be falling victim to the steady rise and ebb of its tides. It was difficult to keep track of how many sunsets he had seen turn the water fiery orange or how often he had stepped out to sit on the beach and gaze up at the stars. In truth, he hated it because he felt it made him indolent—while at the same time it was something he desperately needed. Marcellus had thrown a noose around his neck, and Tybalt was just waiting for the stool to be kicked out from underneath him. His crew was scattered beyond his immediate reach, and the city was growing increasingly unsafe for Avralaenians. He heard through the grapevine that a priest had been attacked. A *priest*.

There were talks of war and of a new king's rise to the throne. He needed a new ship, and he needed to get his people home. He could not do any of that with Lord Marcellus' crony breathing down the back of his neck.

Another thing he liked about the beach was that it was quiet. It gave him space to think. He knew that when he went back inside the tavern, Sweeney would be telling stories vile enough to make Tarquin blush. Cahal would probably be arguing with Sweeney about the accuracy of his depictions and so on. Tarquin would be enthralled and well-entertained.

Tybalt groaned and pushed his fingers against his eyelids, wishing he could dig a little deeper and pop his eyes out altogether. It would not solve all of his problems, but it may put an end to a few of them.

He loved Quin. He truly, truly loved that boy with all of his heart, and he did not understand him at all. He was still wrapping his mind around the fact that in the process of running from the Gilded Lily, Quin had gotten it into his head that finding Tybalt would be the *safer* option.

Tybalt had already run through a dozen different scenarios in his mind, with at least three of them ending in some sort of conversation with Florindel. It never went well when he played it out, although Florindel of real life was a far more reasonable person than Tybalt ever gave anyone credit for being. Then again, no matter how reasonable or unreasonable Florindel might be, Tybalt had promised Quin that he did not have to go back. And Tybalt held fast to being a man of his word.

He knew he had to go back inside, but he did not want to leave the beach. Tybalt allowed himself a few more quiet minutes, watching froth-capped waves swell and crash, dragging pebbles and shattered shells back with them when they withdrew.

Steel touched his throat. The cold razor edge of a dagger bit into his skin, and Tybalt held his breath—not tempting fate by either speaking or swallowing. He stayed perfectly still, waiting either for the sting of having his throat slashed open or for his visitor to identify themselves.

Lips pressed against his ear, and a voice he did not recognize spoke with whispery softness. "Tybalt Carideo?"

He did not speak; he only made a noncommittal grunt. The steel edge was warming quickly to his hot skin.

"If you are not," the voice continued, "I will cut your throat here and be done with it."

"This Tybalt seems damned either way," he managed to say. He did not like the way the blade rested just below his larynx. It made him feel like he was choking. "If you do not want to slash his throat, then what is your intent? To set up a picnic?"

"I am thinking of killing you anyway and telling the prince regent that I found you floating face-down in the river."

His blood went cold. *Prince regent?* He did not want to get entangled with royals, and the fact that he had been noticed by one of them enough to attract this sort of attention set off a deep anxiety. "Depending on what he wants with me, that may be preferable."

The voice next to his ear scoffed. "Stand up with me. Slowly." A hand gripped his arm. Tybalt thought about the knife in his boot, but he was not fool enough to risk reaching for it.

"All right," he said. He felt a tug on his arm, and he rose slowly, following the blade all the way up. Once he was on his feet, the blade moved away from his throat, and he turned immediately on his heel to face his captor.

'*Balshett's hands and eyes,*' was his only thought. He was not a very tall man, and the person standing before him was about his height. The moonlight made their skin look darker than obsidian and lit up the facets of their blood-red eyes, bringing sparks of orange and gold to his attention. Their slim frame was swathed in blue and grey with a cowl pulled up over their head, obscuring most of their features. He would have preferred to meet someone like them in a bar, where he could buy them a drink and marvel at their beauty under warm lamplight.

Their eyes were captivating. His gaze kept wandering back up to meet them. If it were not so dark, he could have sworn that this person had more than two from the way he always seemed to find them no matter which direction he turned his head.

"You do not really want to kill me," Tybalt said, a bit breathless. It was worth a try.

"Not especially," his captor replied. "And if my assignment were to kill you, I would have never given you the chance to speak."

Tybalt swallowed. "Fair enough."

"Will you cooperate, or must I compel you?"

"What does the prince regent want with me?" He did not know if he hoped for Cahal or Sweeney to come to his aid, or if he wanted them to stay put and not run the risk of either getting hurt.

"I will not speak for him. If there is anything he wants you to know, he will not hesitate to say it himself." They tilted their head, and Tybalt was finding their gaze even more difficult to avoid. "Walk with me."

Their words filled his head, echoing through every chamber, leaving behind a dull ache. Tybalt felt compelled to do as he was told, despite every nerve in his body screaming in protest. When they started walking, he followed them, despite panic rising in his chest at his own lack of control.

"Who are you?" he asked helplessly.

They were quiet for a moment before they replied. "Nkiru."

"Ah. I am surprised that you answered me."

"I would not have," Nkiru shrugged, "were you not practically a dead man already."

◆—···———···—◆

"Y OU SAID HE WAS walking the beach?" Tarquin peered out the window for what felt like the hundredth time. He could not see out very far, but worry was eating him alive.

"Supposedly," Sweeney replied. "I did not see him when I went out. He could have walked over toward the coves."

"Or something could have happened to him." Tarquin pulled his blanket tighter around his shoulders. "It has been hours."

"There are a lot of hungry creatures there after dark." Sweeney flashed a smile full of abnormally sharp teeth. "You know, if you are not careful, then a siren may just crawl out of the water and snatch your heart right out of your chest."

Tarquin squirmed. Cahal made a sound that was something between a scoff and a muffled laugh.

"Are there many sirens out there?" the boy asked. "You are the only one I have ever met."

"Oh, yes. There are hundreds. And they will crack open your ribcage like it is a lobster and dig through the meat until they find your delicious heart."

Tarquin cringed. "Just the heart?"

"The naiads eat the rest." Sweeney's smile broadened. "Bottom feeders."

Cahal shot him a look. Sweeney laughed gaily.

"Do not worry," the siren amended. "I will not eat *your* heart. I doubt it would be big enough to satisfy me."

Tarquin pursed his lips. "That is comforting," he muttered.

"I make no promises for Cahal." The siren combed his fingers through his long black hair. "That is between the two of you."

Tarquin shivered. He looked out the window again, hoping against hope that he might see Tybalt walking up over the dune. He was so tired, but he could not bring himself to sleep. "Maybe I should go look for him."

"A good idea," Sweeney said. "That way, whatever ate him will have a second course."

"Sweeney," Cahal said, his words clipped.

Sweeney huffed and rolled his eyes. "I went looking for him once. There is no sense in doing so a second time. If he is alive, he will come back. Perhaps he just wants to be alone."

"And perhaps," Cahal said, "I will spit poison into your mouth if you do not do as you are told."

"No need to *bribe* me," Sweeney purred. He uncrossed his legs and stood up, taking one last long drink from his cup. "I will be back. I am only doing this *once more.*"

Cahal nodded. Sweeney made his exit, humming a sea shanty as he went.

The old tavern slumped into silence. Tarquin would not have minded so much, except Cahal made him feel very unsettled. He curled up in his seat, pulling his knees to his chest. He locked his eyes on the naiad, who was busying himself by chopping leeks.

"Where did you learn to cook?" Tarquin asked. He had to fill the silence somehow.

"You pick up things walking around land long enough." Cahal dropped the leeks into a bowl. "My palate is different from that of a human's. That has been the most difficult thing to navigate."

"I see." Tarquin rested his chin on his knees. "Do you miss... the ocean?"

"No." Cahal looked at him. "Do you miss the Lily?"

"A little," Tarquin replied. "I am scared to go back. And I miss the other boys, but I never quite fit in with them."

"It seems like it was only a matter of time before you left, then."

"Maybe." Tarquin bit his bottom lip, picking at a sore spot. "I had hoped it would be with Tybalt."

Cahal raised an eyebrow at that. "You have bad taste."

Tarquin gave him a small smile. "I cannot help it. It has been ever since we met, even before the Gilded Lily."

"I cannot pretend to see what you do. My palate is different... in more ways than one." Cahal moved on to potatoes, slicing them quickly into circles with a thin, sharp knife.

"I have always wanted to leave with him. Whether it was to go back to West Avralaen or to travel somewhere new entirely—I did not care. I am so sick of this place."

"There is more to Dragoloth than just Seravell," Cahal reminded him. "And more to the world than following around an arms dealer who can barely sail."

Tarquin pursed his lips. "You sound as though you have never loved someone before."

Cahal's knife stopped moving. Tarquin folded himself up a little tighter, thinking he had gone too far.

"I have not," Cahal admitted after a long pause. "I could never bring myself to bother. Why would I? If anyone were to try and touch me, they would die. And from what I have read and seen over the years, what is love without the occasional kiss or caress? What even is the point, if you cannot pull someone close, even fully clothed, for fear that they may touch their cheek to yours and pay the price in choking on their own vomit?"

Tarquin had no answer. He could not imagine love without touch. Love without sex, maybe—but without any physical affection at all? He could not wrap his head around it. "But... do you want to?"

"Do I want to?" Cahal echoed back.

"Do you want to love someone?"

"Whether I want to or not," the naiad said tersely, "is irrelevant."

Tarquin looked at him for a long moment before uncurling from his position. Cahal turned his attention back to his task, paying no mind to the boy as he stood. Tarquin walked over to the counter and propped his hip against it, looking up.

"Have you ever had anyone offer?" he asked. "Has anyone ever wanted to try?"

"To love me?" Cahal snorted.

"To touch you," Tarquin said.

Cahal made a face. "Once or twice," he said. "My kind—naiads—are considered undesirable at best, dangerous at worst. Curiosity has led one or two to offer. I have never bothered to see them through."

"Undesirable?" Tarquin furrowed his brow. "Is your allure not part of your make?"

"We are one thing to a sailor who cannot see through the fog, who has not eaten properly in days, and who is dizzy from the waves. We are another thing entirely to the people who dwell on land. Even the sailors, once they throw themselves overboard, see that we are monsters."

"I do not find you monstrous," Tarquin said, softening his voice a little.

"You do," Cahal said. "And I find pity more repelling than disgust."

Tarquin's cheeks flushed red. He dipped his head to try and hide it, rubbing at the back of his neck. "I meant no offense... I simply wanted to offer you something." He looked up at Cahal again. "You said it yourself; I have bad taste."

A bare smile touched the naiad's lips at that. "Yes," he said. "Bad taste—and a death wish."

"I do not intend to poison myself," Tarquin said, tugging on his shirtsleeves just enough to free up his hands. "It is entirely at your discretion, but I am creative enough to make it worth your while."

Cahal's gleaming red eyes darkened just a bit as they moved up and down Tarquin's frame, as if sizing him up. "What do you propose?"

Feeling a little victorious, Tarquin smiled. "Let me straddle your leg," he said. "Neither of us has to remove our clothes. I can touch you through your trousers—trust me, it has worked before."

"I see." Cahal moved a little closer, reaching out with gloved hands to take hold of Tarquin's hips. Having the naiad so close caused Tarquin's nerves to flutter in his stomach again, but he pushed them down, determined. He spread his legs and let Cahal put his knee between them. He clamped down around Cahal's thigh and patted the naiad's arm, urging him to lift him up a little higher. Cahal did, and Tarquin was able to slide up his thigh, the countertop hitting him mid-back and offering a little support. It helped, because Tarquin did not want to lean against him and risk touching any exposed skin on the naiad's neck and face.

Tarquin reached down and cupped Cahal through his trousers, searching with his fingers until he found the firm bulge. He made a soft, pleased sound and started stroking the naiad through the fabric, squeezing a little and rubbing firmly with his palm, making certain that Cahal could feel it. He was so focused on his work, and Cahal was so much taller, that he could not search his face to see his expression. He could only assume, from the deep growl that rolled up the naiad's throat, that he was doing well.

Cahal brought his leg up a little higher, and Tarquin started to feel his own passion stirring. He ground his hips down against Cahal's thigh, the burst of pleasure pulling a moan from his throat as he worked his hips back and forth, rubbing his hand more vigorously as his own desire took over. Cahal was getting firmer in his hands, and Tarquin was dizzy with desire, the barrier of so much fabric both infuriating and intoxicating, the idea of climaxing while barely being touched was exhilarating.

Cahal pushed Tarquin's hips against the counter, pinning him in place, and Tarquin groaned headily—-trying not to be so distracted by his own pleasure that he neglected his partner. He threw his free hand back, trying to steady himself on the counter. His hand landed on Cahal's knife, and cold steel sliced open his palm. Hot blood collecting in his hand sobered him up a bit, and he pulled his hand around to evaluate the damage, although he kept his thighs tight around Cahal's, not willing to let the pleasure go.

Blood was streaming between his fingers and running down his arm. Tarquin swore under his breath, the hand that was on Cahal's groin going up to touch his chest, asking for a pause. Cahal caught his hand mid-air, what seemed to be a reflex, and stopped what he was doing to look at Tarquin's face.

"I just need a moment," Tarquin said breathlessly. "I cut my hand."

"Ah." Cahal reached out and took Tarquin's hand to inspect the damage. Tarquin swallowed, still feeling a little dizzy, but mostly out of the mood now that his palm was starting to sting.

"I can take care of it," Tarquin said.

When Cahal spoke again, there was something strange about his voice. "I will."

Tarquin furrowed his brow, searching the naiad's face. When he looked into Cahal's eyes, they had turned completely black.

Panic made his stomach drop. Tarquin squirmed, trying to pull away, but Cahal's grip on his bleeding hand was unrelenting. "Please," Tarquin gasped, unable to stop his voice from climbing out of fear. "Cahal, let me go, please!"

His words fell on deaf ears. Cahal caught the tips of his glove between his teeth and pulled it free, exposing his hand—the same bright, warning blue as the rest of his skin. He lowered his face to Tarquin's wound, his purple tongue snaking out to lap at the blood, latching onto the sylph's skin and sucking off the rest. Tarquin opened his mouth to scream, but no sound had the chance to escape. Cahal's fingers filled his mouth, forcing themselves down his throat, and

Tarquin gagged. His throat swelled almost instantly, closing around the naiad's fingers, and he could not breathe. He tried to force some air through his nose, but nothing could be summoned, and his lungs constricted painfully. Tarquin tried to grab at Cahal's wrist, but the contact just made his own hand go numb, and he could feel it spreading down his arm with such rapidity he could barely register what was happening. He heard, rather than felt, his arm drop and bang against the counter. The world was turning black with bursts of color like fireworks exploding across his vision.

His last thought was of Tybalt. His face was wet, and he could not tell if there were tears in his eyes, or if there was too much foam streaming out of his mouth.

The door to the Laughing Albatross slammed shut. "Well," Sweeney said, "I could not find him. Either he is hiding very well, or he decided to leave. He could be dead, I suppose. We will find out if he decides to come back..." The siren trailed off at the sight of Tarquin's body. Cahal's work was unmistakable in the way that all of his victims looked bloated and discolored by the time he was done with them.

Sweeney made a face.

"That was an accident." He pointed at the corpse slumped over on a table. "Right?"

"Yes," Cahal said. He was putting potatoes in a pot with some leeks.

"I do not believe you." Sweeney walked over to the body and pulled up a chair, spinning it around so that he could sit with his legs splayed around the back. He pulled out his dagger and cut a slit down the back of Tarquin's shirt to open it up. "I suppose no sense in it going to waste."

Cahal gestured to the pot. "My thoughts exactly."

"You can cook what you want," Sweeney said as he plunged his dagger into Tarquin's back, twisting it viciously to create a bigger opening. "I am taking his heart."

"You said you could not find Tybalt?"

"Maybe he threw himself into the sea."

"Resting at the bottom with his ship?" Cahal shook his head. "It would be a little dramatic, even for him."

Sweeney shrugged. "I am not his keeper." He pushed his hand through the opening he carved, searching for the dead boy's heart. "You should send a note to Florindel."

"'I found your missing boy. Sorry he is dead'?" Cahal snorted.

"Something of that kind." Sweeney smiled in satisfaction as he found his prize, closing his hand around it and bracing himself against the boy's back so he could tear it free.

"I suppose it is only courteous." Cahal brooded, watching his companion work. "I should send back something of him. Else they may not believe me."

"You think Florindel believes you are a liar?" Sweeney wrapped his ankles around the legs of his chair, holding Tarquin's heart aloft, its gore glistening in the light. "I cannot imagine why he would."

"Is the head too gruesome?"

"Not really. You cannot eat it anyway."

"I will do that, then," Cahal said. "While you are down there, if you would be so kind as to start carving the rest."

"I will need a better knife," Sweeney answered, even as Cahal tossed one onto the table.

"It seems small," Cahal said.

"I knew it would be." Sweeney put it to his mouth. "I should save it for Tybalt," he mused. "It was his anyway."

"He did not want it." Cahal rolled his eyes. Sweeney laughed and took his first bite.

16

PHARUN

The Casualties that Pave the Road to Power

THE MORNING SUN HAD already started to warm up the garden. Spring was drawing ever closer, even if the snow was not going to melt for some time. Breakfast was kept simple: golden pastries filled with spiced nuts and black currant tea. Pharun reveled in the quiet that was only broken by faint birdsongs and the sound of Olympia's spoon clinking against the sides of her cup as she stirred her tea.

"Do you have any doubts about the funeral?" She finally interrupted the silence. Pharun pulled a pastry apart with the tips of his long nails.

"Should I?" he asked. "I feel we are well prepared." He placed a shred of pastry on his tongue. The crisp, flaky crust melted almost instantly.

"As well as we can be." She seemed to agree. "I am still coming to terms with the fact that any of it is real."

"I understand," he said. "I spent so many years praying for him to drop and dreaming about what would happen when he did. Now that he is gone, I must admit that it feels hollow."

"Hollow?" She twisted a lock of her raven hair around her finger. "I loved him, and I feel empty. You hated him... and you say you feel the same?"

"Not quite. I have not lost anything. I stand to gain a great deal; it is the victory that does not feel satisfying." He tore apart another piece of pastry. "You build up something in your mind enough that it becomes unattainable in reality. I always thought that he would have something more to say to me than he did."

"He could not breathe," Olympia said blandly. "That is probably why."

Pharun smiled. "Yes," he said. "I suppose there is something to be said for that."

Olympia rolled her eyes and sipped from the rim of her teacup. "You say that you have not lost anything. Is your family nothing to you?"

"You are my sister," Pharun deflected. "Are you nothing to me?"

"I am still alive," Olympia said. "I must be worth something."

"Shrukian is still alive," Pharun pointed out mildly. "For the time being at least."

"That is different, you and I both know." Olympia's teacup clinked against the saucer as she set it back down. "I am not standing in your way."

"You could, easily. But you are too clever for that." Pharun touched his nail against his bottom lip. "And your suitors are too bountiful. I could have my pick of allies."

"I would choose carefully," Olympia warned. "If your pick does not suit me, I will not tolerate it long, and there have been enough royal funerals for one year."

"So I must find someone who is a suitable match for us both. We have very different tastes in men."

"Not so different," Olympia said pointedly. "I can think of one we have shared."

Pharun's face turned a stormier shade of grey, although he kept quiet until the moment passed. "I was thinking," he said, his voice as smooth as glass, "of Adriel Ercole."

"That would be like you," Olympia said. "You know how I feel about him."

"We will have war on our hands very soon, and his mother's purse runs deep."

"I have no interest in an Ercole purse, his or hers. Not that it matters, as I said. It is your choice, and you will have to write the eulogy."

"One thing I have always enjoyed about you is your way of butchering the Dragolothian language." Pharun waved his fingers for a servant, who stepped forward to pour him another cup of tea. "One would think that you would have a greater care for your brother, now that I am reportedly all you have."

"I am rethinking my position," Olympia said. "Perhaps I will leave. I have toyed with the idea of finding my way to Simisola."

"If it is a princess you would rather have, sister, you need only say so," Pharun said calmly, halving a fig with his delicate knife. "I am not entirely unreasonable."

Olympia gave him a long look. "You do not mean that?"

"Why would I not? A firm alliance with Simisola would be invaluable. And I know for a fact that Queen

Efemena has three daughters, only one of whom is married already."

Olympia was quiet for a bit as she sipped her tea, seeming to consider his words, unsure if she could trust him. "If you are serious, and it can be arranged, you may find me far more agreeable. From my position, it is the best outcome I could ask for."

"Yes," Pharun agreed. "And you know, I find it wonderful that we can communicate with one another so candidly."

She sucked on her teeth. "I find you disagreeable."

"I find you reprehensible. At least we have some common ground."

Olympia scoffed under her breath, lifting her teacup again to her lips. "So you will speak to the Simisolan ambassador?"

"I am meeting with her tomorrow after the funeral."

"Mm." She swept a drop of tea up from her lips with her tongue. "Very good."

THE CHEST THAT ARRIVED at the Gilded Lily was weathered almost beyond functioning. It looked like something that had been pulled up from the bottom of the ocean or else had been buried for decades. Even the locks had rusted off; the only thing that was keeping the lid down were two leather straps that had been wrapped around either end.

Franciscus and Florindel exchanged a look. It was too early for the boys to be awake, and the chest had been there when Franciscus arrived. After searching every tavern and crooked drug den he could think of to find Tarquin, he had arrived back home empty-handed. He knew that Florindel would understand—that the master of the house had not expected much to come of the search—but he still felt like a failure. He had not made it all the way out to the coast as he had planned; he had simply run out of time.

"Do you want me to open it?" Franciscus asked, already kneeling down and turning the heavy chest to face him.

"Do so out here," Florindel said. "I do not want whatever is in there to get into the house."

Franciscus nodded his agreement. He pulled a knife from his belt and cut the leather straps, sliding them off the ends before taking hold of the lid. He looked to Florindel, who nodded his permission, and then lifted the lid.

The smell that emanated from inside was putrid. Franciscus gagged as his stomach flopped, and it was all he could do to keep from dropping the lid. Florindel's brow furrowed, and he covered his nose with his sleeve, gesturing for Franciscus to open the chest all of the way. Franciscus flipped the lid up all the way and leaned back, horror and disgust fueling a surge of bile up his throat.

Tarquin's head rested at the bottom of the chest. It was already turning sallow with decay. His mouth had been pried open and his jaw looked like it had been broken in the process. He was resting on a bed of his clothes, which had been folded neatly and tucked inside. Franciscus had to look away; he could not take it.

"There is something in his mouth," Florindel said. He sounded equal parts mortified and furious. He stepped closer to the chest, but Franciscus reached up immediately, holding out his hand in a plaintive gesture.

"No, please," he said, sitting up properly on his knees once again. "I will." He did not want his beautiful master coming close to such vile wretchedness. Franciscus reached into the chest and found the corner of a paper sticking out of Tarquin's mouth. He tugged, and the paper came free easily.

There was a bit of blood on the corners, but otherwise the writing was dry and legible.

The handwriting itself he did not recognize. He handed it to Florindel who read it aloud.

"*We found him. This was all we had to send back. Condolences.*" Florindel's voice was flat.

There was no name, no signature. Of course, there would not be.

"It is worse than we feared," Franciscus said. He grabbed the lid and closed it again. He could not keep staring at Tarquin's distorted, dead features.

"Far worse. He ran to the wrong people." Florindel shook his head. "My heart is broken."

"The boys will be beside themselves," Franciscus said. "We cannot let them see this."

"No, absolutely not." Florindel agreed, swiping his thumb at the corners of his eyes. "We must dispose of this so that they do not ever see what has happened. If they ask about Tarquin, I would rather have them think that he could not be found than know the truth."

Franciscus nodded. He kept his eyes on Florindel, because just looking at the closed chest made him sick. "The people that are responsible... Do you think they can be found?"

"Anyone can be found," Florindel said, his tone laced with venom. "And believe me that I will."

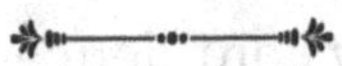

THE QUEEN SAT PERCHED on a brocade settee, her green satin taffeta skirt spilling over the side and nearly covering her feet. The reports that Marcellus had handed her had been written late into the night, and his handwriting got steadily worse as the pages went on. She was accustomed to his method, but there were points where it became unbearable.

"You think the mages are heading into the Red Spine?" she asked, flipping back to the first few pages of what he had written.

"If they have not ventured forward already," Marcellus replied. "You can see where I have narrowed down their possible entry points and marked them. If they follow a reasonable trajectory, they should come out at one of these three points on the other side." He gestured to them on a map as he spoke.

Robin nodded. "What is their likelihood of survival?"

"In the Spine?" He stroked his chin. "Ringo has been through it before."

"So, fair?"

"I would say a bit better than the common person, but not by much. My confidence is not soaring."

"So we may have lost them." She did not seem pleased. She moved a few more pages for the ones she had bent the corners of and marked. "That is not ideal."

"I believe the objective was to squash the rebellion," Marcellus said dryly. "The forest may do that effectively on your behalf."

She cut him a glare. "Do not patronize me." She pulled out another page. "And King Encarz is dead. You think there will be a declaration of war."

"There are many variables," he said. "As noted-, Encarz had two sons. His last days were spent trying to secure an alliance with us. I believe Shrukian would honor that and make attempts to establish what his father began."

"And the other son?" she asked.

"Less so. Conquest seems to be his main objective, and our continent looms as a more enticing prize. There are added complications as he is also *Choeir Ri Saggarthe*, and while he should not be able to reign as king for that reason, my sources inform me that, in so many words, he does not care."

"I see." Robin traced her thumb over her bottom lip thoughtfully. "What was his name again?"

"Pharun Mahtrador."

"He came to East Avralaen for a time, did he not? I remember. I did not see much of him, as he was conducting some rather intensive study at the temple."

"I believe the last you spoke to him was when you gave him and High Priest Felix d'Artion your blessing for their journey back to Dragoloth. That was for his naming ceremony."

"I see." Robin sat back in her settee, looking up at him. "When I asked you to cripple them, I did not mean for you to hobble us as well."

Marcellus raised his chin. "It is what comes with having so many moving parts, Your Majesty. Lystra's death was timely enough to have spurred them into war with Simisola, Encarz's death was not what we planned."

"All the more reason for us to have a vested interest in making certain the *right* son inherits," Robin said. "I assume that your connections in Dragoloth are still reliable."

"We have many anchors throughout the country," Marcellus confirmed. "My information is good; we will be able to know everything as it happens."

"Excellent." Robin pushed the papers back together in a stack. "Have your sources been in contact with Prince Shrukian at all?"

"Yes," Marcellus said. "The situation in Dragoloth is somewhat unstable, so we must proceed with the utmost caution. Prince Pharun is not pardoning."

"I agree with you that we must be careful," the queen said. "We must bring Shrukian back to Avralaenian shores as quickly as possible."

Marcellus inclined his head. "I have already made some arrangements."

"I leave them in your hands," Robin said. "I know you are more than capable. Once he is here, and we are reassured of his loyalties, we will make further plans."

Marcellus bowed. "As you wish, Your Majesty."

THE PALACE PRISON WAS hardly a cushy accommodation. Tybalt had been in worse holes, but none that had quite left him with such an unyielding sense of dread. His cell was bigger than most, which really just left him with more room to pace. There was a small, barred window that was too high up for him to look out of, and not much daylight or breeze could get through either way.

Nkiru had passed him off to the guard without a word once they arrived. She seemed ready to wash her hands of the entire situation, and Tybalt could not blame her.

There was space for a cot but nothing for him to lay on. Tybalt had to stop pacing. It was not doing him any good, and his feet already ached. He pressed his back against the wall of the cell and slid down to the floor, sighing heavily as he rested his arms on his knees and tilted his head back. He stared up at the little window above his head, wondering what the prince regent could want with him—wondering what would happen if he could not provide satisfaction.

He rubbed at his face, exhaustion fighting against his anxiety. He had to stay awake; anything could happen while he slept. By the same token, he wanted nothing more than to close his eyes and let sleep overtake him.

He wondered what Quin would think when he did not come home. He muttered a prayer to Balshett, asking Him to grant the boy some common sense. If

Quin stayed put, Sweeney and Cahal would take care of him. Tybalt was certain of that. They were ruthless mercenaries, but they took care of their own. They would not let anyone go hungry or abandoned.

He also sent up a prayer for Florindel. For whatever reason he was here, Tybalt did not want the prince to go after the Gilded Lily. The thought of any one of those innocent boys suffering was enough to make his heart ache.

His mind kept running away from him. With every passing moment, he thought of something new that could occur, someone he did not want to see hurt. He worried less about himself. He would be all right. Even if he was not, he did not want suffering to spread.

It was ages before he heard the prison door clink. Tybalt picked up his head and sat up a little straighter against the wall. His instinct was to loosen up his body in case he needed to spring for the entrance, but at the bottom of his heart he knew he was not going to escape so easily.

The first person to walk in carried with them an unsettlingly large case. It looked like something a surgeon might use. In their other hand was a bowl——very similar to the kind Tybalt had seen used for bloodlettings—and a small jar with a looped handle that dangled from their finger. Tybalt watched as they set it all down, his mouth too dry to formulate something clever. The person popped open the latches on their case and opened it up, the contents immediately making Tybalt's stomach drop. Thumbscrews. Pins. Something that looked like a boot but was made of iron and had a key-shaped screw at the ankle.

There was absolutely no way he was getting out of here alive. Tybalt tried to steel himself, but he could tell his hands were shaking. He just hoped that no one else would notice.

The cell door opened again. This time, Tybalt knew who he was seeing. It was hard to mistake Pharun Mahtrador, who never missed a chance to dress for any occasion—even a bloody one.

The prince regent, the Crowned Priest, the soon-to-be sole sovereign of all Dragoloth, called for a chair to be brought and took his seat.

Tybalt was finding it difficult to swallow past the lump in his throat. "You sent for me?" he asked as if they were sitting down for tea. "I would have granted you an audience without the escort."

"I do not find your cheek endearing." Pharun crossed his legs as the cell door closed behind him.

"The first thing I like to do with a glib tongue is cut it out."

Tybalt paled. "I would rather keep it, if it is all the same to you. It can be more useful than you think."

"We shall see," Pharun said. "If you say all of the right things, I may allow you to be buried with it. How does that sound?"

Tybalt tilted his head back again. "More generous than I anticipated."

"I am a generous king."

"Not king yet," Tybalt could not help but bite. It was not wise, and he knew it, but he had to say something to make it look as though he was trembling from something other than fear. "Maybe not ever, with royalty dropping like flies."

Pharun set his jaw. "You would know about that, would you?" He seemed otherwise unbothered. "Coincidentally, that is what we are here to discuss. I know you are involved with the Avralaenian arms trade—and a great many other illegal goods."

"I follow demand. If there is money to be made, I will not turn up my nose. If your people are arming themselves against you, then that seems to be where you should direct your concern."

Pharun's smile was tight. The first person to enter was still unpacking their case. Pharun raised his hand to signal a pause.

"Do not worry about all of that, Syme," he said. "Start with the oil."

Syme seemed unhappy, but they did as they were told. They picked up the jar that they had carried in originally and pulled out the cork. They tipped it over their bowl, and Tybalt watched as they filled it nearly to the top.

There was a candle sitting on the floor. The wick ignited of its own accord, burning brightly with a blue flame. Tybalt's back and shoulders tensed.

Syme brought the bowl and the candle over, setting them both down beside Tybalt. They grabbed the half-sylph by the wrist and pulled his hand over to the bowl. Tybalt tried to resist, but Syme had the advantage of his angle. He submerged Tybalt's hand in the oil, bringing it back up only to dip it one more time. Still holding firmly onto Tybalt's wrist, he moved the bowl out from underneath and pulled the candle over by its holder. Tybalt's breathing was getting increasingly shallow. He tried not to think about the pain and keep his eyes fixed on Pharun instead, but that was not helping.

"This cannot be about arms," Tybalt said a little desperately.

"We will start there, certainly," Pharun replied. "And we will eventually move on to your more hangable offenses."

"Which include?" Tybalt's voice pitched a little higher as Syme moved his hand over the candle flame.

"Do you wish to start there, instead? All right. You can tell me about your involvement with the movement that led to the deaths of Queen Lystra Marya Mahtrador and King Encarz Priam Mahtrador."

If he had been panicked before, he was terrified now as realization struck him. "Nothing," he said, even knowing the truth did not matter. "I was not involved with anything that led up to their deaths."

"You seem so earnest. It is a shame I do not believe you."

The oil was heating up. Tybalt's breaths were coming faster. He felt like he was going to pass out.

"I never—!" he began. "Never once... I am not an assassin!"

"You know quite a few assassins, though, do you not? Just because you are a low, filthy, disgusting creature does not mean that you would be the one to get your hands dirty. You would have found someone else for the job, and you did. You had the money to pay them well, you had the weapons and the poisons to get the job done. What troubles me, though, is that I simply cannot understand your motivation. If you can give me names of the people who are *actually* responsible, I may have a reason to keep you alive."

"There are no others!"

"You would take all of the blame? That is not enough to redeem you in the eyes of Azrael, Balshett, or whatever deity whose grubby altar you prostrate yourself before."

"On my life, on my life, I swear, I am not who you want!" The oil was bubbling on his skin. The searing pain and the heat was unbearable. Tybalt bit his tongue to keep from crying out again, and all he could taste was blood.

Pharun allowed Tybalt's hand to stay there until his skin started to turn red and peel. The prince held up his hand then, and Syme pulled the candle away.

Tybalt's chest was heaving. Sweat glistened in his hair and on his brow. He moaned in pain, his unharmed hand clenching at his side.

"Your life is not very much to swear by," Pharun said, "or bargain with."

Tybalt swallowed again, his words coming out on a hot breath. "Fuck you."

"Hm." Pharun leaned back in his seat, curling his finger around his chin. "Let us switch tactics."

Suddenly, Tybalt felt like his chest was being crushed—like weights had been piled on top of his sternum and he could not breathe. He gasped, and Syme let go of his hand. Tybalt clawed at his throat as if he dug deep enough, it would help.

Darkness was closing in. White spots danced across his vision. His ears were ringing, and he felt his head dropping toward his chest, the ground rising up to meet him.

Something stopped him. Pharun's cool hand pressed against his forehead, holding him up, and then tilted him back slowly until his back was resting against the wall once more.

The prince met his gaze with rich blue eyes—as beautiful as sapphires and just as cold.

Tybalt could breathe again. His breaths were still shallow, but it was enough.

"So," Pharun said, "once again. Are you ready to discuss the infractions of your queen?"

END OF BOOK ONE

CHARACTER INDEX

DRAGOLOTH

The Court
ENCARZ, king of Dragoloth
LYSTRA, queen of Dragoloth
PHARUN, eldest prince
SHRUKIAN, heir to Dragoloth's throne
OLYMPIA, princess of Dragoloth
MERIDITH, a baron
THYRON, master of archives
HORUS, secretary of the treasury
CHARLEMAGNE, naval commander
SOKAIRE, captain of the royal guard
SYME, a torture master
ADRIEL, an assassin, heir to a barony

SIRIUS

The Gilded Lily
FLORINDEL, a brothel master
FRANCISCUS, his bookkeeper
TARQUIN, a prostitute
KELLY, prostitute
CHRISTOS, a prostitute
JOSSE, a prostitute

The Temples
MALHII, high priest of Azrael
MELCHIORRE, high priest of Saldon

The City
SWEENEY, a pirate
CAHAL, a former admiral
RODERIC, a tavern owner
PHESEUS, a slaver

✦———•••———✦

EAST AVRALAEN
ROBIN, queen of East Avralaen
MARCELLUS, her ambassador
AMNAS, a dreamweaver
ELZBET, a mage

356

UNCROWNED

RINGO, a mage
FELIX, high priest of Morcant *(abroad)*
CILLIAN, naval commander

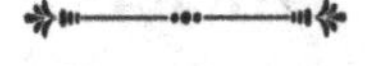

WEST AVRALAEN

TYBALT, an arms dealer *(abroad)*
MERCURY, his husband
FIONE, his crew member *(abroad)*

SIMISOLA

EFEMENA, queen of Simisola
ARENDSE, her ambassador *(abroad)*
NKIRU, her spy *(abroad)*

THE GODS

SALDON, the god of creation
MORCANT, the god of death
AZRAEL, the god of chaos

SIRIUS

ANAIS, the goddess of creation

❖———••———❖

THE PAST
JARIAN, Meridith's father
DAPHNE, Olympia's mother
ANASTASIA, Pharun's mother

GLOSSARY

Known words.

DRAGOLOTHIAN

FADIR
'father'

KREN VEISTEN
'crowned priest'

MIN MAMMA
'my mama'

MAMMA
'mother/mama'

DORMEZ SALVUT
'gods be with us'

DORMECHE SALVE
'gods be with you'

MIN KREN DREGG
'my crowned dragon'

FADIR MORCANHEIM
'father death'

AVRALAENIAN

KEIRLEIGH SOELENMBAUM
'gods be with us'

CHOEIR RI SAGGARTHE
'crowned priest'

GRAGETUS
a dance

AUTHOR'S NOTE

I would like to thank the Pitt County Arts Center for the generous grant that allowed Uncrowned to carve out a place for itself in the world.

I would also like to thank Laura Hope-Gill for her advocacy and endless support.

And I would like to thank Gary Barnum for his tireless work editing.

ABOUT THE AUTHOR

My name is Sirius. I write glory, gore, and monsters and I am the author of *The Draonir Saga*.

I like to make art and I am a professional drag artist. I take a great deal of pleasure in cosplaying the characters I write.

I am a queer nonbinary creature living in the hot and bothered South, in what has been dubbed 'Halloweentown', North Carolina. I currently live with my husband, son, a hypervigilant Australian shepherd, two snakes, two geckos, and a tarantula named Dr. Lecter.

www.ingramcontent.com/pod-product-compliance
Lightning Source LLC
Chambersburg PA
CBHW010631100726
47900CB00011B/2784